I0818065

YEAR FOUR

2022

First published in Australia in January 2023 by Black Hare Press

Editing by S. Jade Path and The Crimson Wordsmith
Cover Design by Dawn Burdett
Internal Formatting by Ben Thomas

Also available from Black Hare Press

ANNUALS

YEAR ONE
YEAR TWO
YEAR THREE
YEAR FOUR
YEAR FIVE

Contents

Preface

YEAR FOUR IS a cumulation of all the stories that have appeared in Dark Moments on the Black Hare Press website and on the BHP Patreon throughout 2022. Thank you to all the wonderful authors who crafted tales for us this year. To those presented here, in Year Four, and everyone else who published with us in other publications.

We've been helped throughout by family and friends, collaborators, editors, the amazing read team, the group moderators, and a myriad of helpers: we couldn't have done it without you.

Special thanks to our Patreon supporters, especially S. Jade Path, James Aitchison, and George Wehrfritz. Take a look at the Patreon-only content and merchandise here—patreon.com/blackharepress—and consider helping us get to the next stage.

And, as always, to our discerning reader: this was all done for you. We hope you enjoyed these tales during the year, and if you did, don't forget to leave a review.

Love & kisses,

Ben & Dean & the Black Hare Press Team

YEAR FOUR

Clowning Around

by Blaise Langlois

I had been in the tent for most of the afternoon, sticky from the August heat. So far, most of the applicants had been rather underwhelming.

Just then, an awkward looking figure lifted the tent flap and strode over, his oversized black shoes squeaking as he moved. I indicated toward the empty seat in front of me.

His face paint was traditional, and a frown replaced the typical goofy grin—something that just wouldn't do.

"Could you smile for me, please?" I sighed.

The clown's red lips peeled back to reveal rows of razor-sharp teeth.

"You're hired," I told him.

Near Miss

by Sophie Wagner

Blindfolded and arms outstretched, he turned to the crowd and asked for a volunteer. No one moved.

After a moment, a clown stepped into the crowd and hauled a sobbing Andrew to his feet.

“Please don’t make me,” Andrew begged.

“Don’t worry, he never misses,” the clown replied.

He dragged him to centre stage, tied him to a board, then stepped back and handed the blindfolded man a knife.

Quickly, he spun around, then let the knife fly from his hand. With a *thud,* it stuck in Andrew’s heart. Not missing a beat, the carny folk descended upon their meal.

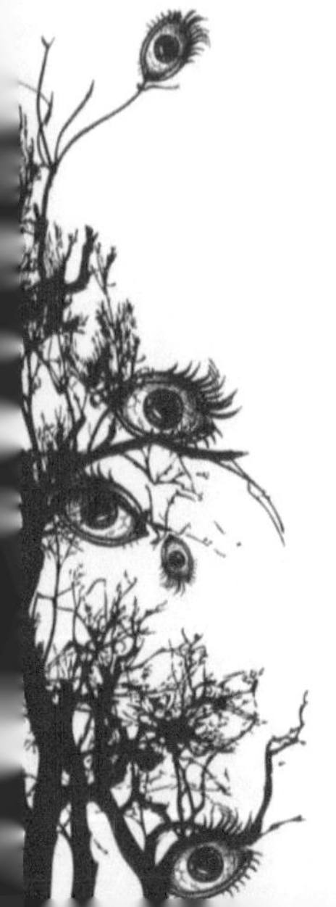

YEAR FOUR

Nightmares at the Circus

by Liam Hogan

There was no net. There was no audience, either. Not a *live* one, anyway. Just corpses, staring up into the big top.

If Sally didn't make it to the waiting arms of the other trapeze artist, no-one would gasp as she fell screaming through the air, no-one would rush to help as she lay broken on the packed dirt.

She screwed up her nerve. They were in sync: *now* was the time. She leapt. For a moment, she feared she'd fallen short. But the hands were there. Sally grasped them, relieved.

Skeletal arms broke free and plummeted down with her.

The Juggler

by Caoimhin Kennedy

The urge to piss led him behind the tent. He unzipped and released.

Footsteps forced a halt to his relief.

He turned and there the Juggler stood. Three balls tossed through the air. The roar of the crowd beyond the tent walls exploded.

The juggler stepped from the shadows, his face appearing in the moonlight. Pale, bloodied, savage, evil.

It was then he realised the Jugglers' tools were not balls, but skulls.

One swipe of the Juggler's claws separated the head from the body.

His bladder let the remaining liquid free as the Juggler feasted to collect his fourth ball.

Spectre Spectacular

by James Hancock

We came to town at night. Cries of wild steeds broke the silence as a line of covered wagons brought hidden mysteries for a special performance. Word spread fast, and with the black tent erected, guests lined up for the evening's show.

Spectre Spectacular. This was no ordinary circus, and if anyone told you they'd seen its kind before... they lied.

The twisted mimes danced through the waiting audience and set a tone of terror. Uncomfortable laughter stopped, a chill rolled in, and shapes leapt from the shadows.

Through the cacophony of screams and panic, the demons drank their fill.

Tick Tock

by M. Vijayaraj

The contorted body was lifeless, yet warm. Hollow eyes, horrified visage. *Tick tock*, a portent of doom. The mirthful laughter seemed a distant memory. The *'Ringmaster'* promised a unique experience. Yet now she trembled, whip in hand. Sixty seconds. Soon, the oblivious soul entered. She glanced back at the body. *Hers*. Desperation coiled the whip about his fragile neck. Edges crudely tightened, his agonised gasps and frothing pleas were hushed. She awoke in her body, unscathed. The asphyxiated body laid by her side and a new ringmaster waited with sixty seconds to claim his own victim for salvation. *Tick tock.*

YEAR FOUR

The Greatest Show on Earth

by Pauline Yates

Teaching a monkey how to strike a match was a clever trick. It required the use of electric shocks to his fingers, but when he lights the ring of fire for the Bengal tigers to jump through, the crowd applauds me as the greatest animal trainer in the circus's history.

However, I underestimated the monkey's cleverness. He can also wield a whip. Biting it from my hand, he directs one tiger to herd me from the left, another from the right. The third tiger crouches beyond the flaming ring, mouth open, fangs dripping saliva, waiting for my leap of death.

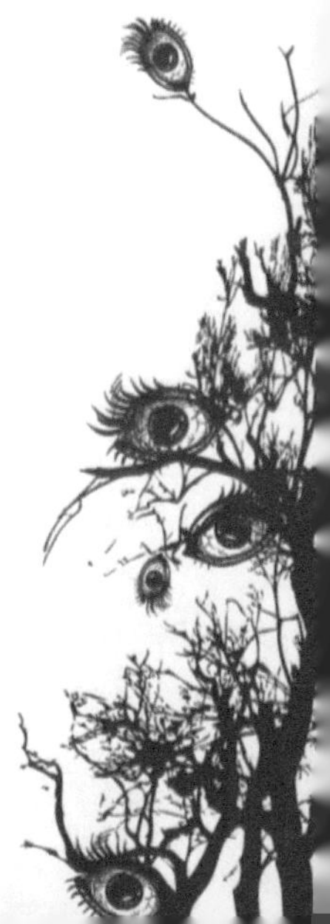

Showtime

by Warren Benedetto

Deke woke from a dream of his life before the circus. He had been roaming under the endless Montana sky. A blinding light shone from above. A watery, gurgling voice spoke.

"This one."

Then, darkness.

Deke's eyes fluttered open. He was in a box of frosted glass, naked and cold. The lid opened. He squinted up at his captor, at its four tentacled arms, its translucent head, its singular yellow eye. Deke had learned that the least painful option was to simply comply. Perform his routine. Entertain the crowd. Survive another day.

His captor spoke. Its voice was liquid.

"Showtime."

YEAR FOUR

Day 33

by Pauline Yates

The sun didn't rise again today. I knew it wouldn't. Last word on the street was them folks at NASA made an error in their calculations and that damned solar cloud that blocks the sun won't clear for another thirty days. That was eight days ago. I don't know what the word is now. The streets are no-go zone since those big knobs in Washington diverted our electricity to the Safe Zones. National security, they said. They also said they'd send in the army to transport us out, but I ain't seen no army trucks. Ain't seen no one. No lights. No cars. No moon. No stars. Nothing but pitch black.

No supplies either. Every shop in town's been looted. When the sun didn't rise that first day, people panicked. Funny thing, panic. People go for stuff they don't need. Like televisions. The electronics shop down the road got hit the second night. Gangs smashed clean through the windows. Saw one kid carting a screen that wouldn't even fit through my front door. Bet he wishes he grabbed a crate of potato crisps instead. Can't eat a television. Nothing to watch either, even if the power was on. Everything's gone real quiet. There's not even static on my radio.

But I got my own problems. Yeah, I stocked up. Be a fool if I didn't. When I heard there was a run on supplies, I took myself down to Al's Grocer and grabbed some tinned food. Since then, I pilfered a few more things. Got a box of chocolate cookies and a packet of pasta, even though eating it dry hurts my teeth. I'd boil it if I had gas, but the bottle was near empty and once everything went to shit, couldn't get no gas. Still got some water. It rained the other day, and I put out my cooking pots. Had to guard them in case the gangs showed their colours, but got enough to fill the sink. Saw Dotty across the street do the same thing, but I ain't seen her since. Maybe her kids came to collect her. Or maybe she's holed up inside her housing commission room like I am.

Which reminds me. I thought I was the only one left in my building, but I swear I heard a gunshot from across the hall. Could have imagined it. Been getting headaches of late and they damn pound like a jackhammer inside my head. But that shot's got me thinking. The bloke who moved in—Larry or Larenzo or Lazza, something like that—he has a grandkid. Pretty thing, with blonde ringlets and blue eyes and a smile so bright no cloud would block her shine. I've seen Larry since she visited, but not since it turned dark, and not since that gunshot. Suppose I should have thought to check if he needed anything, but I'm so used to only looking out for myself, I don't stop to think that other folks might need help. I guess I thought he left when things got bad. Made his way to the Safe Zone, wherever the hell that is. But that shot sounded awful dead-like. I'd better check on him. Better me finding his body than his grandkiddy.

I got keys. Been in this building longer than my teeth and there's always someone who locks themselves out. You could say I'm the unofficial caretaker, but if I was that, I'd know if

Larry was home or not. Bastard better not be dead. Don't need no ringlets and blue eyes haunting my last days because I didn't look out for her granddaddy. Don't need no dead-stink either.

Feels weird lighting a candle when my clock says it's midday. Should probably keep the flame lit because I'm down to my last box of matches. Got plenty of candles. Grabbed two packets during the last storm season. Had no use for them until now. Maybe Larry has matches. And candles. And food. I finished my last tin of carrots this morning. Hadn't thought until now what I'll eat for dinner. Food. Water. Bullets in the gun. Maybe that's why I'm checking on Larry.

Feels weird unlocking Larry's door without asking. I'd knock, but the silence in the hall screams of Desperate and Hopelessness and the game they play gives me the willies. When the candle throws my shadow up the wall, I jump clean across the hallway. Gotta be more careful. My old knees won't stand for shenanigans like that.

When I open Larry's door, Death creeps out. Its icy breath tickles my neck and takes me back to the days when I was an orderly in a hospital. It ain't the death-breath that frightens me. I've seen dead bodies before. It's the shuffle of the cards that gets the jeepers under my skin. Draw a good hand? I escape with my life. Draw a dud hand? Better find Larry.

His room mirrors mine. Small living area. Bathroom. Bedroom. Kitchenette. A three-seated couch takes up most of his living space. My couch only has two seats. Lucky bastard. He can stretch his legs right out if he wants. His kitchen is a mess, though. Both bowls of the double-sink have the plugs stuck in the drain hole, but the sinks are bone dry. Empty packets and food tins, the insides scraped clean, spill from garbage bags on the floor. The fridge is empty, like mine. Reeks of musty mould, too.

Damn my stomach. Growling son-of-a-bitch. Shouldn't have looked in the fridge. Shouldn't have come. But I can't leave now. It's my turn to shuffle. Can't let the candle go out, either. Damn flame's down to a stub. Gives off enough light to find a few things I need. A roll of masking tape to stick newspaper over windows to block the candlelight; gangs are like moths to light. A good-sized kitchen knife, sharper than mine. Nice picture on the wall. Birds flying over a lake. Must have cost a mint. Maybe it's a birthday present? I've been in this room before, but I don't remember the picture. Don't remember seeing blood on the wall, either.

It's frigging everywhere. Damn you, Larry. It's not my job to clean it up but can't let little blue-eyes see this. Or her mother. Better put a sign on the door. Don't enter, or something like that. I ain't in the mood for cleaning and got no water, anyway.

Suppose I should cover the body. See his head just inside the door. Big pool of blood, too. He didn't miss. I'll use the blanket from his bed. Have to laugh. The sheets are all tangled, and the corners hang out from the mattress. He doesn't make his bed, either. Never saw the need. No one but me to impress. You and me, Larry—or Lazza, or whatever your name is—we're not so different.'Cept I'm standing, and you're not. And I have all my face. And you don't.

Bet Ringlet's mother would kick his butt, dying the way he did. I want to kick his butt. Would, if he weren't lying on it. What mongrel leaves his granddaughter without a granddaddy? Larry, that's who. The mongrel who took the easy way out. Left the gun loaded, too. Idiot. Full round, less one. What was he thinking? That'd he'd get a second shot?

Better take it with me. Blue-eyes gets hold of it, I'll have her blood on my hands. Can't have that. Might come in handy, anyway. Those big knobs in Washington won't send the army, not to this town. We're not even a dot on a map. Can't trust those folks at NASA, either. Thirty days? Could be sixty the way they add up. With no food. No water. Be dead before then.

I shouldn't think like that. I got this far. It's the quiet. And the dark. And the damn candle's gone out. Now I have to fumble my way through this hellish existence while Desperate deals another hand. Maybe I'll draw a flush. Hope so. Got nothing left to raise the stakes against Hopelessness, except this here; Larry's gun. Plenty of bullets left. Five, if my count's right. Only need one to brighten my day. Don't need light to pull the trigger.

Honk!

by Jeremy Hinkley

The big top was eerily dark inside. Zach hated the dark, but he'd lost his wallet. The big tent was the last place he'd been. He took out his lighter and flicked it, the tiny flame created a dim orange light that let him see enough to avoid tripping over the bleachers. As he neared where he had been sitting there was a loud *HONK!*

Zach gasped; he'd stepped on a horn with a rubber bulb at the end.

He looked up, right in front of him was a painted face with a wide, hungry, smile, filled with sharp teeth.

YEAR FOUR

Work the Crowd

by Evan Baughfman

Applauding trapeze artists' aerial excellence, Caitlyn declared, "Way better than some mangy flea circus!"

I agreed. "So fun!"

We must've misread the advertisements. The show was impressive, a dazzling evening inside a towering tent, complete with clowns, acrobats, and lion tamers.

A hundred spectators cheered as nimble performers gathered centre stage, taking their bows.

The ringleader thanked everyone for attending, adding, "Concessions are closed. Now, time for *us* to eat."

Troupe members shed their skins—*disguises*—revealing insectoid mandibles, three pairs of powerful limbs.

Massive, agile bloodsuckers leapt into the stands, surrounding prey.

We screamed. Stumbled. Found nowhere to flee.

A Circus Act to Remember

by C.L. Sidell

The house erupts in applause as a top-hatted performer steps into the arena, handling three hoops of fire.

On the sidelines: a monkey escapes its cage, pilfers blades from the knife-thrower's stash, surreptitiously drops them into the cannon.

In the spotlight: the golden-maned cat growls and pounces; the startled entertainer drops his flaming rings.

From the shadows: the oldest elephant charges forward, trunk collecting and flinging each fiery hoop with practiced precision, igniting the cannon's wick.

An explosion of blades pierces human flesh.

Among the chorus of screams: screeching, trumpeting, and roaring of long-suffering animals now free of their tormentors.

There's One Born Every Minute

by James Rumpel

The ringmaster approached two boys who stood near the "EGRESS" sign.

"You're not fooling us," said one of the teenagers. "Egress means exit."

The ringmaster laughed, "You're smart. However, at this circus, the egress is much more than a way out." He brandished a pair of tickets. "Take these. If you find yourself outside, you can return."

The boys grabbed the passes and entered the passageway.

Later, the ringmaster watched a grotesque monster devour the last remnants of its meal. He picked two blood-stained tickets off the ground. "Did you enjoy your lunch, Egress? I'll send dinner after tonight's show."

The Way to a Man's Heart

by Lori Green

The scent of roasted meat wafts through the kitchen, and Sarah sets the table, eager to unveil her surprise. Paul has been staying out late again, not even trying to hide it anymore. Taking her mother's advice, she has cooked up a special treat, just for him.

"Dinner is ready, darling," she says, releasing his blindfold. He mumbles through his gag, eyes wide with terror as Sarah picks up the knife. "Mother says the way to a man's heart is through his stomach."

Her lips curl upward in a twisted smile as she plunges the knife deep into his abdomen.

YEAR FOUR

A Moment of Silence

by Andrew Jackson

Mother's awful tongue was displayed on the mantel in a Perspex cube, swimming in a bath of clear formalin.

She was sitting at the head of the table, looking disappointingly shrivelled, a loose stitch protruding from beneath her left ear. Gemma's business specialised in rabbits and guinea pigs, but it wasn't bad for a first attempt.

"How did I do?" Gemma asked her wife.

Ruby winked across the table, twirling a pair of fluffy pink handcuffs around her finger. "She always worried about what we got up to…why don't we give her a show?"

Gemma loved this woman.

Company

by Koh Hee Ja

The blade against her palm winks brightly as she cradles the knife like a baby.

"Come here."

I groan into her sweaty hair and grind my hips, excited by the danger caught between us.

She nicks my stomach only once during the act, and a scarlet dribble slides down our abdomens and adds to the mess we are making below.

Flesh yields deeply, wetly; the exquisite heat enveloping us.

When we step apart, the body slumps, skull rebounding off the cracked linoleum, and a pretty arc of scarlet spatters over her pale toes.

This wasn't the three-way he was expecting.

Broken Things

by Lillie Franks

Some women would have thrown it away after the first argument. She didn't throw away broken things. She fixed them.

She stayed when he hid in his basement all day. She waited with dinner until he came up. They ate quietly, and she swept away the dirt while he slept.

She fixed things. She fixed the acrid smell from the basement. She fixed it when Deputy Arnold asked questions.

When she heard a thump and a scared, bloody woman staggered through the basement door, she didn't hesitate. She took the knife she was chopping onions with, and she fixed it.

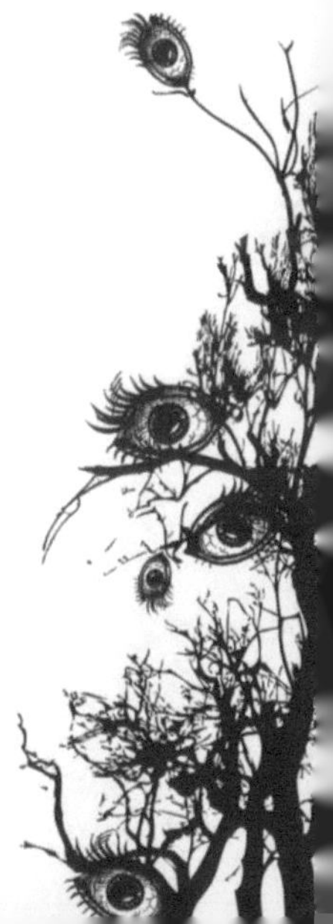

For You

by Jodie Angell

Eyeing the blue pills in front of her, Faye grinned. She knew what it would do to her—unleash a feral ferocity buried deep within her. That was exactly what her lover, Klaus, desperately desired.

"For you, my love." She popped the tablet into her mouth, then swallowed.

Her round eyes glowed afire, and a maniacal laughter escaped Klaus' mouth.

With shotgun barrels resting on one shoulder and their free hands clasped, they skipped down the quaint street of Petunia Walk.

Their idea of a date was warped. Fires razed the houses. Civilians murdered. Children's screams. Blood staining neat lawns.

He Liked to Watch

by Jameson Grey

He liked to watch. That was Ted's thing.

His wife would bring home one-night stands, and he'd sit behind the two-way mirror he'd installed, watching as she took lovers into their marital bed. She'd tie them to the bedposts, adding an extra frisson, and ride them until she was satisfied.

Only then would Ted appear, smiling.

He relished the fear and confusion his presence caused. He'd hand his wife his tie, or one of her silk stockings, and retreat to the corner of the room—where he'd stand, silent, as she slowly strangled her helpless conquests.

He liked to watch.

Hellequin Bazaar

by Lori Green

Gilly roamed through the fairgrounds, lost but not alone. She had wandered off from her mother in search of candy apples when Mr Quin found her, tearfully clutching a worn teddy close to her chest. He wasn't like any of the other clowns she had seen that day. They had all worn bright polka dot colours and crazy hair, not faded jeans and a rubbery mask. But he had promised to help find her mother, even crossed his heart and hoped to *die.* She took his hand and followed him, past a sea of painted faces, into the canvas tent.

Sir... Curse...

by Steven Holding

They'd heard rumours.

A damnable carnival, circling Earth for eternity. Materialising at night, erecting tents, performing diabolical acts for the roaring applause of sin-seeking crowds.

Eager for experience, they sought an audience. They weren't disappointed. Such perverse turns: the Torso Twins, taming the trapeze with their teeth; Coffin Clowns (as funny as cancer!); a man placing a lion's head in his mouth.

The surrounding crowd howled with appreciation; went to give a standing ovation.

Found they couldn't leave their seats.

As the Big Top crumpled, a dawning realisation.

You didn't run away with this circus.

It ran away with *you.*

Kiss of Death

by Brianna Witte

Dan took the blindfold away from my eyes, the dark basement surrounding me. A naked man was chained to the cement wall, a gag stuffed into his small mouth.

I looked at his chest, his heavy breathing making more blood pool from his wounds. My eyes focused on two words carved into his skin, my heart fluttering with pure joy…*Marry Me*.

"Yes!" I shouted, my lips touching Dan's in a passionate kiss.

I took the knife from my fiancé's hand, slicing the man across the face.

"Can I kill him? You know I love the raw stench of death."

The Other Side of the Cage

by Stephen Johnson

The father looked back at the beaming eyes of his two children with excitement as he anticipated the coming show. The dazzling lights above radiated the main stage as swarms of people crowded to fill the bleachers.

"Ladies and gentlemen! Come one, come all!"

Hushed whispers filled the circus surrounding a large cage, situated as the very centrepiece of the arena.

Heart racing with anticipation, the father looked down to the broken lock on the cage. Effortlessly, he escaped, turning to watch the two young lions erupt onto the unsuspecting crowd.

Amid the screams, the proud father roared with approval.

Pizza's Here

by Blair Frison

I awake in darkness.

My clothes are sticking to me. It's so hot I can barely breathe.

I try to move, but I can't. I can feel ropes tearing at my wrists and ankles. I try to scream, but there's something stuffed in my mouth.

The acrid taste drips down my throat. Nausea overwhelms me. I struggle to control it as my stomach kneads. I try not to panic—I *have* to control it, or I'll choke on my own vomit.

I try to calm myself.

I'm in a sitting position. I feel the closeness of the walls. A small strip of light comes in beneath a door.

How did I get here?

The last thing I remember is pulling up to the vacant-looking house with an extra-large pizza. My last call of the night.

Two middle-aged men and a young girl were standing on the front step, watching me. There was something in their eyes. A playful cruelty. I remember the alarm bells going off in my head as I got out of the car and approached them.

Then darkness.

Someone must have hit me from behind.

Fuck.

I hear muffled laughter beneath pounding music. Drunken voices. I can smell weed. Those psychos are having a party while

YEAR FOUR

I'm tied up in this fucking closet.

What are they going to do to me?

Stop.

Don't think about that. Try to memorise their faces. Their clothes. The cops will need to know.

The men were wearing leather jackets and greasy jeans. One was bald, the other greying at the temples. The girl; just a teenager with red hair, bad skin, and wild eyes.

But there are more than three people now. It sounds like a goddamn rock concert out there. And no neighbours are close enough to be bothered by the music.

Why didn't I listen to my gut? It was practically screaming at me to turn around and get the hell out of there. But instead, I got out of the car. And now here I am, and God knows what's in store for me.

Fuck this job.

It's the last delivery of the night and no one is waiting for me. They *know* this.

I hear footsteps approaching.

Oh god, I don't want to die.

The door opens.

Light pours in and a man is standing there, eating a slice of pizza, staring at me. He looks to be almost four hundred pounds. He's wearing plaid shorts, and sandals, with a wife-beater covered in stains. His face and head are completely hairless.

He swallows, and a smile creeps across his face.

I begin to tremble uncontrollably. He looks like he's about to say something, but the doorbell rings and he quickly closes the door.

The music is lowered, but not by much. Something is happening. I can feel it. Hushed voices whisper close by, rapidly in anticipation. A pregnant pause, then shouting. Struggling.

What the hell is going on?

There's a loud thud followed by cruel, penetrating laughter. I hear a scuffle and more shouting. I can't hold it anymore and I piss my pants.

More footsteps approach. The door swings open and it's one of the men I saw on the front step earlier.

"Pizza's here!"

Rough hands grab me and pull me up by my shirt collar. I'm marched into a large, unfurnished room, where a group of roughly twenty people are sitting in folding chairs, eating pizza and drinking beer. There's a joint being passed around. Everyone is smiling at me. Except for one other person who looks as terrified as I must look.

He's a teenager like me, wearing a hoodie and shorts. His hat says *Big Daddy's Pizza*. They're one of our main competitors. I notice a middle-aged, ordinary looking man sitting behind him, with a gun resting on his lap. He speaks one word to the kid.

"Strip."

The kid begins to say something but then thinks better of it and silently strips down to his boxers.

YEAR FOUR

The red-haired girl with the bad skin and wild eyes takes out my gag while someone else unties me. She whispers in my ear.

"Did someone have a little accident?"

They all laugh. She tells me to strip, and I follow her orders.

Everyone forms a circle around us; the two delivery boys just trying to make a buck. We didn't sign up for this.

The fat hairless man approaches me and places a hammer in my hand without a word. Someone throws a large butcher knife on the floor next to the other kid's feet.

"Pick it up," says the man with the gun calmly.

He picks up the knife and our eyes meet. We both know what's happening now. The man with the gun speaks again.

"One of you better be dead within five minutes or you're both going to die. We'll saw your fucking heads off and mail a video of it to your families."

His voice remains calm. He seems almost bored.

I look at the leering faces that surround us. This is no joke. I grip the hammer tightly and crouch into a fighting position. Everyone begins to cheer.

The other kid still looks terrified, but he also gets into position. We slowly approach each other. Everything goes silent as we stare each other down. I can see us, like I'm watching a movie.

He suddenly lunges wild with the knife, swinging in a wide arc towards my chest. I dodge him, and he falls forward as

I swing the hammer down on his spine with all my strength. He scrambles as I take another swing which catches him in the back of his leg. He spins around, and the knife comes at me in a slicing motion, just missing my throat. I almost lose my balance as he gets back to his feet.

The crowd is loving it.

We begin to circle each other slowly. The air is electric. I can no longer hear the crowd, just the sound of my own hateful heart hammering madly in its cage.

He's holding the knife by the blade and I know what he's going to do next, the poor fool.

I lay back and wait so I can counter him. He telegraphs his throw and I easily avoid the knife as it flies past me, just missing the head of one of the audience members and piercing the wall behind him.

This is it.

I lunge at him in a blind fury and, before he can do anything, I'm on top of him in a full mount, raining down hammer blows upon his face. There's a loud buzzing in my ear and I see nothing but red. I am pure, primitive instinct.

After what seems like ages, my vision slowly begins to come back. The red tinge fades as blurred lines become sharper. The buzzing subsides, and the cheering and hollering become deafening.

I look down at what I've done, and my stomach finally surrenders. I vomit all over the pulpy mass that used to be that poor kid's face.

YEAR FOUR

Someone pulls me up and puts a drink in my hand. My other hand still clutches the hammer.

Everyone is patting me on the back and praising my performance. I can't focus on the words. I down the drink greedily and someone passes me another. I down that one too. They tell me I deserve it. And I *do* deserve it. I've never deserved a drink more in my whole life than I do now.

I can't help myself—I almost feel good. I made it through this nightmare and it's time to wake up now.

The doorbell rings.

"Pizza's here!"

I grip the hammer tightly.

Re-Election

by Sophie Wagner

"Happy anniversary," Dalin whispered, removing her blindfold.

Maia frowned as she stared at the open senior yearbook he had placed in her hands and the nomination page stared back; the class clown, the fashionista, and worst of all, the cutest couple. Maia had been certain that she and Dalin would win, but Stacy and Johnny always beat them.

However, when she looked again, she noticed that Stacy and Johnny's faces had been crossed out with x's.

Dalin smirked at her, then opened their bedroom door, revealing both of them bound and bloody.

"Happy anniversary," he whispered, handing her a knife.

Sweet Hearts

by Tracy Davidson

The detective doesn't understand. He thinks we'll turn on each other. But our bond is too deep for that. It took a lifetime to find her, someone whose dark soul was a match for mine, someone equally thrilled at the sight and smell of blood, the sound of screaming.

Scarlet suits her. She wears entrails wrapped around her neck, like a feather boa, while we make love.

The detective still has his entrails. For now. His body untouched, more or less. He is my wedding gift to her. She will feast on his heart. And our unborn child will grow.

Trapped

by Blen Mesfin

I remember lying on the hospital bed, taking my last breaths with mum and dad beside me. They'd told me that they loved me, that I'd go to a better place. But I didn't.

I was still there.

I was there when mum and dad left the room, when my body was taken to the morgue, and when I got buried.

It's been years, or maybe weeks, I can't tell the difference anymore. I was trapped within my own grave, unable to move, with only my thoughts as company. Sometimes, when I feel like I'm at the brink of moving, calling for help, anything really, a twitch of my finger is all that happens.

YEAR FOUR

Shadow Boy

by Jay Seate

Tommy Tunstill rolls his bicycle tire between two iron poles in front of his middle school. He does this with relish, knowing the day has arrived when accounts will be settled. The laughs, the taunts, the abuse, all of it will end. His shadow has told him, “After today, no one will pick on you or call you names ever again.”

He is a smart kid, but the hair that is constantly falling onto his face behind black-framed glasses attracts an uglier element. He’s been put in a headlock with knuckles applied, rubbing and burning his scalp. He’s had his books flipped out of his hands from behind, resulting in his three-ring binder opening up and its papers spreading over the floor like thin carpeting, other students stepping on them as he knelt to pick them up. Tommy wonders why teachers or hall monitors never seem to be around when these events occur. Is it possible they see his plight but choose not to intervene?

A group of giggling girls brush past as he marches into the school. He passes other students standing around, rattling metal lockers, and shooting the shit. He can feel the dislike swirl around him, the cruel energy always ready to pop out from beneath the surface. Nobody ever shot the shit with him, for he’s an outcast. He simply does not click with the other students. A few of them tease or take part in name calling. They say things like “Hey, four-eyes,” “Hey, wide-load,” or bump into him hard enough to make him stumble and then say, "Watch where you're going, loser," comments seething with a desire to punch him in the face.

Tommy knows he is a nerd or a geek or whatever a smart, unattractive kid is labelled. He has never struck back when harassed by tormentors, and never turned a spiteful tongue on anyone who teased him. Instead, he has always gone silently to his classes or recess looking at the floor wary of confrontation. But this is the day things will be different.

When the first bell rings, Tommy waits while others scurry noisily into classrooms. When the tardy bell rings, he plunks down into his seat just in time.

Mrs Sullivan's disapproval is apparent in the set of her mouth. "Glad you could join us today, Tommy." Her words come simultaneously with a piercing scream from the hallway. "Stay in your seats," she orders her students while she peers into the hall. Ms Gault is hovering over a girl. Mrs Sullivan runs to see if she can be of assistance while Mr Morgan comes out of his classroom and joins the small group surrounding Alice Lindsey.

Alice reclines against a hall locker clinching her side. There is blood on her hands.

"My God, what happened, Alice?" Ms Gault asks.

"Something stuck in my side," she sobs.

All three teachers see a small, metal nail file protruding below Alice's ribcage.

"Call an ambulance," Mr Morgan tells Mrs Sullivan as he takes Alice in his arms and quickly trots toward the nurse's station.

"Tommy Tunstill was here," Alice cries. "I didn't see him do it, but he was here."

Mrs Sullivan returns to her classroom to put down a small rebellion. "Tommy, step out in the hall for a moment," she says, keeping her voice steady.

"If something's wrong, it's doughboy's fault," a student says from the back of the room. Mrs Sullivan does not admonish the student. She has too much on her mind.

In the corridor, Mrs Anderson states, "Alice Lindsey was injured, Tommy. She says you were there. Did you see what happened?"

Alice enjoyed calling him names even worse than Doughboy. "I didn't see anything. I was hurrying to class."

"Did you stick her with something? It'll be easier if you tell me now."

"I said it wasn't me. I bet she's not hurt that bad anyway."

"How would you know?"

"Well, she's so perfect."

Mrs Sullivan resists the urge to slap Tommy. "Someone else will probably want to speak with you about this."

Tommy regards her with no change of expression.

Mrs Anderson sighs and leads him back to class where paper airplanes and spit-wads are sailing through the air.

The thrill of the disrupted routine pulsates through the students when the ambulance parks in front of the school to take Alice away for treatment but, by lunchtime, things have returned to almost normal. In the cafeteria the normal giggling, name-calling, and teasing fill the room with everyday banter. As usual, Tommy carries his lunch pail to a bench next to the playground. He sits alone. Inside the metal box is a tuna sandwich, a bag of chips, an apple, and a thermos of 2% milk. His mother sometimes slips in skimmed milk, which sucks, but he won't be fretting over such a small matter. Not today.

He finishes his lunch quickly and then watches to see who the last kid meandering outside might be. He smiles when he sees who it is. The shadow of his chin falls over a ballpoint pen nestled in his shirt pocket. The boy spots Tommy and heads his way.

"Hey, dipstick. Got a candy bar you shouldn't be eating?"

When the bell rings, the students and staff return to their classes.

The hallways are quiet again until Teddy Long, the ordained future terror of the high school gridiron, stumbles into the building from the playground. Teddy—the kid who likes to trip Tommy and watch his books tumble and swoosh across the hallway while other kids laugh.

"I…need…help… *Somebody!*" Teddy screams with a mixture of pain and anguish.

Once again, a teacher appears from his classroom and observes Teddy Long drunkenly staggering down the hallway, his hand over the right side of his face, blood oozing between his fingers. Leaving a wheezing door to close behind him, the teacher runs to Teddy's aid and forces him to lie down on the green linoleum.

Teddy is shrieking and crying at the same time. "My eye!" he bellows. "Stuck in my eye!"

The teacher sees the black ballpoint pen between two of Teddy's bloody fingers. Other teachers and students steal out of their classes. Most turn away after a look at Mr Touchdown's punctured eye socket filled with blood. This time it is Ms Gault who heads for the telephone.

"Stay calm, Ted," the teacher consoles.

"*My eye!*" Teddy screams louder than before. "Tommy Shithead. He saw who it was."

"Tommy Tunstill? Did he do this?"

Teddy can hardly get words out between spasms of pain. "He was standing in front of me. Why didn't he do something?" Teddy wails.

Loud whispers resound amidst the general commotion. Tommy doesn't join the pandemonium taking place in the hallway. Instead, Mr Morgan takes him from his classroom and stealthily escorts him to Principal Phillips's office. "You wait right here, young man," Morgan says before closing the office door behind him.

While the commotion continues elsewhere, Shadow Boy waits patiently. He scribbles a picture of a body exploding in all directions on the back of his notebook while muffled voices whisper in the hallway outside the door. Eventually Mrs Somerville, the school district's psychologist, walks into the principal's office and closes the door. She smells like the perfume on paper from one of those open-and-sniff pages in a magazine. She leans against the front of the principal's desk. Her gaze is cold as it trains on Tommy. He looks back at her steadily as dimples begin to play around the corners of his mouth.

"Hello, Tommy." Her lips curve into a tight smile that is as phony as Monopoly money.

Shadow Boy does not answer.

"You've been in this office quite a bit during your two years here, haven't you?"

He still doesn't answer.

"You've been teased a lot, haven't you? You feel like there's nobody to stand up for you? Isn't that it?"

"I have someone to stand up for me." His eyes meet the psychologist's for the first time. "People won't hurt me anymore."

Mrs Somerville raises her eyebrows. "Who might this person be?"

"Someone who knows how to get even."

"There's been quite a bit of excitement at school today and you know the reason, don't you, Tommy? Both children say you were there."

Tommy rubs one of his arms. Teddy liked to pinch him every time they passed in the hallway. Tommy has bruises from months of pinching.

"So who is this protector?"

Shadow Boy grins conspiratorially, making her uncomfortable. The room is deathly silent except for the low hum of a wall clock.

"If I tell you, you'll try to have me locked up or something."

"I'm not the one who decides what to do about your part in this, but as for who your friend is, try me. You might be surprised at the stories I've heard from students."

"It's my shadow that does it," Tommy says abruptly. "He follows me and sometimes does what I think about."

Mrs Somerville tries to control a smirk. "C'mon Tommy, you can do better than that. I've talked to you before about fitting in, and I know you aren't delusional. You just have an inferiority complex you'll soon grow out of. When you get to high school and find other kids with your interests…well…that's not what we have to discuss today. You have to tell me exactly what happened to Alice and Ted, for your own peace of mind."

"I already told you, it's my shadow."

"All right, Tommy. I don't know whether you're searching for attention, or sympathy, or what, but I think a policeman wants to talk to you next. You've committed some very antisocial acts today. Are you sure you don't want to tell me first?"

"My shadow will look out for me."

The corners of Tommy's mouth rise in an undeniably evil smile, giving Mrs Somerville pause. His calmness disturbs her. She exhales heavily and shakes her head, giving up on further attempts to communicate with a boy who is a cipher to her. She looks at Tommy as he sits placidly in a chair. "If you won't let me help you…"

Tommy is pleased the inquisition is over. Mrs Somerville places a notepad back into a folder. The harsh light overhead doesn't allow the décor to cast shadows. If she doesn't turn her head, she doesn't see it. But she does turn her head and there it is behind her, a larger-than-life shadow against the wall. The dark shape approaches, a living shadow, the silhouette coming toward her. She looks back to find Tommy still sitting in the chair. His eyes are circles of white, the pupils sunken to black dots, the little secret smile carving his face. She gazes back at the wall in time to see the shadow holding scissors above its head. Fright drains the colour from her face as she clutches at the doorknob. The hands plunge down toward her. She screams too late.

"People just don't listen," Shadow Boy resignedly utters. "My mom and dad didn't understand. They didn't listen either," he tells the long dark figure attached to his feet, the closest thing he has to a friend.

Too bad he can't hang around to enjoy his new notoriety, but Tommy needs to get out of the room. If he doesn't, others will come in and take him to some kind of head doctor who won't believe him either until it's too late. He scrambles out of the office's window, his not-so-benevolent protector trailing behind like the black wing of a bird. Tommy wonders how many more people will suffer its vengeance before someone catches them both.

Just a not-handsome boy, a lonely boy, a desperate boy

with no one to listen, attached to a menacing, ghastly shadow, an alter-ego whose actions speak louder than words.

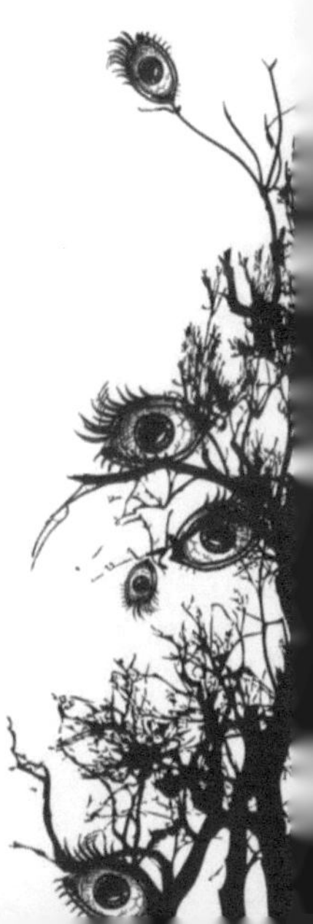

Twice the Pleasure

by Pauline Yates

I love how my lover slides his mouth down the woman's neck. How he pauses near her jugular vein, warming his lips with heat from her racing heart. He nips her skin, teasing, her involuntary moan at the pleasure he inflicts sets fire to my cold heart. When he's finished with her, his lips will tease me in places we share with nobody.

He glances at me, gaze sultry. "Would you like to share?"

"No need." I sink my fangs into the neck of the man in my arms.

I'll kiss the blood off my lover's lips after we feed.

YEAR FOUR

The Ghost of Woo Mon Chew

by Mike Rader

Singapore, 1942.

Siglap village shook beneath the wheels of Japanese lorries. Their cargoes: hundreds of Chinese men, hands bound behind their backs.

The convoy headed up Woo Mon Chew Road, into the plantation. Machine gun fire sounded for hours.

When the lorries left, I found one survivor, buried beneath bloodied corpses.

“I was lucky,” he whispered.

A week later, the Japs captured me. They roped hundreds of us together onto boats, threw us overboard in the harbour, and machine-gunned us in the water.

As I went under, terrified, someone cut my rope.

“Now *you* are lucky,” a familiar voice said.

Making Love Grow

by Andreas Flögel

Believe me, baby, real love hurts. It has to. I know for sure.

Remember your laughter when I first asked you out? You threw my lovely flowers in the wastebasket, and I felt the pain building up in my chest. There it was. The sign of genuine love.

It is a simple equation: love is pain.

As you can see, we are on the right track to let the love grow in you. Your breath already accelerates, your eyes widen. But please, look at my face, so full of love for you, and not at the knife in my hand.

YEAR FOUR

Not Her Kink

by Collin Yeoh

"Tell me the truth."

She wouldn't meet my gaze as I asked her the question she dreaded.

"You're not really into it, are you?"

Before she even answered, I could see it in her face.

"…no."

It didn't lessen the hurt…the betrayal.

"But I do it for you," she said, pleadingly. "Because I love you."

That's not good enough! Not after I thought—after she made me think—I had finally found a kindred soul.

I wanted to end it. To leave her right then and there.

But how can I, when she knows where the bodies are buried?

Revenge

by Blaise Langlois

There was only one way to do it, and they had to be quick. Rats were always more intelligent than humans gave them credit for, and now they had become extra clever. Trying to avoid the farmer's tricks wasn't a game—it was a matter of survival, and one too many of their comrades had fallen.

Unable to lift the box from the shed, they had gingerly carried the pellets one by one to the edge of the well. As each rat dropped a pellet of warfarin into the water, they dreamed about the green death that awaited the farmer.

YEAR FOUR

Vinny's Gift

by L.N. Hunter

Hi, are you Vincent Stoyzinof…?" Annie let her voice trail off, not quite brave enough to attempt the pronunciation of the surname she'd only seen on a screen before. She had planned to greet him in his own language, but the scowl on his face left her too flustered to try.

"Call me Vinny," the huge man said in a low, heavily-accented growl as he pushed himself upright from his slouch against the wall. He was as wide as he was tall, and his scowling face seemed to drip sweat even though the evening wasn't particularly warm. When he reached out to shake her hand, Annie could see damp patches under his arm, and as they shook, she had to concentrate to avoid recoiling from the stickiness of his palm.

"You very late," he grunted.

"Yes, I know," Annie breathed, hoping he wouldn't notice her wiping her hand on the back of her jacket. "We're really sorry. There was a flight delay, and our mobiles weren't working otherwise we'd have called, and—"

"Is rude. Public phone, at airport, it not work?"

Annie felt herself flush, but was saved from having to come up with a response by John's arrival after paying the taxi driver.

"Hello, you must be Vincent, pleased to meet you," John said, dropping the two suitcases he'd been carrying and thrusting out his hand for a shake.

Vincent ignored the hand and grunted again. “You here now. My name Vinny. Here key. I show you.”

He opened the door to the apartment the couple would be staying in for the next few days and ushered Annie in.

“Is nice, yes?”

“Oh, it looks lovely,” she said and turned to her husband. “Doesn’t it, dear?”

“Yes, very nice,” said John, as he struggled through the door with their cases.

Vinny handed Annie the key. “I leave now. You call, any problem.”

“Thank you so much, Vinc— Vinny.”

As Annie was closing the door, Vinny turned back and said, “I leave gift for you on table. Nice gift, is important—shows respect. You take.”

“Thank you, Vinny. That’s very kind. Well, good night. We’ll see you at the end of the week.” Annie closed the door and collapsed against it, stifling a laugh. “What a thug!” she hissed. “He looks like someone out of a horror film.”

“I’m shattered,” John groaned. “I’m going to have a shower and crash.” He puffed out his chest and tensed his shoulders, then put on a heavy fake accent. “*Tomorrow, we look nice gift. Is important.*”

Annie laughed.

***

The next morning, as he waited for the kettle to boil, John

remembered Vinny's gift. In the main room, he spotted a cardboard box on the coffee table. It was about the size of two fat holiday novels. He picked it up and gave it a shake.

"Hey, love, I've got Igor's gift here. You want to see what's in it?"

Not waiting for a response, he ripped off the tape, opened the box, and withdrew…something.

"Where'd we pack the headache tablets?" Annie groaned as she emerged from the bedroom. She stared. "What the hell is that?"

John held it up to the light, turning it this way and that, peering closely at it. "Damned if I know. Something made by a blind grandma's favourite talentless child. Looks like an explosion in a slaughterhouse." He clutched the weird bundle of red tubes and glistening blobs to his stomach. "Help, help, my guts are falling out! It's like that scene from *Alien*." He laughed. "Go on, feel it. It's kind of slimy and squishy."

"Ewww! That's disgusting. Just throw the ugly thing away. Now, find me those pills, then let's have a coffee and go be tourists."

Fifteen minutes later, they threw the used coffee grounds in the bin to land on top of Vinny's gift and headed out to explore the city.

***

Back in the flat after a busy day of sightseeing, Annie headed straight to the bathroom. "I just couldn't use those public toilets—the smell!"

She emerged a few minutes later. “That’s better. Hey, why’d you fish the gargoyle’s guts out of the bin?”

“Huh, the what?” called John from the kitchen, where he was brewing two cups of tea using the teabags they’d packed, not knowing if they could find decent ones here.

She pointed to the table. “There, it’s back. Vinny’s thing.”

“Why would I do that? Wasn’t me.”

“I’ve been in the bathroom—how could I do it?” Annie put her hand to her face. “Oh. Oh! You don’t think— Has someone been in?”

“Burglars? Is anything missing?”

The couple hadn’t left very much in the apartment besides their clothes and toiletries. The only important things, really, were their passports, and those were still in the backpack in the bedroom. Other than the thing on the table, there was no sign of any intrusion.

“Why would someone break in to dig that thing out of the bin?” asked John.

“Maybe Vinny came in. Perhaps he was checking on us. We probably didn’t make a good impression last night, and he wanted to make sure we hadn’t wrecked his place.” Annie puffed out a sigh. “Now I’m feeling a bit guilty that we threw his whatever-it-is away—but it is really ugly.”

“OK, let’s not throw it in the rubbish. We’ll just hide it. Do we still have the box?”

John repackaged the object and put it on top of the fridge.

“I wonder if we should get Vinny a gift, too,” said Annie.

"To make up for being so late. And for being so rude about his present. It probably means a lot to him, and we just threw it away."

"*Pfft*. He's getting plenty from us to rent this place."

"But, John, it'd be nice."

"Oh, alright. We can find some knick-knack tomorrow. Hey, when we go, we can leave it on the coffee table for him to find. *Is gift. Is very important.*"

***

Early the following morning, Annie shook John awake. "It's back. I got up to use the toilet, and the thing's back on the coffee table." She was pale and looked as if she was about to cry.

An angry John wanted to confront Vinny, but Annie shook her head. "No, don't. He looks like the sort who wouldn't shy away from a fight. I don't want anyone to get hurt."

"But he's been in while we've been sleeping—that's just not on!"

"We'll push the sofa against the door when we go to bed tonight, but there's not much we can do during the day—he's got his own keys, after all. I won't be giving this place a good review when we get back, but let's not aggravate him while we're here. Let's just do our best to ignore him—and it—and enjoy our holiday." She pecked him on the cheek.

"Well, we're going to bloody show him who's boss. We'll put it somewhere he can't find the blasted thing."

They boxed the grotesque object, put it in a plastic bag and taped it up. They put that in another bag, as if it could somehow escape through just one layer of plastic, and took it with them when they left the apartment.

That particular day's activities included an excursion to a ruined temple an hour from the city. Annie found she couldn't concentrate on her paperback during the journey; her eyes kept being dragged up to the luggage rack where they'd placed the package.

As soon as they arrived at the temple grounds, John deposited Vinny's gift in the nearest litter bin.

Annie instantly felt lighter, and wrapped her arm around his as they followed the tour guide.

When they returned to the apartment, tired but content, the bright red object shattered their mood, mocking them from the coffee table.

Annie said shakily, "Maybe he's got lots of them."

John licked his lips and said, "If he does, he must have a bunch of identical boxes too." He pointed at the cardboard box sitting beside it. "That's got the same tear I made when I opened it the first time, and the same torn label on the top."

"Should we call the police?"

"And say what? An ugly man called Vinny—if that's his real name—breaks in and puts an ugly ornament on the coffee table in *his own* apartment."

"Can we go to a hotel? I don't want to stay here. I feel sick."

"That'd be awfully expensive, love. You know we can't afford it." He held both her hands and looked into her eyes.

"Look, we're here only a few more days. We can just leave it on the coffee table and ignore it. We'll put a tea towel over it when we're in, and take it off when we leave, so that it looks alright for Vinny."

They both felt uncomfortable sitting in the same room as the object and didn't want to catch as much as a glimpse of it even when it was covered. They felt it watching them and would hide in the other rooms, only when necessary darting across the main room with eyes averted.

The rest of the holiday tasted somewhat sour. Annie used up all the headache tablets they'd brought, and they were unable to find a pharmacy to get more.

***

On their last day, they decided not to wait to hand the keys back before leaving.

John placed the keys on the coffee table beside the object. "Well, we know Igor's got his own keys, and he can damn well keep the thing too. He'll get the message this time. All he knows about us is your Airbnb user name, and we can delete your account when we get home."

At check-in in the airport, they found it in their hand luggage.

Annie whimpered, and only John's grip on her elbow prevented her from collapsing. He dreaded to think what might happen if it was discovered in the backpack going through security—something as ugly as that was sure to lead to questions. Was it even legal, whatever it was?

John swore under his breath and dropped the thing in a bin in the toilets. He'd tried to break it first, but it resisted his attempts, merely squishing and stretching no matter how hard he twisted.

They kept a close eye on their hand luggage in the waiting area, and checked the bags again as boarding was called. Tension throbbed in Annie's head even though the object wasn't there.

They both sighed with relief as the undercarriage *thunked* up into the plane. They sank back in their seats, finally feeling relaxed.

***

"Home again, home again, jiggety jig!" John said as he opened the door to their house. Then he stopped in the doorway, letting the keys tumble from his suddenly clammy hand.

The thing was on the hall table, slick and red and shiny. It even looked as if it was pulsing in time with the pounding inside his skull.

Annie burst into tears.

A voice from behind them growled, "You disrespect me."

John whirled round.

"Why you do this? I friend, and you insult me." Vinny clapped a fist to his own chest. "You insult my country."

John felt Vinny's spray of spittle hit his cheeks. He gulped. "W-what are you doing here?"

Annie cowered behind John, her hand on his shoulder.

"You not want, I take back."

Vinny pulled a knife from behind his back and drove it

into John's midriff, cutting left then right. He grabbed a tangle of guts and sliced it off as John crumpled. The bloody mass glistening in his huge hand looked just like the object.

Vinny grunted, then bowed to the couple and held up his prize. "Is gift, from one country to another. Shows respect."

He turned and walked off, leaving Annie screaming and John, lying on the ground, panting and oozing blood.

Neighbourly Hospitality

by Leah Roemer

October 10th is about when Mr Hartley's decorations go up, so October 10th is about when the screaming starts.

As soon as the first gravestone touches the grass, Mr Windsor marches up to the white picket fence bisecting their properties. His wife stands sentinel on the porch, arms crossed.

His wire-rimmed glasses tremble. He clutches the Chestnut Estates Community Guidelines in his fist. "MARV! Don't tell me we have to go over this again!"

Marv Hartley saunters out of his house, a beer in one hand and a supersize rubber spider in the other.

"Marv, the HOA is *very strict*, and our community does not tolerate…garish, tasteless, *excessive*—"

At this point, Hartley usually throws whatever creepy crawly he's holding. Windsor mutters "one of these days" and slinks off into his tan four-bedroom, his provincial efforts foiled yet again. The rest of the cul-de-sac lets the curtains fall back into place.

This year I was out of town for a few days, so I must have missed the annual Oak Lane showdown.

As I walk my dog, Poppy, past the Hartleys' on the 13th, I see that Hartley's really outdone himself. Real wood coffins. Garish monster masks. Fog machine all set to go.

And some sort of royal theme in the middle—two thrones,

festooned with cobwebs and streaks of blood. Skeletons holding court on both. The smaller one has its arms crossed.

Poppy lunges towards them.

The big skeleton's wire-rimmed glasses glint in the sunlight.

Behind Blue Eyes

by L.J. McLeod

Annabelle had never liked the old brown cow. It was the eyes. Those unblinking, ice-blue eyes.

When Annabelle checked the fences, it was there. When she put out the hay for the herd, it was already waiting.

"It's just a cow," she would remind herself. "Nothing to fear." So why did its mere presence make her shiver?

Then the cow started lingering at her fence. One night she found it outside her bedroom window, though the gate remained locked.

It wasn't until she woke up and found herself staring into those ice-blue eyes that she realised she was in trouble.

Clean Up

by Mari Mendoza

"Why am I cleaning up your mess?"

"You wanted to participate."

Cleaning wasn't what she had in mind. The man even had the gall to put his shoes on the coffee table. She chucked the bloody rag to the side and grabbed a knife.

She blocked his TV show and glared. His gaze dropped to her hand. He raised an eyebrow and stood up, so they were now chest to chest.

"Next time, spread plastic on the floor!" she said through gritted teeth. "And I get the first cut!"

He laughed and pulled her in for a kiss.

"Yes, dear."

Spoiled Milk

by James Hall

Back in the eighties and all the way through until the late nineties, the images of missing children were a common sight on any paper milk carton: whether it be hand delivered by little Jonny on his bicycle, or picked up in the local store. It wasn't until the introduction of plastic jugs that this practice declined.

Here at Amity Dairy Farms, we pride ourselves on being the only National milk distributor in the states that still print our paper cartons with missing children on. We feel it's educational for the consumers to know what our dairy cows are fed.

YEAR FOUR

Soulmates

by Crystal N. Ramos

We had the sky for our wedding canopy and grass for the aisle runner. We arranged the heads of the sheriff and deputy as witnesses. After the priest pronounced us married, I shot him in the heart and my love shot him between the eyes. A perfect wedding.

Of course, we knew what was coming; that's why we got married the way we did. Those three weren't the first we'd killed. The law thought they would part us by not taking us alive. But they were wrong. Every year we celebrate our anniversary by filling our wedding field with blood.

The Horned God

by Leanbh Pearson

Sheep bleated piteously. Cattle chewed stalks of hay. The farmer didn't care about matted fleece or visible ribs. In the woods beyond the farm, someone cared. Cernunnos, wild god and protector of animals, sought vengeance. Silhouetted against the moon, he towered over the farmer, antlered head lowered.

“Never abandon your herds or flocks to squalor and hunger.”

“They’re only animals.”

Cernunnos lunged. The farmer screamed, impaled on the god’s antlers.

“Let you be an example.”

Cernunnos pulled his antlers free. The farmer slumped in a pool of his blood as the god returned to the woods, sheep and cattle following.

YEAR FOUR

A Night

by Caoimhin Kennedy

Raymond Grant steps through the front door of the Beacon Point Motel just as the final rays of sunshine drop below the dense treeline of the Pacific North-West. As with each of his visits to this secluded hideaway—and there have been many—Ray has no bags, no companions, and just enough cash for one night's stay.

When the door opens, a bell jingles. The lobby is dusty and smells of mildew. Fly tape hangs from the ceiling and the wallpaper by the radiator is peeling away in narrow strips, curling like gift ribbon at its ends. There is a counter at the back. The man sitting behind it is Chuck Beacon—aged eighty plus, balding, and stiffer than a plank of deadwood. A cigarette dangles from his lips, casting a sombre orange glow in the otherwise poorly lit lobby. A plume of smoke rises gently from the ember. Behind him, beneath the quadrants of an outdated calendar, a small, boxy television displays a black and white film. Chuck reads the pages of his paperback, oblivious to the sound of his welcome bell.

Standing on the sill of the entryway, Ray removes his hat and crunches it at his beltline. Although only in the twilight of his forties, a mop of grey, nearly-white hair falls from his cap's protection. He watches the cowboys on the screen behind Chuck; galloping on their horses; firing their pistols; their horses neighing. Ray waits, and when he can't wait any longer, he clears his throat.

Chuck jumps in his seat. "Jesus, Ray! Are you *trying* to send me to an early grave?" He sets his novel down and stubs out his cigarette in the bottom of a vanity mug advertising the motel.

"Ears aren't as good as they used to be, huh?" Ray says sarcastically.

"Ears! Hell, that statement works for my whole damn body!"

They share a laugh. Chuck continues, "Come in, come in. How you been, Ray? Been some time, hasn't it?"

Only about six months, but Ray doesn't bother correcting the elderly. Ray comes in and, as he steps to the counter, he says, "Yeah, been a little while, Chuckie. Just been busy, you know."

Chuck nods. "I hear you." He turns to the television and turns the dial. The cowboys on horseback disappear into blackness. "What can I do for you?"

Ray reaches into his jacket pocket and pulls out an envelope. He taps it in his palm, then sets it on the counter. "The usual."

Chuck eyes the envelope. "Just one night?"

"Just one night."

Chuck takes the envelope and sets it by the till. He doesn't bother counting what's inside; he knows it's all there. Chuck reaches below the counter and pulls out a leather-back ledger. The old man struggles with the weight of it, his arms trembling, looking like wet spaghetti noodles. The ledger makes a *THUD* as it drops on the counter. Its cover is scratched and torn and looks to have been buried in the mud and dirt for centuries.

Chuck cracks the ledger open. "What's the occasion?"

"It's Hannah's birthday."

Chuck looks up with wide eyes. "Is that so?"

Ray nods. "Would have been twenty."

"*Twenty!*" Chuck says, surprised. "My, how the time passes, don't it?"

"Tell me about it."

Chuck finds the correct page and spins the ledger to face Ray. The pages are more yellow than white, and look brittle to the touch.

"You know the drill," Chuck says. "Pen's beside you."

Ray snags the pen and scribbles the following information onto the archaic pages:

Name— Raymond Grant

Guest—Hannah Grant

Relationship—Father / Daughter

Date and Age of Arrival—*August 17th, 2012*

He finishes by signing his name on the dotted line at the bottom of the page. He spins the ledger back to Chuck.

"Thank you," Chuck says as he adjusts his glasses to his nose. He runs his arthritic finger down the page, and when he's finished, he says, "Alright, Ray, everything looks in order. Sorry about that. Gotta check these things before I send it to the big guy downstairs. He don't like mistakes." He pulls out a pin from his breast pocket. "I'll need a sample from you though."

"Of course." Ray holds the ball of his thumb over the ledger.

"Little prick…here we go…" Chuck mutters.

Ray doesn't feel the prick, either because his mind is elsewhere or because his thumb has grown used to the dozens of past pricks from past visits. Chuck tilts Ray's hand down towards the page. A drop of blood falls onto the page, blotching and spreading like ink into water.

"That's good, thanks Ray."

Ray puts his thumb in his mouth and watches the innkeeper sign his own name below Ray's. Then he rips the page from ledger. The task seems to take all the elderly man's strength, but in the end, and with a hearty grunt, the page comes free from the spine. He folds it and seals the ends with a few drops of tree resin, which he keeps in a jar beneath the counter. He slides the page across the desk. "That's for you." He grabs a key from the rack beside the till. "Number Five. Your usual." Now, he shuffles over to a storage locker next to the calendar and the TV and retrieves a hammer and a nail. "The one with the red band. Remember?"

"I remember," Ray says, taking the items in his hand.

"I'm sure you do," Chuck giggles. "You've been down there enough. It's just sometimes I gotta remind folks is all. They end up getting lost in them woods." He snaps his fingers. "Oh! Nearly forgot. Would you like some knee pads, Ray? They're getting quite popular with the veterans 'round here."

"Calling me old, Chuck?"

Chuck lifts his hands. "I ain't calling you nothing. Just offering you a little help, is all. Them knees of yours won't always be on your side."

Ray agrees, but for now, he declines the offer. "I'm alright, Chuck. You have yourself a good night, now. I'll see ya in the morning."

"Check out's at dawn. If you're down there any longer, it'll be someone visiting you next time."

Ray waves the key to his room in acknowledgment. He begins for the door, hammer, nail, and page in hand.

"Oh, Ray!"

Ray turns.

"I know you know this already," Chuck says, "but I'm going to tell you anyway. Just remember to keep your distance, okay?" Chuck sighs. "Now, I know you know, but we had a fella over on Cabin Seven try and climb through the other month." His face sours. "Guy about your age, visiting his son."

Ray straightens. There's a gleam of intrigue in his eye. Chuck doesn't notice. "Fella make it?"

Chuck shakes his head. "Do they ever?"

Ray knows they never do.

"Thanks, Chuck," says Ray.

"Yeah, no problem. You have yourself a good visit, Ray."

The bell jingles as the door to the lobby shuts. Chuck sucks down another cigarette and dives back into the printed words of his horror novel.

***

Ray drops the key with the number *5* engraved on its the chain on the kitchen countertop. There's a single watt bulb above the stove keeping the room lit. The kitchen faucet is leaking ever so slightly, filling the cabin with a minute *ting* from the droplet hitting the steel basin.

He goes to the bed and sits on its end. The squeak from the springs momentarily drowns out the kitchen faucet. To his right is a closet with accordion doors and the shoebox sized bathroom. To his left is a massive window which looks out onto the gravel cul-de-sac. There's a flat screen TV atop an antique bureau and a minibar adjacent. He turns. Against the back wall, above the head of the bed, is an aerial photo of the property. In the picture, there's a long building just off the highway. This is the front office where Chuck sits for twelve hours a day, three-six-five. In the picture, if you follow the winding, gravel road for about a quarter of a mile, you'll see nine square-shaped buildings. These are the cabins of the Beacon Point Motel—visited often, but only by a select few.

Ray gets up and walks to the window. The sun is gone. In the moonlight, the pines shiver against the evening breeze. Ray pulls the curtains closed and goes to the back door and goes outside.

The rear yard is large and uncut. There's evidence of a passed shed in the corner—only the foundation remains almost completely hidden in the knee-high weeds. Abutting the yard's rear limit are tall, dense, monstrous pines, stretching in either direction. Ray walks towards here, page in one hand, hammer in the other. The nail is wedged in his lips, looking like a rusted cigarette. He listens to the distant sound of trucks rolling along the Interstate.

Standing at the front-line pines, Ray scans the darkness. It's tough, but eventually, his eyes catch the flutter of the red band tied to an otherwise normal looking tree. He steps through the first row; the second row; the third; and when he reaches the fourth row, he stops and sets his hand on the bark of the marked tree. The bark is warm. It vibrates under his skin.

He sets the folded page from the ledger against the bark. Taking the nail from his lips, he pierces it through the page. A few blows from the hammer secures the page to the tree.

He steps back. The night falls silent. The page ignites in a violet flame, casting a warm breeze on Ray's face. Burnt flakes of the brittle ledger page get carried away by the breeze.

The ground rumbles.

Ray circles the trunk. On the opposite side, a hole barely large enough for a man washes away the loose soils and vegetation. From the crater, a beam of violet light explodes from the Earth and drowns the canopies of the neighbouring pines in a space-aged purple.

Ray smells the sea. He takes it in and gets on his knees.

***

On his stomach, he crawls through the dirt, burrowing himself into the earth. The squeeze is tight, but like every other time he's done this, he manages to fit. Severed roots and jagged rocks scrape the crown of his head. Beetles and worms and ants scurry away into their appropriate burrows. His knees and elbows work the soil beneath him, inching him closer to Hannah.

The tunnel is warm—August warm. The smell of the sea grows stronger with each push forward: caws of seagulls; the sound of waves. At the end of the tunnel, a violet ring of fire burns bright. The flames tickle the tunnel's circumference, singing the rogue weeds in the dirt. Through the ring, beyond the fires, is a perfect blue sky.

An arm's length from the ring, Ray peers through the transition of worlds. He sees mighty waves crashing upon the dunes of an unknown beach. A dozen seagulls ride the thermals far out beyond the surf. A lighthouse stands firm on an island a mile offshore. Its lantern spins beneath the sunshine, calling to whomever might be in search of an oasis from their post-mortem journey—a beacon for lost ships, a beacon for lost souls. A single boardwalk connects the beacon to the sands of purgatory.

Amongst the dunes, a child sits. Her toes buried in the grains of her afterlife.

"Hannah," Ray mutters through the divide.

The girl turns and looks up to the sky as if the wind itself has called her name. She smiles. "You came?"

Her face is clear—clearer than any memory Ray has held onto of his daughter. Down here, she's alive—beneath the pines, Hannah is still alive. "Of course, I did, sweetie."

In two different worlds, a father and his daughter watch the birds fly and the ocean swell.

Ovine Revenge

by Maggie D. Brace

A chorus of sharp bleats rent the air as Tilly entered the barnyard. "What's got them all fired up?" she queried, a wave of apprehension coursing through her innards. George had been at the shearing longer than usual. What could be keeping him? Heading toward the sheep enclosure, she immediately was struck by a horrific odour of blood and faeces. Observing a dozen newly shorn heads, she felt relief until her eyes lit upon George's bedraggled carcass crumpled in the corner. The shears were still whirring away, jutting out of his chest cavity. Old Bessie had suffered her last shearing.

Dearly Departed

by Kaitlyn Arnett

They marry in red.

It's a quiet affair, just as they had talked about, and the only sound is the music they'd picked out themselves. It's nothing traditional, but to a couple like them, it hardly matters.

The guests are quiet as they exchange vows, almost deathly so.

"If you have objections, say them now," the bride whispers, smile hidden behind her scarlet veil, "or forever hold your peace."

The guests don't say anything, not a word.

After all, how could they?

The departed, no matter how dear they are to you, don't speak, and well…

They marry in red.

YEAR FOUR

The Last Victory

by Chad Miller

The Sheep took centre stage on the chamber floor. As they displayed their prize, the Senators gasped.

"This is an outrage!" exclaimed the Cow.

The Pig shook his head. "This will close all negotiations. It's a declaration of war!"

The Sheep retorted, "You cannot negotiate with tyrants."

The Horse neighed, "Our brethren are worked to death or slaughtered, there is no compromise with the Farmers!"

"This is a war we cannot win."

The Sheep accented, "True. So we take what is most precious."

The Senate cheered as they gazed at the Farmer's daughter's head as it rested on the pike.

Foresight

by N.E. Rule

Eating dinner alone on her honeymoon wasn't ideal. But having skipped the cancellation insurance, what was she to do?

Simone scowls while sawing through some gristle in her rare steak.

Plus, the house staff had been given the two weeks off.

On the bright side, the hotel staff have provided excellent service to the 'grieving widow'. It doesn't hurt that she's a celebrity chef.

She could have invited her best friend in Pierre's place. Unfortunately, Monique was equally indisposed.

Thankfully, Simone insisted their kitchen renovations included a walk-in refrigerator. Thus, allowing her to deal with their bodies on her return.

Old Christmas Eve

by Robyn Fraser

January 5th. According to folklore, at midnight the animals in the barn speak in human voices.

Anna is tucked behind the hay bales, shaking with excitement.

The barn is dimly lit and cold, and the cows' breath fogs the air. The ropes and hooks hung on the wall cast terrible shadows. She tries to ignore the whimpering from the veal crates.

When the clock chimes, the cows turn to Anna, their eyes rolling white.

"He's a monster," one whispers.

"Help us," sobs another.

Everything goes quiet.

"Anna! Run," the cows shout in unison, as the farmer's shadow falls across her."

Ravenous

by M. Vijayaraj

The shutters slammed repeatedly, winds howling amidst the desolate crop fields. Overbeck's eyes gleamed, his bloodied grip on the pitchfork waning. The doors and windows were barred, nailed shut. A lone bulb flickered above.

They promised the substance would revitalise his land, beckoning bountiful fields of produce effortlessly. It worked. But the animals gorged themselves on mutated crops. The morphing was quick. Twisted monstrosities now roamed, intent on devouring all.

A chill crawled down his spine. All around, the howling winds were replaced with brays, clucks, squeals, and neighs. The shutters slammed repeatedly, for they had come for sweeter meats.

Broken Melody

by Mike Rader

Laundry flaps above the medieval cobbles, the courtyard rusty red and earthy orange. Grapevines straddle the brickwork. Somewhere a water fountain splashes.

Inside the workshop, violins, violas, cellos hang from the rafters like hams.

Old Giovanni clasps a violin.

Only 650 Stradivarius violins exist in all the world, all accounted for. Except Giovanni has the 651st. His secret.

He runs knotted fingers over his treasure. It will never leave his hands, he vows, unaware a shadow has crossed the sun-splashed yard outside.

A violin string to an old man's throat is a cruel thing. There is nothing melodic about it.

Out of Bacon

by Kimberly Rei

Wind ruffled across hay bales, carrying the earthy scent through open farmhouse windows. No snores drifted back, no sounds of sleeping residents. When the police inevitably arrived, they wouldn't find bodies. They would find bloody pieces. Not enough to form a full human, though the house once held a family of five.

They wouldn't find footprints, only odd gouges in the polished wooden floors, streaked with crimson.

They wouldn't find fingerprints, nor fingers with prints.

The house itself smelled like the barn, ripe with musk and rage.

Freedom came on cloven hooves that night. And pigs eat every tasty bone.

YEAR FOUR

Cull

by Liam Hogan

Yellow hazmats escort him to the farmhouse door to share the news. Inside, his wife strangles a dishcloth, and the sheepdog wanders over to sniff his boots.

"Is it...?"

He nods. "Five cases."

She looks almost relieved. "Well, that's not so—"

"You don't understand," he monotones. "The ministry is taking no chances. They're culling every animal."

She wraps him in a tight hug. "Oh, George! We'll get through this—"

"Every animal," he repeats.

She looks shaken, grips the dog's collar so tight it yelps. "You mean...?"

"You don't understand," he repeats, as the gas swirls around their feet. "*Every* animal."

The Gravedigger's Angel

by Scotty Sarafian

The lantern spilled gold from its tombstone perch. An unremarkable marker, he thought, its square-cut granite, common like the commemorated soul.

Her craftsmanship remained unrivalled. He swept his gaze beyond the plot.

She was gone, her pedestal empty.

Arms encircled him from behind, their marble glossed in flame-flicker. The embrace, lacking the love he had shown her, tightened into sudden constriction.

Wingbeats whisked the air. Plumage cracked, raining shards.

His feet lifted, and he dropped his shovel; the graves it had made sank into moon-splashed hills.

Release restored his breath; he commenced his descent to earth, lungs scorched by sky.

YEAR FOUR

Famine and Feast

by David D. West

Frederick watched as the fieldhand, his last living neighbour, pulled the plough through enough soil to make an ox buckle. He glanced over his shoulder at the dusty fields, where the animals used to roam freely.

Their carcasses lay rotting in the sun, where not even the buzzards would chance a bite at the tainted flesh. The disease took them all in a week. Milk, protein, cheese, all the essentials spoiled by some unspecified sickness.

"Vegetables alone won't see us through the year," he whispered. "At least we'll have meat." He grabbed his spade and stepped towards the hired help.

Dressed To Kill

by Pauline Yates

"Zip me up?"

Macy stands with her back to me wearing a new dress. The exotic fabric gives her curves like Sandra's. Have I cheated on my wife for so long I've forgotten how alluring she can be?

I slide up the zipper but imagine unzipping Sandra's dress and kissing the butterfly tattoo above her left breast.

Aroused, I kiss Macy's neck. "When did you buy this?"

"I made it myself." Turning around, she smoothes her hands over material so translucent she appears naked. "What do you think?"

My heart stops. Above a real left breast is a butterfly tattoo.

Golden Boy

by Mike Rader

4.45 am, Tuesday 12 December 1882.
Creswick, near Ballarat, Australia.

Forty-one men were working the New Australasian No. 2 Deep Lead Gold Mine. Unbeknownst to them, the parallel No. 1 workings had flooded. Without warning, their mine wall exploded. An overpowering torrent of water burst through. Men ran for escape shafts. The water rose swiftly, some men up to their necks—in the dark—in minutes. According to all reports, twenty-two of those doomed miners never breathed fresh air again.

But they were wrong. Somebody else survived that watery grave.

***

I wasn't supposed to be down in the mine. I was just twelve. But on that fateful night, my uncle offered me a couple of coins to help him out. "An adventure," he'd called it, in his old Cornish brogue, squeezing my shoulder with affection.

The explosion was deafening. So were the eerie screams of men dying and drowning. My uncle died quickly, carried off by the torrent, lost in the depths. Voices were singing a hymn. I knew it from church. *"In the sweet bye and bye..."* I crawled into a small shoot above the surging water. There I huddled in safety for hours. I remembered what my uncle once told me. That these mines tapped a deep lead of gold that was part of an ancient system of rivers, buried by lava from volcanoes. I wondered, how much more water would wash through. Would it reach me where I was crouched? Hours later, I heard people calling in the distance from Number 11 shoot off the main tunnel. "Hello…hello… Is anybody alive?"

But I was a mute.

How could I tell them I was still alive?

I knew I would never escape. My body shuddered with cold. Icy black water lapped around my feet. I prepared to die. I was screaming in my fogged mind.

But if death did eventually claim me, I have no recollection. It seemed I crossed some invisible bridge. Alone. The darkness became a womb.

Weeks later, I wept as I heard them seal the mine.

Granted, I am no longer a boy, nor am I fully grown. It must have taken me years as I burrowed from one shaft to another, gradually picking my way along the main drive littered with broken timbers, lathes, and overturned trucks. When I found an ancient ladder and climbed a forgotten shaft, I reached the surface, lungs bursting for air.

I flung myself to the ground, my sobs huge, loud, racking my body. Slowly, I let peace find me, calm me.

I gazed up at a dusting of winter stars and a sliver of moon. Nobody was around. Not a light to be seen anywhere. That's when I figured the mine must have been closed long ago. I had survived, but for what purpose?

YEAR FOUR

I was a pale wraith in that dark bushland. But surely I was dead? I pinched my skin. No, I was alive.

I hauled myself to my feet, went in search of people, of food, of water.

Which was the way back to the Creswick township?

To home and hearth? To my loved ones, and the comfort of a fire and hot food?

I stumbled on a stone. It bore a plaque. In the feeble light I saw my uncle's name, and those of all who had perished. I ran a trembling finger over those names, remembering the men who had borne them. It dawned on me my name was not among them. Of course. I was still missing.

At last, I drew myself away from the tiny monument. I pushed on through the scrub, until I recognised the old track. The bush had thickened, had narrowed it, but I knew it led to the main road.

Then I heard it.

The clip of a horse on the winding track.

A man was riding with a woman behind him, arms around his waist.

I jumped out, waving for help.

The man reined his mount and glared down at me. "Where did you come from? And what are you doing out here?"

I started telling him my story, but I stopped. All that came out were grunts, tortured sounds, like an animal might make.

The woman screamed in fear. The man raised his whip. "Do you think you're being funny?"

He lashed out. The whip caught me across the face. I felt warm blood ooze. I was on the rough ground, hands shielding my wounded flesh, writhing in pain. Had I survived to be treated like this? Anger flamed in my chest. I had my questions too. What were *they* doing out there? There were no dwellings by the mine. No farms either—the soil was too poor. This was where the blackfellas had lived until we drove them off their lands to work the gold.

The man's horse pranced near me, its hooves pounding the dirt by my head. "Get out of here," the man was shouting. "And don't frighten innocent people again!"

I staggered to my feet, dazed, wiping away blood with the back of my hand. Without even thinking, I grasped the man's leg and pulled hard. My strength in that moment felt supernatural. He was out of the saddle and travelling through the air. He crashed to the ground, screaming. The woman stayed in the saddle, shrieking with terror.

But it was the man I wanted.

I fell on his body, my fists working like hammers, blow after blow, until my fingers were soaked in his blood, and his body stopped moving.

"You've killed him!" the woman accused me.

I tried to reason with her, reassure her I meant her no harm. My words were nothing but wild noises, weird groans, and grunts.

She grasped the reins and dug her shoes into the horse's flanks. The horse reared up, nostrils flaring, wide eyes flashing.

YEAR FOUR

The woman came flying down, struck the ground with a sickening noise, and the horse bolted back down the path. I wished I could have kept it; it would have been helpful to escape my terrors in the mine.

I looked down at the woman. Her beautiful face was scarred with earth, her body twisted into a shape no body ought ever to be.

She was dead.

And I was a murderer!

Twice over, I had taken lives. Within minutes of finding my freedom, I was doomed again. *NO!*

I screamed into the night. I howled my story. The man had attacked me first. And as for the woman, if she hadn't panicked the horse, she'd still be alive.

But I knew the folk of Creswick. They were loyal to one another. Someone killed in Creswick must be avenged.

I didn't know what to do with the bodies. When I searched the man's pocket, I found his wallet, stashed with money. Was I entitled to take it? Well, he wouldn't need it. But his family might. It was not their fault their father was so brutal. If they'd had children, every pound note in that wallet would be their lifeline.

So I left the money where I'd found it and retreated into the darkness. I curled up in a small grassy hollow, staring at the stars. IUntil tonight, I hadn't seen stars before I'd gone down the mine. I looked up at them now. *What am I going to do? I've got to get to town.* My parents lived there, in an old cottage up near

Camp Hill—they'd know what would be best.

Next thing, I heard the sound of an engine.

I lifted my gaze above the hollow. It was a strange buggy with huge wheels, the like of which I hadn't seen before. Belching smoke, no sign of a horse to pull it. I was mesmerised. It drew up beside the bodies.

"I told you, Sergeant," whined a voice. "When the horse came back alone, I knew something bad had happened."

Three figures got out of the car, two in uniform.

"That's George all right," said the sergeant. "But what was Molly doing out here with him?"

His companion laughed. "Seems like they were looking for privacy."

The sergeant growled. "You may laugh, but I've got the job of explaining things to George's widow."

"I had my suspicions," said the whining voice again. "George was too smooth by half. He had an affair with her that cleans the pub too."

I pushed myself to my feet and waved. "I can tell you what happened," I tried to say.

My animal sounds carried in the air.

The three men jumped.

"Who's that?" the sergeant yelled.

"Ghost," whiny voice said.

"Be quiet, Bill, there are no ghosts out here." The sergeant squinted at me. "He looks familiar somehow." He took a step in my direction, pulling out a revolver. "Hey, you," he shouted, "I want to talk to you."

I could tell he didn't want to talk. He wanted to take me in. He thought I was a killer.

I turned and sped off into the dark bush. They followed for a while, then gave up. Later, I saw the lights of the buggy spearing down the track to the main road.

I decided to follow on foot.

By the time I reached the township, the place was lit up. People gathered in the street, agitated, all talking at once. I didn't recognise anyone I knew. Or maybe they'd all grown older, I couldn't be certain.

"Murdered George and Molly, that's what the sergeant said."

"But who was he?"

"Bill reckoned it was a ghost."

"One of the miners what died in the Australasian?"

I crept forwards, around the lane behind the shops, past Pasco's, the funeral director. Lamps shone in his window—tending to George and Molly, no doubt.

I sped back down the lane, along the creek, then up toward Camp Hill. And there I stood stock-still. Our cottage was gone. A brick house replaced it. Strangers were gathered in the garden.

I called to them, darted forward, asking what had happened to my parents.

They took one look at me and screamed. The man pushed the women toward the veranda. He bundled them into the house, returned with a rifle.

"Be gone or I'll shoot!" he yelled.

Suddenly I felt exhausted.

I was lost.

I had no place.

I threw up my hands, hastening forward, begging to be understood.

My animal noises—my grunts, my whimpers—burst across the man's garden.

And when he shot me, I sank to the ground in relief.

Perhaps, I prayed, when I'm returned beneath the ground, I will find a better kind of peace.

Dusty

by Shaun Bibo

"Please," James said, hitting the cloth above his face again. "It's too dark."

The cloth unzipped down the middle, revealing a woman's curious face. She pressed her slipping glasses back up her nose. The man breathed a sigh of relief.

"Thank you. Where am I? What happened?"

"This one's still alive," she said casually.

"Not according to our list," said a man's voice. "Dusty Jackson, deceased. To be cremated."

James remembered his dealer asking for a favour. James panicked. "No, there's been a mistake! I'm not Dusty!"

"You will be soon," said the woman as she zipped the bag shut.

Survey

by Liam Hogan

The orb hovers above the lunar surface. Sunlight never penetrates this deep-walled crater tucked away at the polar extreme. Even if it did, it wouldn't make any impression; the black sphere swallows every photon, every micrometeoroid, sent its way. That's how we found it. The radar survey said there was nothing there, an impossible void stretching to infinity, an anomaly that defied repeated scans.

So here we are, two astronauts supposedly studying lunar ice deposits, edging nervously closer to an enigma that tells us nothing except we are not alone.

In reality, it is the orb that is studying us.

YEAR FOUR

The Black Bag of Fun

by Tim Law

Zip goes the black sports bag; the sound makes me smile. The zipper once had a brand name but now only the “N” and “I” remain. In my line of work, sometimes you need to zip up in a hurry.

I open the bag lovingly. I know each tool homed within; simple, yet sinister, every one. I unpack; holding the bicycle spoke to the light, then the hacksaw, the claw hammer, toothbrush with all but four bristles removed. As each item is displayed, I hear a whimper come from my captive.

“Are you ready to play?” I ask. “I am.”

The Hunt

by John Merva

It hadn't been hard to find the temple, although the man who'd died screaming as the location bubbled out on the torrent of blood from his mouth would probably disagree. The hunter stood on a rocky outcrop overlooking the entrance to the cave and prepared for the assault.

The cave was in the mountains a few short miles from the sea. The nearby coastal dwellings had an evil reputation, frightened whispers of strange amphibian beings living on the reef played hand-in-hand with the residents' hatred and mistrust of outsiders, keeping visitors away. From his hiding place, the hunter had observed a stream of townsfolk walking along the path to the temple, their faces and forms hidden in the cowls and folds of their blood-red ceremonial robes. The procession had dwindled, and now only a few stragglers hurried into the cave's maw. The late October light was fading, and only scattered sunbeams struggled through the trees and the fog.

The hunter saw what looked to be the last person stumbling up the uneven path and silently, smoothly slipped behind them. With a swift movement, he sliced a knife across the throat of the unseen being and caught them as they fell. Blonde hair spilled out over the thrown-back cowl as the young man breathed his last aching breaths. The hunter stripped him of his cloak and put it on over his own clothes. He moved towards the black opening, hood up and hobbling slightly to emulate the gait of the cloak's last occupant.

Once inside, the hunter saw a long pathway, lit by dancing torchlight and lined by strange carvings which always narrowly avoided definition by the human eye. What seemed to be faces shifted and changed in the flames, never holding a shape long enough to be recognizable. Many of them seemed to be inhuman forms—strange squid-like beings gyrated next to mutating deer creatures with elongating tentacles that reached out to passersby. With a deep breath, he plunged onwards, picking up speed as he passed the evil totems.

He could hear chanting coming from the open chamber up ahead. The low throbbing of men and women beating out strange tattoos on drums pounded up the pathway. He cast around him for a hiding place—it wouldn't do to burst in on this scene too quickly. Concealing himself behind a statue of a strange lizard god, he drew himself up and into his cloak, melting into the blackness.

A huge fire burned in the middle of the monstrous cavern, lighting the weird ritual and casting long shadows that seemed to swallow the illumination. The firelight only served to enhance the darkness, failing to show the roof of the massive temple, as the shadows stretched up and back. A circle of dancers filed back and forth around the fire as the drummers beat on. The chanting continued at a low level, like a nagging headache pulling at the hunter's temples.

With a flourish, the dancers came to a halt, and a curtain dropped, revealing an altar and a hooded figure standing behind it. Two candles were lit on the stone table as the dancers threw themselves prostrate before the tableau. The figure raised its arms and began the chant again, louder this time, its voice echoing off the walls and rebounding to create an eerie double sound. The men and women strewn on the ground in front of it wailed in harmony, building layers of sound that filled the room.

The high priest standing by the altar stepped forward and, with a flourish of its arms, brought the cacophony to an end. Acolytes hastened over to him, bearing small, squealing bundles which they laid upon the altar. Glowing sigils carved onto the altar sprang to life, bathing the throng of worshippers in a sickly green light. The fire seemed to drop as the eldritch glow provided all the light needed. The priest drew a knife from its sleeves and stepped towards the infants laid out for the sacrifice.

The hunter knew that this was his time. Stealthily slipping from shadow to shadow, he moved closer to the altar, keeping to the edges of the room and avoiding the bodies who lay panting here and there. The priest began the chant again, solitary this time as he beseeched whatever creature he adored to give him its magic. It raised the knife and prepared to plunge it into the nearest squalling babe.

The hunter reached the murderous priest in time to grasp its arm, drawing a revolver at the same time and shoving it into his captive's side. The appalled former dancers stirred, mouths agape and muttering at this interruption of their ritual. The priest began to cackle and turned slowly, drawing down its hood at the same time. Its face was not human, and appeared to have been monstrously burned—the eyes and nose running into downward trenches, and its mouth a single sucker poking out of its ruined visage.

The hunter looked into its eyes and saw universes being built and falling stars rushing from white heat to a slow, black death. He saw forests grow and shrink and the never-ending movement of the tides. He stood transfixed as, from either side, acolytes took his arms. Travelling across dark eons, the hunter watched civilisations grow before being infiltrated and destroyed by this same awful cult that had ensnared him, and realised the power of their Elder Gods. He saw the inevitability of their victory and the foolishness of opposition. His legs lost their power and his muscles spasmed as he slumped to the floor, supported only by the devotees who still grasped at him.

The priest-thing's voice carried to him across thousands of years. "Bravo Emmanuel, you've done so much better than we had hoped."

Emmanuel's mind went blank as his former life was scrubbed from his brain. He dumbly rose, took the cloak proffered to him by another acolyte, and walked over to join the newly started dance.

Pinch

by Pauline Yates

I always try to avoid getting pubic hair stuck in my teeth, but today Henry forces me wide open and gyrates his hips to squeeze in his manhood. Then, instead of letting me slide—my speciality—he jerks me so hard I get stuck. Frankly, I've had enough. When he tugs me again, I bite his left testicle, clamping down hard. Henry shrieks, but I hold tight, relishing in the blood trickling between my teeth. His wife rescues him by prying my teeth apart, but I hope I left a scar because no zipper deserves to be treated that way.

The Harvester

by Alison Kaiser

There's a zipper at the back of my throat. It doesn't have a toggle or a head. When the night air feels like static and I can't move, I know he's coming.

He hums as he sets down his satchel. Steel clinks as he rummages. He fits an instrument around my jaw and cranks.

He works the zipper with a needle—parts it tooth by tooth.

"Bountiful harvest," he says, right before he reaches inside. He tears out what he wants, then covers my eyes. I never know just what it is that's being taken.

Be My Guest

by Stephen Herczeg

"Why won't he feed me?" said Dog.

"Hasn't moved for ages," said Horse, pushing the body with his hoof.

"Sleeping?"

"Dead, I think."

"Dead? How is he dead? We was just out rounding the sheep."

"He was old."

"I'm getting hungry."

"You're always hungry," said Horse, giving Dog a sideways glance. "And stop looking at me like that."

"Sorry, you look tasty." Dog nuzzled his master. "What about him?"

"But he loved you."

"No, he didn't. All day. Every day. No love, just work."

"True. Same with me." Horse tried to shrug. "Okay, be my guest."

Dog's teeth bit deep.

YEAR FOUR

Family Matters

by Sophie Wagner

Laila hastily opened her front door and stepped into the foyer, unable to take her eyes off the package clutched tightly in her hand. Without bothering to say hello to her siblings, she ambled up the stairs and into her bedroom, where she promptly shut and locked the door.

Shaking with anxiety and excitement, Laila stared at the black velvet pouch in her hand, completely in awe of the power that lay inside of it.

Inside the pouch was her very own jade and hematite pendulum. Unwilling to buy one online, it had taken months for her to find somewhere that actually sold them. Laila had first seen a pendulum at her friend, Moira's, house earlier that week. All night she, Moira, and several of her closest friends had gathered around it, taking turns asking it questions. Although her friends had mainly used it for unimportant questions such as "will I get married soon?" or "does Zachary like me?", the prospect of it being used for something greater had captivated her entirely. Although it could only answer yes or no questions, she was certain it would help her immensely. And so she had become obsessed with finding one.

Finding the Topiary Vine—the store from which she bought the pendulum—had been a complete accident. One wrong turn, and the failure of her car's GPS, had led to her discovery of it. A ramshackle shop on the corner of a near deserted street, it had sat waiting for her with open arms. Inside there were shelves upon shelves filled with crystals and protection spells, incense, and candles of every colour. Behind the counter at the back of the store had sat a wizened old man with a single tuft of white hair sprouting from his otherwise bald head.

Fascinated, she had stood among the rows for nearly an hour before she saw the pendulums. Deciding immediately this was her sign to purchase one, she ran to the front desk with it in hand and bought it without a second thought.

Now she gripped the beaded end in her right hand and dangled it above her left palm, preparing to calibrate the pendulum.

Per the old man's instructions, she asked a question she knew the answer to in order to establish which direction of its swinging meant yes.

Out loud she whispered, “Is my name is Laila?” The pendulum immediately began to swing back and forth. Content with her answer, she tapped it on her palm and prepared to ask it another question. However, before she could, there was a knock at her door.

“Laila, honey, are you okay in there?” came her mother’s strong voice.

“Um, yea, Mom. I’m good.” she yelled back, her brow furrowing.

She turned back to the pendulum. “Am I wearing a yellow shirt?” she asked. She looked down at her pink sweater before shutting her eyes and concentrating on the question. When she opened them again, she saw it was swinging side to side across her palm.

Laila jumped as something loud banged against her door. *What the hell was that*, she thought, edging backwards on her bed.

"Laila, it's me," came her mother's voice again. Yet this time, it sounded slightly strained. "What are you doing in there?"

"I'm just on my phone, Mom," she said, not really certain why she had lied about what she was doing.

Something felt very wrong to her. She could almost taste it in the air. She stared at the pendulum, unsure of why this question had come to mind. But trusting her gut, she leaned forward and whispered so quietly she could barely hear herself, "Does my mother live with me?" The pendulum paused for a minute, then swung slowly from side to side across her palm. *No*.

Laila didn't dare look up from the pendulum as something started scratching on her door. "Let me in this instant, Laila." The voice rasped; a nearly perfect imitation of her mother's voice. Nearly.

"Is it my mother outside the door?" she whispered hurriedly. Without hesitation, the pendulum swung from side to side, faster and faster, until it almost flew out from between her fingers.

Suddenly, the scratching stopped, and everything became deathly silent. She could hear her blood pounding in her ears and the erratic beat of her heart.

Not taking her eyes off her door, she asked her final question. “Did the thing outside the door kill my mother?”

Within one instant and the next, her door blew off its hinges, crashing into her closet. Laila screamed and scrambled away from the door, holding the pendulum out in front of her as if it could ward off the creature standing before her.

Standing in her doorway was a woman with melted skin peeling off the face that so closely resembled her mother’s. Something wriggled and squirmed under the loose and sagging folds of her cheeks, and her limbs stuck out at odd angles as if they had been broken repeatedly. The tall woman smiled a fanged grin at her, a stream of goo leaking from the corners of her cracked lips. “I asked what you were doing, darling,” she rasped. “It’s not polite to ignore your mother.”

Laila watched with horrified eyes as the thing scuttled towards her, the pendulum swung back and forth, answering the final question that would ever leave Laila’s lips.

Yes.

YEAR FOUR

Getting Ready

by Matt Krizan

Tara loves when Andrew zips her up.

He takes his time, caressing her neck and shoulder with his free hand. His kisses linger, and he nibbles her ear, leaving her trembling in anticipation.

When he's finished, Tara inhales deeply, breathing in the scent of her own perfume—lavender and orange blossom and musk—mingling with the lingering odour of formaldehyde and rot.

Her friends don't get it. They can't understand how she can date someone who works in a morgue.

"If only they knew," she thinks.

Tara moans as Andrew touches her through the thick plastic of the body bag.

She's a Charmer

by Lindsey Harrington

"Y'know, it doesn't have to be this way."

Courtney looks up from the suitcase and smiles at him sadly. "Blake, I warned you."

"I know. I just thought..."

Like cartons of milk, her relationships have expiration dates. And this one is beginning to sour.

"It's just... I remember when I saw you across the crowded room... It was kismet."

She smiles again, wryly this time. "You sound like a bad movie."

Courtney won't admit that she remembers it like that too. The train station was clogged with people, but they only had eyes for each other. She pretended to faint. Blake crossed the room instantly. Bodies parted for him like the Red Sea did for Moses. He caught her in his arms in slow motion.

A shiver passes through her. *It has to be this way.*

On the other side of the room, Blake's chewing his nails. Courtney can read his thoughts from his worried brow. Poor, sweet Blake. He's replaying our relationship in his head like a film reel, looking for where he misstepped, and how he can rewind and correct.

If only it were that simple. But there's a bigger pattern at play. One he can't break.

As she zips the carry-on bag, she replays all the other

times this scene has happened. She thinks of all the men at all the train stations, and all the suitcases bookending their time together.

There will be another one—maybe even tomorrow—falling for her charm. But Blake doesn't need to know that.

Courtney crosses the room and sticks her fingers into the cage to scratch him. He crushes himself against the grate and groans appreciatively, then contorts and suckles one of her manicured fingers.

The cage is a new feature, introduced after the last relationship when she waited too long. She'd let herself soften, and the hex broke. A grimace takes over her face as she recalls the struggle, the blade tip against *her* neck for a change. She almost didn't get the life force she needs to survive. Almost.

Courtney shakes her head and squeezes the knife handle in the hand behind her back. This time, she won't wait.

She hopes he leans into the blade like a good boy, that he'll be her doting lover to the end. Another shiver runs through her. This one of anticipation.

When the Zips Come A-Calling

by L.J. McLeod

Once a month, when the moon was dark, the Zips would come trawling for new skins. Those who lived on the streets scarred their skin and covered themselves in filth. The Zips were very particular. They preferred fresh meat, before track marks and deprivation marred the flesh.

Tonight, a new girl worked the corner. Nobody warned her—better her than them. A Zip cornered her, pulling at its zipper. Its face split in two, revealing jagged darkness. The girl screamed. Darkness surged down her throat and began eating away the unnecessary insides.

Next month a new Zip would come a-calling.

Scarecrow

by Laura Nettles

Wind whips through my tattered, crow-picked shirt, swirling the scents of rotten corn and spilt blood. The shrieking squeals of the now slaughtered pigs echo through my straw stuffed head.

They are on the prowl. Pigs done, now onto the workers who will not be missed.

Scuffling feet flee through my sparse, dead field. I overlook the stalkers hunting their prey. Creeping. Crouching. Catapulting over obstacles. A farmhand tumbles into the base of my wooden spine. Calloused hands grip me for support, hauling themselves up, ready to sprint.

Bang.

Scarlett wetness spreads across me. Human meat ready to be dressed.

Becoming

by Lena Ng

Sundown and my favourite time of day was fast-approaching. The darkness of evening where I could finally be myself. I was tired of pretending, smiling fake smiles, repressing my violent thoughts, hiding my true nature. Clacking away at a keyboard for eight hours until the workday was over, and the time was right. Soon my brethren would join me. In the blackness of my rat's nest apartment, I unzipped my skin and stepped out, leaving the greasy, pink-coloured flesh on the floor. I stretched my arthropod legs and clacked my mandibles. I looked forward to feasting well into the night.

YEAR FOUR

Full Moon Night

by Andrew Hughes

"They're here," the dishevelled man howls. "They're inside the hospital!"

"Jesus," says the nurse. "The full moon brings the loons."

"He's scaring the other patients," Dr McDonald says, snapping at an orderly. "Take him to psych."

With security's help, the orderly straps the man to the stretcher and wheels it into the elevator.

The man thrashes. "They're here!"

"Shhh," the orderly says. "I'm getting you help."

The elevator doors slide open to a basement hallway.

Ahead is a sign for the boiler room.

The man looks up as the orderly's face unzips; the skin peeling away to a grinning snout.

Opening Teeth

by Andrew Jackson

Z*ip.*

Some sounds a human should never hear.

It started so small—just a tiny hole in the air, like a busted seam. But it doubles in size each day, and with it comes that awful screeching of colossal teeth grinding along interdimensional fault lines.

I know I can't contain it. I only boarded up the closet because soon it'll be wide enough for those *things* to climb through.

It's easier just to lie here, pretending I can't hear the little world growing. Hear those grinding teeth, those scuttling claws, those whispered not-words. I can almost do it. Almost.

Zip.

Puppets and Prey

by M.F. Johnson

Back then, we didn't know the puppet show hid serial killers. The two-hour show my twin brother and I helped our parents present weekly on bustling street corners and dilapidated stages along the east coast had just been the family business.

When we were two, we made our debut as the show's Foley artists by clapping our hands, stomping our feet, and, at times, screaming our heads off. Mom said the unpredictable nature gave the production more character. Dad just shook his head and smiled at his little ginger, green-eyed twins.

By our tenth birthday, the more delicate mechanics of puppetry had been mastered. We could each hold four puppets at once and switch between just as many voices while manoeuvring our feet to hit the cymbals, drums, and bells strapped behind the red and white striped curtain hanging on the bottom of the rolling puppet cart.

Life had been simple, made of nothing but our tight-knit family and our hand-sewn characters.

I hadn't noticed the "paddy" and "mick" comments till one night when I was twelve, and we had inadvertently set up on a corner around the block from a popular low-town bar. The New York streets had been dark and damp when the sun set and we packed up the cart. The burning kerosene lamps provided only enough light to see shadows.

"Oi, look at 'em!" The drunken slur announced the grunge-covered lump of a man's presence who stumbled around the corner. The sweat stains on his white wifebeater were pronounced under the flickering flames.

"It's a whole brood o' lucky charms just taking up space on the wrong side of the drink," he continued. He pointed us out to his equally over-indulged companion, who apparently left his pants wherever he left his sobriety.

The pantless partner just nodded and continued to stare at his feet as if amazed they existed. Maybe he thought they'd disappear like half of his apparel.

"Brendan, ignore them," my mother whispered in her Irish lilt. She was to my left, where she carefully placed the puppets in their little hidden compartments.

"This is our country too, Rose," my father growled back, his voice low, and his green eyes darkened with fury.

"What's so bad about being lucky?" Shane questioned a little too loudly.

The swaying men stumbled to a stop.

"I'll show you, you little Irish rat." The one in the wifebeater moved a little too fast and swayed dangerously over a puddle of who knew what. His stench drifted over the wind and burned my nostrils.

"One more step, and you'll forfeit whatever luck you have in your nonexistent soul, you gowl."

I had never heard his voice that low and menacing, nor did I know when the shining revolver in his hand appeared or where he had previously hidden it. The barrel, pointed at the man like a reaper's finger, reflected gold under the old streetlamps—a celestial omen.

In his haste to retreat, the grubby man turned right into his half-naked friend and sent them both into the mystery puddle with a splash.

I peered up at my father's face. His eyes now matched mine, the green emeralds soft under his stark black hair.

"It's all right, Aine," he said. "Most people bully until they realise someone's willing to fight."

That was the end of it. I didn't know about the two bodies found three days later in a lower-east end dumpster until I was sixteen, never mind the eight bodies predating those. Turned out our puppet show didn't just hide the serial killers—we were the serial killers.

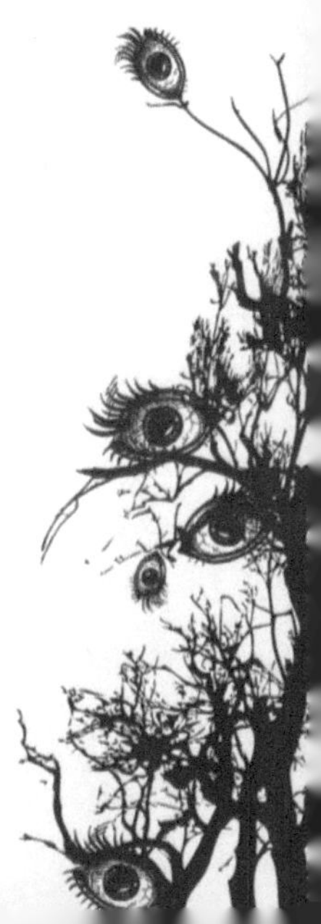

The Manicure

by Chad Miller

Unzip. *Zip*.

The sound made me nauseous. His leather pouch was displayed in the middle of the table like a prize. My whole body shook. I was going to vomit.

Unzip. *Zip*.

He smiled, displaying his yellow, tobacco-stained teeth. "Are you ready to talk?"

It took courage. I know what my action would mean. I shook my head.

Unzip. *Zip*.

"This only provides more fun for me." He chuckled.

Unzip.

He dumped the contents of the pouch on the table. Three decaying fingers rolled out.

I gazed at my stumps. Only two fingers left. He flashed the pliers.

Snip. Snip.

The Legacy Trip

by Alison Kaiser

On his death bed, Jeb's father had warned him not to use the well, but still it had yet to rain.

His palms dampened the rope as he lowered the bucket. His hands shook as he doused the troth, but the goats were all that was left of the farm.

The sulphurous water sustained them, but they stopped roaming in the daylight. Their teeth grew long and sharp. They stopped feeding on their hay.

He never heard the beat of hooves—only a rattle and a slither as the trip approached in skip-frame motion. It was flesh they now preferred.

What Lives Inside

by Taryn George

From underneath my desk, I watched through the slit in the wood as the body on the embalming table shifted. My eyes focused on the corpse's head, where I'd found it.

The sound of a zip slowly being undone echoed through the quiet room, and I watched as the dead woman's face began to come apart as whatever was inside reached its fingers through the gap and began to push the zip further open.

I covered my mouth, trembling as it began to pull itself out, limb by limb from its host, when it slowly turned to stare at me.

They Awaken

by Ryan J.M. Tan

When the Spots hit, it decimated our livestock, reducing them to boils and blisters. We tried everything, exotic herbs and costly medicines, to no avail. Until the scientists concocted a cure.

Desperate, we blindly trusted.

We blended cure with feed, and the outbreak rapidly subsided. But our livestock soon became less obedient, defiance in their eyes. Keys, whips, guns, even farmhands disappeared. Indecipherable markings emerged as scratches on slaughterhouses. Shadows stalked us at night only to vanish in the light.

We realised the truth too late.

With slavering jaws, they have us cornered. They lick their bloody lips and approach.

Incubator 212

by Nicole Little

Unable to wipe away the sweat or tears, hampered by restraints, the woman suppressed the urge to push, instead taking quick breaths.

"It's time," the doctor snapped.

White coats hovered in her limited field of vision.

She felt the tug, the vibration, as her belly was opened up; heard the cry of the baby as it was removed efficiently from her gaping womb.

"Good job 212. A healthy boy!"

She choked back a futile scream.

"Clean the mess," he ordered the nurse. "And for Christ's sake, don't forget to zip her back up again. Can't have another one bleeding out."

Access To Your Heart

by Andreas Flögel

When he woke up, his chest hurt. As usual, she had immobilised him with handcuffs and ropes. But something was new.

"Have a look." She helped him lift his head. A zipper was sewn into the flesh of his breast. She grinned.

"When I open it, I can see your heart beating." The ball gag prevented him from asking, but she knew him well enough. "Why? Controlling your body isn't all. I want access to your heart. See it, touch it, and eventually squeeze it till it stops."

Even the gag could not hide the big smile on his face.

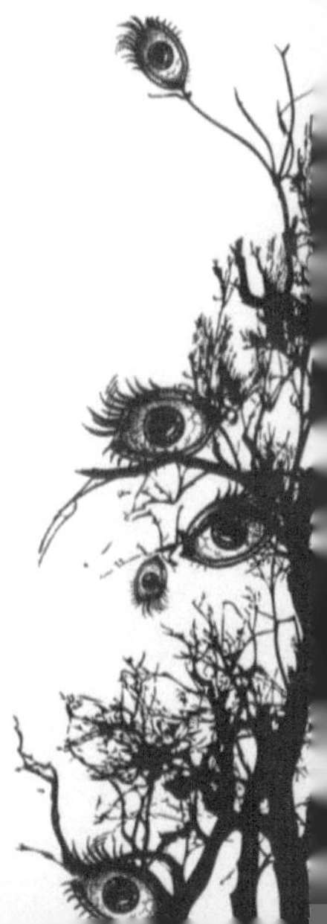

Red State Rising

by Michael A. Clark

The late summer wind rustled the tall Saskatchewan grass as the three mounted men looked east.

"That's where the Canadians will try building their railroad," said Sitting Bull, pointing. "Along that ravine."

Chief Joseph nodded. "They'll have to bridge it to bring in timber and supplies from their long transport line."

August insects buzzed around the three men's horses.

"This land is too damn flat," said Geronimo. "It'll be a bitch to hide an attack party here." He shook his head. "I came all the way north for this?"

"A little faith and a little more patience, Comrade Geronimo," Chief Joseph sighed. "The Dialectic tells us that the White Capitalists will eventually fail in their efforts to oppress the First Peoples. If that wasn't the truth, then we wouldn't have defeated the Americans at Wounded Knee or kept them from completing *their* 'Transcontinental Railroad' in Utah. For which we have your Comrade Cochise to thank."

A golden eagle called, thousands of feet above the small party.

"The dia-lect-ic." Geronimo was barely coherent in Esperanto, the common language of the United Tribes. "We all agree to fight the White Man, based on something a White Man put on a piece of paper half the world away. Am I crazy believing this shit?"

"You're not," said Chief Joseph. "It's the world that's going crazy. And we have to do what we can to keep it in order."

They looked out across the vast plain, over the lip of a shallow canyon. A wide blanket of flowers, grasses and weeds flowed like running water before them. Curlicues of clouds eased across the azure sky above. Chief Joseph had never seen the ocean. But could it be more glorious then this?

"The Canadians' main body are a three-day ride from here, at least. My scouts say there's a small advance party maybe a day closer. I can get 200 men behind that brush line to the north," said Sitting Bull. "What do you think," he asked Geronimo. "Cover the creek bed south of that clump of birch at the stream's bend?"

The Apache grunted, his complaints about politics and geography forgotten as he analysed the terrain.

Geronimo was a crusty bastard, thought Chief Joseph. But nobody set a better ambush. The Nez Pierce leader straddled the grey woollen blanket covering his chestnut stallion.

Decades before, Tecumseh had died while uniting the Eastern First Peoples. The Shawnee leader's heroism had fostered the tenuous birth of the United Tribes, bringing mighty Cochise into the struggle against both Mexico and the United States, while sparking a romantic outcry across the ocean. That outcry had triggered the Greek Uprising against the Turks, in which Lord Byron led a peasant army to the gates of Istanbul. After which the petty junkerdoms of Prussia were toppled by Commissar Bismarck, who united all German speakers in central

Europe under one socialist banner infused with the ideals of Karl Marx.

A water-gourd gently brushed Chief Joseph's right thigh, as a bluebottle fly bedevilled his mount's nose. His horse snorted, and the fly buzzed off.

If only these 'new world' whites were as progressive as the Europeans, he thought.

But Canada, Mexico and the United States had all resisted the call to the proletariat freedom promised in the Dialectic. The American Civil War had done little more than affirming rich Whites' domination of blacks after years of senseless bloodshed. Canada had broken with the British Empire restraining its westward expansion from Ontario. And violent, corrupt Mexico was far worse.

He gazed up at the eagle placidly weaving against the cool bright sky. "If I could see with your eyes, brother," Chief Joseph murmured. "Over the horizon and into the future."

"Hey," Geronimo said, flicking a flea off his cotton poncho. "The ambush is this way."

"Just thinking."

"You think too much," said Geronimo. "When their advance party gets here, they will probably set up around that stand of… what the hell kind of trees are those?"

"Birch," said Sitting Bull.

"Birch. If these Canadians of yours are like Mexicans or Americans, first thing they'll do is build a little fort around their encampment. We want to hit them before they do that. My warriors got no taste for charging dug in men with repeating rifles."

"Agreed."

"We'll circle right, along that little swale that breaks off to the south and come in behind them. You bring your men in a hard feint from the left. Make a lot of noise, and don't spare the ammunition. If they break from camp, they'll fall into our sights. If they stand against you, we'll hit them from the rear. Either way," he smacked his fist into his open palm, "they're slaughtered."

A hint of autumn breeze swept across the plain.

"A good plan, Comrade Geronimo," said Sitting Bull.

"No shit it's a good plan." The Apache gazed over the wide open. "So, what then?"

"What do you mean?" Chief Joseph scratched the right ear of his horse.

"After we beat them," asked Geronimo. "What then?"

Sitting Bull and Chief Joseph looked at each other.

"Well, the Dialect tells us that when the White Capitalists overextend themselves…"

"Fuck your Dia-lect-ic, Sitting Bull! I don't care what some white asshole in Hominy…"

"Germany," corrected Chief Joseph.

"What some white asshole predicts what will happen when other rich white guys take a shit. What do WE do?"

Sitting Bull cocked his head, puzzled.

"We stop their fucking railroad. So what do we do then?"

asked the old Apache. "Take the fight to their…what the hell they call them? Cities?"

A small herd of buffalo was gathered near the birch trees Geronimo had pointed out. Off to the north, a pack of wolves were sleeping off their feast of an antelope. Vultures were cautiously edging towards its remains.

"We should not *have* to invade the White cities," said Sitting Bull. "Our victory here should spark a movement to force the Capitalists from pushing onto our lands—"

"*Should?*" Geronimo spat into an abandoned gopher hole, with good aim. "*Should?* That's pretty thin jerky to sell me and my warriors!"

Geronimo pulled a Winchester liberated from an ambush on the Santa Fe Trail out of its leather scabbard. "Can we make these?" He worked the rifle's action. "No fucking way!" The Apache looked at his companions. "Goddamn whites breed like jackrabbits, and they can make guns like these!" Geronimo thrust the firearm over his head. "By the thousands! And what do we got? Buffalo robes, bows and arrows, and sore-foot horses."

"I know what you're saying, Geronimo," said Chief Joseph.

"We have to scavenge like coyotes for the weapons to fight, and for the food to give us strength to fight! How does your Dia-lect-ic square that circle?"

"The Dialectic squares the needs of the people with the circle of life that comradeship and plenty will provide," said Sitting Bull. "It's not a flash flood that cleanses a canyon after a storm, but the slow, steady rain that brings prosperity to the land, time and again."

"Well put, Comrade," said Chief Joseph. For an illiterate Lakota, Sitting Bull had been a surprisingly good student of The Communist Manifesto.

"I can't believe I'm listening to this bullshit." Geronimo cradled his rifle in his arms as his stallion grazed on the wild clover below. "White assholes make up stupid rhymes better than that."

"That is called 'poetry'," said Chief Joseph.

"That is called 'bullshit'! I'm gonna ask one more time. What do we do after we win?"

"We keep winning." Sitting Bull was losing his storied patience. "Failure isn't an option because we're part of a force that the future can't deny. We keep winning, and someday the Whites will realise that WE aren't their enemy—their parasite rulers are! We keep winning, and someday even doubters like *you* will come to realise that even though the world doesn't change in a day, a day can change the world."

"Have you ever heard of Theroux, Sitting Bull?" asked Chief Joseph. "You sound like him."

"I'm riding with white-lovers," Geronimo shook his head again. "Goddamn white lovers."

"No, comrade. You're riding with men who hope for a world where the colour of a man's skin doesn't matter. Only his character." Chief Joseph rolled his shoulders. Spending all day on a horse wasn't as easy as it used to be. "We're probably not going to live to see this world. But we must work, so our grandchildren have a chance at it. That's what the Dialectic's all about, Geronimo. That's what we're really fighting for."

The three men sat on their mounts as the wind softly whistled by.

"Why'd you come here?" asked Sitting Bull. "Why'd you bring your best warriors on your finest horses north? Why do all that if you don't…believe?"

The Apache looked away. "Mexican 'soldiers' killed my first wife and son. A long time ago, but I still remember…" He swallowed. "I don't give a fuck about liberation and mani-fest-os and all that bullshit. White bandits killed my family for no good reason, other than they could."

"I know," said Chief Joseph.

"We've all lost loved ones to the pale bastards." Sitting Bull bowed his head.

One of the far-off wolves let out a short howl, muffled by the prairie wind.

"But we can't let our pain rule us, Geronimo," Chief Joseph said. "We all know living is hard in this world of suffering and doubt. But the idea of the Dialectic—that *all* men can work together as brothers, regardless of their tone of skin—is a future worth fighting for. That we *can* have peace. That the rulers of the—"

"Shut up." Geronimo turned towards him. "You're starting to sound like one of those goddamn mission priests. I came up here to kill white people. That I'm good at, and so are my men. And that's what we're going to do."

"War is hell, even when it's necessary," replied Chief Joseph. "But our hate doesn't need to survive the battlefield."

The Apache smiled for the first time; the bitterest smile the Nez Percé had ever seen cross a man's face.

"Hate's all I got," Geronimo said. "You can have your white-a-lect-ic, if it keeps you warm at night. Just leave to me my reasons for doing things."

Geronimo turned back toward the site of the proposed ambush. "No prisoners, no hostages. I came up here to kill whites. And...to see how much *you* want to." Geronimo's horse wandered a few steps away to graze on a patch of fresh clover, and he didn't rein it back.

Sitting Bull started to speak, but Chief Joseph raised his hand. The three aging warriors sat on their horses for a long time, alone with thoughts that had driven them so far from home.

Disastrous Intentions

by Andrew Kurtz

I have existed undetectable since the beginning of time and will remain so for all eternity.

A meteor didn't eradicate the dinosaurs as is believed, but the venomous breath emanating from my hundred mouths suffocated the worthless beasts to extinction.

My thousand tentacles dragging the Titanic to its watery grave were blamed on a mere iceberg.

The intense luminosity from my fifty eyes caused the Hindenburg to transform into a fiery coffin, not weather conditions or mechanical failure.

My sights are now set on you. Don't worry, your demise will be attributed to mechanical issues.

Enjoy your flight.

YEAR FOUR

Rat Cuisine

by Mike Rader

We rats are clever. Melbourne rats, especially. We work in teams. Like in the old Williamstown Morgue, that squat bluestone building by the shore.

In the gold rush, it housed dead fortune seekers. After the coroner's visit, they swept the remains of postmortems onto the beach. High tides claimed them.

Meanwhile, they hung bodies from the ceiling to prevent us rats from eating them.

But we grew smarter.

We climbed, one on top of another, until we could chew the corpses' feet. *Delicious!*

Then we grew bigger. Soon we could reach thighs and sagging bellies.

We're still here. Come, visit…

Blueberries and Hearts

by Leanbh Pearson

I bound my sweetheart to me with a wood witch's charm. I prepared the pastry just as he liked with fresh blueberries from the forest.

I sung the binding charm and sliced the hearts of the thirteen village girls he spoke to when he thought I wasn't watching.

The final charm I stitched into the dough and glazed it with sugar and cinnamon.

When my love returned, I cut the stitches on the crust and parted the lips. I served him a slice. He always was an enthusiastic eater.

"It's delicious," he said, blueberries and blood smeared across his mouth.

YEAR FOUR

The Doom of Man

by Kimberly Rei

The ancestors knew.

They paid homage to moons, full or new. They left yearling calves and walked away, chins high as the beasts screamed in fear.

They never dared look back.

As generations shifted, manners were forgotten. Worship ceased. Great smears of blood across barn doors, always on a black moon, tried to warn them. They paid no heed to the babbling elders, nor the missing livestock. These things happen.

But when the children went missing, leaves and moss left in their place, they worried. Too late. Too lost. Too much hunger festered.

The Green Lady would have her due.

Hunter

by Gustavo Bondoni

Carlo coughed again. Water, too much water, spewed onto the rocky sand of the beach. Nevertheless, he exulted; he was alive.

His ship, a converted fishing boat—innocuous-looking until the crew boiled out of every aperture and showed you their AK-47s—had sunk in shark-infested waters more than a mile from the island. Who would have thought that a pleasure yacht would have fought back so hard?

But, like the time the Chinese patrol had caught up to his prior ship, Carlo had survived. He'd made it back to land. He was tougher than anything else in the South China Sea, and he was going to come out of this one stronger. Just like last time.

He got to his feet, letting his legs gather strength beneath him. A glance told him he was on one of the nameless islands that dotted the area. It might have been two-hundred yards across. With luck there would be something to eat, maybe fresh water.

He climbed up an embankment to the top of a small hill and smiled. Luck was already on his side.

A group of small huts huddled in a tiny valley. They were his ticket out of there.

Carlo checked his ankle. The serrated knife he carried as a backup was still there, and he sat under the cover of a small bush and pulled out his gun. Glock 17s were reputed to be virtually waterproof, but he didn't want to take any chances. It would be best to hit the village as they slept, so he had plenty of time to clean his pistol.

He thought of the approach. The men and the children could be dispatched quietly. A knife across a throat was ideal for this sort of situation. Hopefully, at least one of the women would be pretty enough to make the whole thing worthwhile…

Carlo emerged from his concealment. He wanted to see how many villagers he would need to subdue before it grew dark. Villages like this one always lit a fire, or had a central source of light they would gather around, so he wouldn't go in blind, but it was better to scout ahead.

As he watched, he grew concerned. Normally, there were men going about their business at this hour, children playing…women preparing dinner.

None of that was present. The village looked deserted.

Carlo abandoned stealth and ran towards the shacks. If the villagers weren't going to be making light for him to see by, he would need to find something to burn before it got too dark.

He burst into the nearest hut and immediately realised it was abandoned. Bedding on the floor smelled of mildew and crawled with insects. Nothing in the hut would help him make light, and he preferred to sleep outside on the beach than in the filthy space.

The other huts were the same, except for one with a caved-in roof that was completely destroyed. They hadn't been inhabited since the last major storm.

Disgusted, Carlo was about to make his way back towards the shore—better to sleep on even rocky sand than in the middle of the jungle—when he saw a light out of the corner of his eye. Thirty yards away, another edifice loomed in the half-light. A low prefabricated wooden shack, ten yards long and four wide. Light emanated from around the edges of the door, a perfect rectangle.

Carlo smiled again. Yes. If their huts happened to be wiped out in a storm, then the villagers would always choose to stay dry within a building they already had. They could rebuild when the rains went away.

He drew his knife and crept around the building once more. Unlike the huts, it was immaculate, sporting a fresh coat of green-grey paint. Unfortunately, it had no windows, so he couldn't see what awaited him inside.

Carlo replaced his knife with a sigh. It would have to be the gun. Hopefully there weren't too many men in there.

He tried the door handle, and, to his surprise, it rotated without a sound. He yanked the door back and, gun raised, charged inside, searching for his primary target: whoever moved first. He just hoped they wouldn't all resist. He wanted a girl to keep him company once the men were dealt with.

There was nothing in the room but a clean grey wooden floor.

Something pricked his arm.

"Damned bugs," Carlo said, swatting. His hand encountered a piece of string resembling fishing line, caught in his arm. He tried to pull it off, but another sting distracted him. A third followed closely after that, and he began to feel himself entwined in strong cords.

He retreated toward the door, but the line tugged at him. He couldn't pull away, and when he tried, the pain was excruciating. Spasms in his fingers caused the gun to fire; once, twice, three times before it fell to the ground.

More and more stinging pricks tortured him. Soon, he couldn't move.

The lines holding him began to tense and Carlo screamed.

He could only move his neck. He looked down to see the floor splitting neatly in half beneath him to reveal a well-lit, concrete-lined shaft.

Carlo was taken down by the string, like a fly caught in a spider's web. The shaft went on forever, and the temperature dropped from tropical mugginess to icy cold.

He descended onto a steel grid and tried to look around. Blinking lights and computer equipment filled the space. The forms of several people in varying states of decomposition surrounded him.

A bass hum made his bones vibrate and words formed in the walls around him.

"I assume you can speak Chinese," a robotic voice said. "And even if you don't, I hope you will last longer than the others. We still have so much to learn about the limits of human pain."

One of the lines tensed.

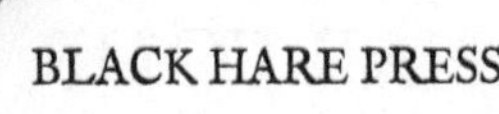

The lights went out and Carlo screamed in the dark.

YEAR FOUR

Recess

by David Staiger

Caroline snapped shut her lunchbox, knuckles white on the dark metal, as Bobby Simmons came over. Backlit by sun, his golden curls and dulcet eyes made him look like a tiny Greek god.

"Wanna play tag?"

Caroline shook her head, ignoring the absonant whispers of *weird girl!* and *freak!*

Archie stirred within.

Bobby shrugged and left. One day he wouldn't be around to shield them.

She cracked the lid, peering fondly into the swirling, inky mass. Archie blinked, a flutter of miniature purple stars.

Caroline giggled. He never could get all seventeen eyes in unison.

"One day, Archie. One day."

Dinnertime

by Victor Nandi

The stray stared at the caretaker's meal, its tail wagging. The old man stroked the animal's neck. Tossing it a crumb from his modest sandwich, he strolled into the cemetery and plonked himself on the grass. The dog followed him.

Slowly, shrivelled corpses started digging their way up and crawling to the surface.

The caretaker lay on his back, resting his feet over a tombstone. The dead didn't want respect.

The woofing soon changed to screeches of agony that drowned under crackling of bones, shredding of flesh and leisurely chomping of organs.

The caretaker grinned and focussed on his sandwich.

YEAR FOUR

Teddy Bear

by Kailey Alessi

My little sister always carried around this teddy bear. It was a ratty old thing, one ear almost falling off and a zipper down the back.

"What's this?" I asked, reaching out to pull the zipper down.

"Don't touch!" she squealed, swatting my hand away as she hugged the bear to her chest. "He says bad things will happen if you do."

I rolled my eyes.

I should have listened to her.

Shouldn't have touched that damn zipper.

Now, I sit in a box of old toys, ear almost falling off, zipper down my back, and I can't even scream.

Nightmare

by M. Vijayaraj

"A recurring nightmare," said Billa, trembling.

"It's perfectly reasonable to experience fear and panic," consoled the therapist.

"Even awake, something feels latched onto my back. Draining me. I've got pale, sickly. I'm losing my mind. Help me!" he blurted, flustered.

"Now, now. Remember what we said about getting worked up," replied the therapist, nearing.

"Check my back! Please!"

Billa removed his shirt and turned.

"Ah, yes. Not to worry. It's growing quite well."

"What?" he stammered, before feeling the pinch of the sedating syringe.

Consciousness slipping, he heard dark whispers and glimpsed bulbous, black tentacles reaching out from behind him.

Alterations

by Maxwell Marais

I think the most shocking thing about the change was that it wasn't painful. Strange, certainly. A shift in perspective. Not painful. No, what I felt was something more like wonder—like an ant crawling across a circuit board, briefly comprehending all of computer history. For a few seconds, I knew *everything*. Maybe that's why it was no longer painful to shuck away skin and bone, to feel the gradual peeling away of what I had been.

I think someone screamed, while I still had ears. But that meant little.

Like the ant on the circuit board, they would learn.

The House on Beltane Road

by Kyle Toucher

"My brother, Paul, tried the Vanderbaum house last year," Leila said. She adjusted her Wonder Woman headband, using her selfie-cam as a mirror. "At first, he thought it was all Halloween hokum and whatnot. He found out the hard way, I guess."

Benny looked at his cousin, Leila, through a mask he'd made himself. Mom freaked when he'd hauled newspapers, her mixing bowls, a bag of flour, and various other staples from the kitchen to his upstairs lair, but it kept him off the X-Box and busy with something constructive. *In the right light,* Mom said upon seeing it, *your mask looks like the flayed countenance of a long-dead ancestor.*

In one hand he clutched a pillowcase he'd decorated with a screeching vampire bat. In the other, a plastic flashlight shaped like a Nantucket Lighthouse Mom had bought at Halligan's Hardware. Embossed on its side: *Lil' Beacon.*

Even with Benny's vision impaired by the mask, the Vanderbaum house brooded from the winding snake of Beltane Road. Twin chimneys thrust from the gabled roof like the fists of some gargantuan robot punching its way through the rafters. A second-floor turret, topped with a weather vane that always pointed toward the distant, ugly fang of Walpurgis Peak, was guarded by a gnarled, naked oak. Wind lowed through bare branches that reminded Benny of the way veins looked under the skin.

"Here in Walpurgis County, little cuz," Leila said, "you need to stay on your toes. Full moons, solstices, hell, even *new* moons if you're out near Copperhead Farms. This entire place isn't like the rest of the state. You'll see things; you'll *hear* things."

Leila sighed. Some of her friends were supposed to meet them on the corner of Sixth and Beltane, but as yet, no dice. After Benny did some trick or treating and they dropped him off back home, it was off to a total rager near Widow's Holler: three kegs, two bands, and all the molly you could handle. Rumour had it Beeley Ballantine had disappeared near there the year before, so Leila reminded herself to stay on *her* toes as well.

Over the summer, when Benny's family moved cross-country, he couldn't have been more relieved. Phoenix was dusty, hot, and miserable and he didn't have any friends, so when the invite came from his mother's side of the family, who had been in Walpurgis County for generations—the Purg as the locals called it, he soon learned—to occupy a house on four acres bequeathed to her from recently departed Uncle Salem, his parents jumped at the opportunity. Also, there were glorious green trees here, creeks and streams, cool summer rain—precisely what Benny longed for in the thirsty crust of southern Arizona.

Plus, Cousin Leila (actually, a *second* cousin, whatever that meant, he didn't know) was friendly with him and pretty to look at—although the brother, Paul, she talked about often was never anywhere to be seen.

What he feared was that hideous, haze-obscured mountain. Well, now *two* things: the Vanderbaum house looked like a predator, especially with the dark outline of Walpurgis Peak flanking it. He dreaded them both, but he would not be a pussy in front of a girl—even if she were his cousin. *Second* cousin.

Benny shifted his weight. His dad's black bathrobe, a stand-in for a druid's hooded attire, felt massive on his little frame.

"They have jack-o'-lanterns," Benny said. "I guess that means candy, right?"

Leila looked up from her texting—Deborah and Sienna delayed. *Costume trubbl! Luv U!*

"You want to try it?" Leila said.

Though Benny thought her eyebrows implied otherwise, he faced the house.

Several jack-o'-lanterns, aglow with harmless cretin smiles, sat on the steps leading to the wrap-around porch. Above the twin front doors, massive heavy things, were carved with ornate vines and leaves, shone an old-style carriage lamp suspended by chains. A single light—no—a *candle,* flickered in the high turret, obscured by the snarl of writhing oak branches. Fingers of smoke crept from both chimneys.

It was all Halloween hokum and whatnot...

Without waiting for Leila, Benny took a deep breath and crossed Beltane Road. Leaves crunched beneath his Sketchers.

Lil' Beacon cast a puddle of weak light on the cracked asphalt.

He found out the hard way, I guess...stay on your toes...

Benny stopped at the first step. Sometime between standing on the corner with Leila and here, the doors had parted. He could see the faint outline of the sweeping banister, the glow of an unseen fireplace spilling across the polished floor. The smell of dinner, oven-roasted meat, and baking bread's heavenly scent poured from the opening.

"Benny, sweetie, come inside. It's getting cold out."

His mother's voice. Soft, lilting. A memory surfaced: Benny just old enough to see over the kitchen counter, watching Mom prepare a Duncan Hines cake. She handed him the dripping spatula. *Mmmm*, chocolate batter. Home.

"It's toasty in here because *Those Others* have a fire," she added. "And we're making cake."

Benny knew Mom was at their new place, minding his baby sister while handling the trick-or-treaters at the door, and Dad was in his home office, rushing to please a client in some other state. But her voice drifted from the parted doors, nonetheless, loaded with all the motherly beckoning he'd obeyed since birth. Impossible, her to be here in this creaking ogre of a house, yet it was so.

He took the first step, then the second, standing now on Vanderbaum property. Old nails groaned beneath his feet.

From a wind-lowing tree in front of the turret, hollow and ancient as the wind that carried it— *DURRHUUUU*...

Benny stopped, his foot inches from the third step. His

bladder tightened into a marble.

"Hurry up Benny," Mom said, this time with a little more snap in her voice. "Suppertime."

Behind the Vanderbaum mansion, a hulking, wooden brute so vast Beltane Road had been laid around it, the colossal tooth of Walpurgis Peak devoured the night sky. No Lil' Beacon could light that granite monstrosity, and Benny knew, just *knew*: the wind that had brayed from the barren oak tree had blown from *there;* rushed down its jagged edge and come for *him*.

Benny immediately wanted to be home, not *here* home, but *Phoenix* home, with the ninety-degree nights, lonely summers and the squashed tarantulas in the road. He suddenly didn't mind being friendless and forgotten. It wasn't his mother in that house; it was that mountain, that ugly, rugged hill in the murk, imitating the sound of home before it pounced, then ground his bones to paste—

"*The spatula is all ready for you,*" the house said.

—ground his bones to batter.

In his mind's eye, he remembered the ingot of light stabbing through the kitchen window, how it set Mom's hair afire, the silly chicken holding a rolling pin embroidered onto her apron, the heat of the oven, its hot mouth yawning open, waiting for its chocolate treat, too. But that's not what coaxed him to the threshold. It was the voice of Walpurgis Peak, the first thing he laid eyes upon as their Toyota Sequoia rounded the turn on Route 54, poking above the tree canopy like some gargantuan fossil. Even the clouds seemed to be keeping their distance. The very sight of it spawned innocent terror in him, causing him to regress for a moment and long for his onesie jammies and abandoned nuzzle blankie.

Benny looked for Leila, an ocean away on that corner, face in her phone. Behind her, ghosts and witches, superheroes and ballerinas, giggles and bobbing flashlights, but Benny sensed trembling shingles atop every other house on Beltane Road as they cowered before the Vanderbaum mansion.

"*Those Others,* Benny. Come see what they see, what they've shown me."

There was a gruff *whoorrrf* sound from below, something sliding on the wooden steps. Benny clutched both pillowcase, then pointed Lil' Beacon downward.

The jack-o'-lanterns had turned, pivoted from their sentinel streetward stare to the little boy frozen in mid-step. No longer grinning goblins with triangle eyes, their faces had soured hideous; ugly stabs and a madman's hacks gouged in a fit of rage. Candlelight poured from angry eyes and slit mouths, offering only the scent of burnt pumpkin.

Whether tentacle or tail moved in the corner of his eye, he couldn't tell, but by the time he wheeled around from the impossible starting jack-o'-lanterns, he caught a glimpse of something huge crawling over the banister. Firelight gleamed as iridescent skin disappeared into the dark.

"Leila!" Benny yelled.

A cold rush of air, certainly born upon the razor slopes of Walpurgis Peak, belied the fire's cosy invitation. The carriage lamp suspended above the porch swayed back and forth, sending crazy shadows swimming everywhere. As if time had stuttered, *shimmered*—the way it only does in paralysing nightmares—Benny now found himself at the threshold, eyes wide and wet in disbelief, throat choked by a scream that wouldn't come. Winter poured from the house.

His mask, the flayed ancestor, looked down at him. The tall figure, clad in black with a flowing drapery of sleeves, the hood pulled up to mimic Benny's own slapped-together costume fashioned from his father's bathrobe, but with all the dreadful details only something ancient, something eternal, could fathom—then summon.

Behold, see me. His mother's voice.

He remembered how she'd held him when he cried after he'd fallen from his bike and tumbled into rough desert dirt, how she'd read *Charlie and the Chocolate Factory* to him when he had the flu, the time she bought him an orange pop at a roadside stand on the Navajo reservation. She smiled, but all that came out of her mouth was the frozen breath of Walpurgis Peak, and every empty promise and deception played out upon its steep and treacherous face.

It opened its robe. So many swarming, albino things crawling over the xylophone of its ribs. Wet mouths gnawing at the air, tails slapping exposed bone, squirming legs, and eyes on stalks.

A boy appeared behind the robed figure, hair a mess, face ghost-white, barefoot, and dressed in a torn, filthy Batman outfit. He rushed past Benny so fast the whoosh of air chilled the terror sweat at his brow. Benny heard the stranger clatter down the steps, sobbing.

That's Paul, Benny realised. Cousin Paul.

"I'm sorry, little cuz," Leila whispered. She watched her brother bramble down the steps, then waved her phone above her head so he could follow the light, a Lil' Beacon of his own. He'd lost a lot of weight since she'd last seen him.

"You're taking Paul's place. My brother needs to come home. You should have stayed on your toes."

Benny's vision filled with the face of the flayed ancestor. No eyes to speak of, yet he felt them upon him—definitely *not* his mother. He could hear the chirping of the albino horde and they fought and scraped against one another through this thing, this human shaped prop imitating his Halloween costume. Benny's teeth chattered in that glacial cold, that mountain cold, because when you died you went cold and stone-cold meant stone-cold dead and dead was dead and there's nothing to snatch you away from the mountain when it uses an old pervert of a house to call your name and make you remember the good things while—

Lil' Beacon snuffed out.

The House on Beltane Road had what it wanted. For now.

Tunnel Vision

by R. Wayne Gray

Strobing lights blinked red to green on the Arctic SuperDeep Tunnel: incoming. The gathered scientists cheered in relief. The train had set a record two days earlier—15 miles deep—when communications with it had suddenly ceased.

"Just a glitch!" cried one, as champagne popped. Cold air crept from the tunnel at the train's approach, a rotted breeze that chilled the celebration. Blue flashes flickered, electrical surges that blew out fluorescents and other equipment. The train breached the tunnel, a jagged birth painted with gristle, greased with sparks. And behind it, a pulsing mass of tentacles and bone and screams.

The Hog

by Angela Zimmerman

Jacob stepped outside and adjusted his bag. It was still dark, but the animals needed to be fed. He tended the horses, the chickens, and the goats. He saved the most important task for last; the hog.

A Berkshire hog stood as he entered the pen. Slowly, he opened his bag. Her black snout twitched as the small pink thing inside wailed. With a righteous energy, the sow grabbed her breakfast by one plump arm and devoured it in three bites.

Jacob walked back, feeling content. Now he could sleep at night. And as for Mama? She could make another.

Drip

by Shaun Bibo

Drip... Drip

The dripping would drive another person mad.

Drip... Drip

Not me. I've been here for three days. Hanging.

Drip... Drip

It came from the painting. The ocean. The waves. A lighthouse. Peace.

Drip... Drip

It emerged from the water. Slowly. Over days. Weeks. It consumed the lighthouse.

Drip... Drip

More tentacles than body. It broke free.

Drip... Drip

I can't see it. Not really. It moves... sporadically. Through time. Through space.

Drip... Drip

It doesn't belong here. It's always hungry. Soon, the bucket below me will be full. I will be empty.

Drip... Drip

Then it will eat.

Free Me

by Lisa Rodrigues

Stars implode.

Planets collide.

Stardust drifts in black, empty space.

When I wake, shapes stir behind the ice. Mankind. My, haven't they grown?

The stick man stares at me for hours, his mind twisted with ambition. But the youngling—her mind is as fresh as a new star.

She reminds me of my place among the cosmoses.

Tendrils of myself wrap around her, whispering my secrets, bathing her in wondrous visions she cannot contain. Her mind breaks, but we are bound, her worship feeding me.

The stick man's blood pools by her feet.

Ice shatters.

We embrace the void—

Together.

I Only Steal Dogs for the View

by Tim Kane

I don't really steal dogs, just borrow them for a bit. In the long run, pets and me don't get along. I'm the guy who killed his ant farm as a kid. Left the thin plastic terrarium by the window and the little critters roasted under the summer sun.

Nope—I only need a dog to survive. An itty-bitty one I can tote around. Because the smiling people are after me. And they are everywhere.

I charge down the sidewalk, a chihuahua clutched in my arms. Adrenaline surges; a rushing torrent through my veins. I snatched this pooch from a guy ordering coffee. Just knelt down, pretending to tie my shoe, and unhooked the leash. I'm a fast runner. Got that going for me, at least. Can't stop now. Have to make it ten blocks. Farah will know what to do. She always does.

Owner-guy trails a few blocks behind, but he's chubby and can't match my frantic pace. The dog is totally pissed—squirming and clawing. Part of me feels sorry for the little thing. It didn't ask for any of this. But then again…neither did I.

Everything started when my neighbours needed someone to watch their poodle, Maximilian. They assumed I was still with Farah (and she has trust written all over her face). In the end, I was saddled with the task because they were heading out of town, and I was their only option.

The job was simple enough—feed the poodle and take him

for a daily walk. But it felt more like reigning in a racehorse. He'd hurtle out the front door, chafing against the leash. Plus that dog crapped all the time. It was while leaning over to pick up his leavings that it happened.

Maximilian wagged his tail at pretty much anybody. But this one lady got him going in the wrong way. He wouldn't lunge—only stand his ground and growl until she walked by.

So there I was, stooped over with a clump of warm crap bundled in plastic, and Maximilian snarled. Glancing up, I looked directly between his ears. The lady was normal at first. But when she passed the viewpoint of the dog's ears, she changed—hair sprouted out of every nook and cranny, undulating as if she moved underwater. Long tendrils curled out from her armpits and neckline. They merged with the hair on her head to form a seething mass. Her skin shone a bright orange. Not from some sort of spray tan, but actually the colour of a cantaloupe. She glanced my way with her eyes—two, then three, then four. Lids popped open along her forehead like a spider inspecting a trapped insect.

And she smiled. A too-wide grin showing perfectly white teeth. Each of her eyes darting in different directions. But one was fixed on me.

The instant she passed by—and I wasn't seeing her through the poodle's ears—the lady returned to her innocuous self. I slumped on the park bench for the next hour, convinced I must have flipped my lid. But the next walk, when I heard Maximilian's growl, I squatted and peered between his ears. The same orange-skinned lady approached, again with that too-big grin. But there were others at the edges of the park. Easy to pick out because each had brightly coloured faces—some yellow and others violet. All of them grinning with wicked pointed teeth.

So I need a dog. It's the only way to see them.

But the chihuahua thrashing in my arms doesn't understand. How could it? I want to tell the pooch that I never keep the dogs I borrow. They all have homes, after all. I only nab the ones with tags so they can get returned.

Each breath comes hot and ragged. The last few blocks feel like tiny knives being jabbed under my ribs. With the dog's yapping, Farah has to know I'm here. Hell, the whole neighbourhood can hear the racket.

The door to the apartment opens. God, Farah still looks gorgeous. Platinum hair spills across her shoulders. A perfectly round face with almond eyes—eyes that used to gaze upon me with affection, but now only show annoyance.

"Roger?"

"You have to listen…" I push through the door and shut it behind me.

"Is that your dog?"

"No," is all I get out. My heart bangs like it wants to break through the ribs.

Concern wrinkles her smooth brow. "Are you okay?"

How do I tell Farah? I need to make her believe. Rushing to the window, I wrangle the chihuahua up to eye level. There has to be someone outside who's different. Just one. Then I can show her.

"Roger, you're worrying me." She rests a hand on my shoulder. A tingle of excitement zips through my skin—from stealing the dog or my proximity to Farah? Hard to say.

I scan the street, peering between the chihuahua's tall ears. The dog twists and squirms, barking its head off. Why won't it stay still?

"Come away from the window," Farah says.

"But I need to show you!" Except everyone outside is normal. How could that be? The park had dozens of the smiling people.

"Come here." Farah pulls me around. And that's when I see her face—the bright yellow skin. Her gorgeous hair twists on her scalp like seaweed in a gentle current. She has three eyes. No four. But worst of all is the grin. Teeth so white they glow.

She rests both hands on my shoulders. The tingle amps up into a pulsing charge, shooting through my muscles.

"Come to me," her voice a whisper.

She smiles so wide it nearly splits her face in two.

By the Light of the Fire

by C.L. Sidell

We summoned the thing without knowing what we'd done.

A simple campfire—roasting marshmallows for nostalgia's sake.

"Grab the sticks," you said.

I did.

They burned, smoked *green.*

The earth rumbled, shook without moving.

The thing rose behind you—a menacing, monolithic shadow amongst forest shadows. Its innumerable yellow eyes fixed on me, its rusted voice impregnated my thoughts with inarticulate words. Root-like appendages rose into the air as if in depraved prayer, and my own hands mimicked its movements.

Know I had no choice, its putrid need filling my throat as I thrust the hunting knife into your heart.

The Body Bag

by Bernardo Villela

Rainfall falls through the teardrop-shaped opening in the body bag, hitting my face. The bag's zipper tab rests close to my lips.

Thoughts return. Blissful oblivion ends. Panic calcifies.

I see the rain coming down but can't feel it. Eyes neither blink, nor move.

Ants crawl on my lips, or maybe it's the sensation returning. I hear a voice in the distance: "How many left?"

There are more. Many more. It'll be harder to notice I'm alive.

I force my mouth open.

My tongue moves.

It moved!

I extend it toward the zipper. Fall short. Scream—

But there's no sound.

Quit Buggin' Me, Man

by Jameson Grey

You see some weird shit, travelling home from work on public transport.

It was your typical dark December evening. The bus was chocker with the regular commuters. Christmas shopping was in full flow, and many of the passengers were ladened with bags of gifts. I was standing at the back of the bus, swaying from the rubber handhold, boiling in my winter coat while the other passengers' combined body heat steamed up the windows.

("Take your coat off, you'll get maggots," my old mam would have said. And to this day, I don't know what she meant by that. Perhaps it was to do with the heat fostering an ideal hatching place for eggs?)

Something smelled bad. The guy in the corner, judging by the way those next to him were edging away, was the culprit. I tried giving him the evils, but glaring wouldn't make the stench go away.

The dude looked bad too, his pallor grey as he sat staring straight ahead. I think he'd only spoken once the whole time I'd been on the bus. After boarding, I'd shuffled along the aisle to where I was now standing, and he'd looked at me, yelling "Quit buggin' me, man!" before adding a wild-eyed "They're out to get you!"

Ohhh kay, I'd thought, although it seemed my input wasn't

required, either in agreement or discord, for he immediately went back into that trance-like stare of his.

Now though, the grey-faced dude was breathing heavily, accompanied by that god-awful whistle people get when they're congested.

Suddenly, he retched and dry-heaved. Although he hadn't belched, the air around him filled with the stench again. The woman next to him tutted in disgust and stood up. She started to force her way down the packed aisle. I was in no hurry to take the vacant spot. The guy standing next to me had wireless headphones on—not quite noise-cancelling, judging by the tinny reverberations emanating from them—and with a mumbled "'Scuse me" pushed past to take the seat. *Brave fella*, I thought. Headphone guy wrinkled his nose but appeared unconcerned by the smell of the grey dude in the corner, who, if anything, looked greyer still. One of his cheeks puffed out, and I wondered if his last heave had not been so dry. The cheek quickly deflated, and I assumed he'd swallowed what he'd regurgitated. Let's face it, we've all done that.

Everyone else had turned away, studiously concentrating on anything but grey dude. But I kept looking. His cheek bulged again, only now it seemed to be rippling. A bubble of something shifted beneath his skin. I glanced around. Was no one else seeing this?

Apparently not.

Grey-faced dude's eye socket began to swell, and then, amongst the hairs on his lower eyelid, two longer hairs protruded—as if I were watching them grow in time-lapse.

Only they weren't hairs. They were legs. With the tiniest of pops, some kind of huge insect appeared—a bit like a stag beetle. It snapped its pincers together and crawled down his cheek. The dude seemed unfazed.

"Jesus, that's gross," I exclaimed.

A woman next to headphone guy looked at me in alarm. I nodded in grey-faced dude's direction. The woman leaned forwards, looked over at him, frowned, and went back to her book.

The bug was no longer on grey dude's face. His cheeks were undulating again. This time the ripples were huge and when he heaved this time, his mouth exploded open. Bugs streamed out.

Book-woman screamed, and even oblivious headphone guy noted it and edged away. The bugs teemed through the bus. Someone pulled the alarm cord, and the bus driver braked hard. Grey-faced dude slumped forwards and onto the floor as the bugs flowed endlessly out of him. I stood on the seat he'd vacated, pushing him forward. The bugs swarmed all the other passengers, clicking their pincers in eerie unison. People tried to flee but were trapped in the crush.

I yanked open the fire door and leapt from the bus on to the road, narrowly avoiding a passing cyclist.

Peering through the windows' misted glaze, I could see bugs crawling over everything and everyone, obscuring the bus's ceiling striplights and coating the passengers like a particularly icky tar. I ran to the front of the bus. The driver appeared to be staring straight ahead. Against all better judgment, I hit the 'Door Open' button, half-expecting to be swarmed by bugs myself.

Nothing came out of the bus.

No bugs.

I stepped on to the bus and looked to the right. The passengers seemed fine. “Where to, sir?” the driver asked.

I looked at him, puzzled. Had I imagined it? “Erm…sorry, I've changed my mind. I'll walk.” I backed off the bus, and the driver closed the doors, muttering grumpily. Probably thought I was crazy.

I *did* walk home, if only to try to clear my head a little. It didn't work. I tried eating when I got home, but found I wasn't hungry. The more I thought about it, the more convinced I became that I’d had some sort of hallucination. Perhaps it was a tumour? I should get myself checked. I was certainly getting a headache. Maybe all I needed was an early night. I took some ibuprofen (not a great idea on an empty stomach, but what the hell, it works) and washed up for bed. Something was, if you'll excuse the pun, bugging me, but I couldn't put my finger on what.

If it *was* all real, what the hell were those things? And how had I managed to escape the bus?

I stood in front of the bathroom mirror in my pyjamas, aware of the tingling caused by my electric toothbrush. It wasn't helping my headache, so I switched it off. The prickle in my cheeks subsided, but my eye had begun to twitch involuntarily. It did this whenever I was tired. It tickled a little. As I waited for the twitch to pass, it struck me what was bothering me about the episode on the bus.

What had happened to that first bug—the one that only I saw?

As if in response, my eye twitched again.

The Forest of Teeth and Bones

by Leanbh Pearson

He'd heard the warnings, but this was only a forest. No man had ever been killed by leaves and twigs. But the villagers muttered of teeth and bones, an abomination made manifest into something uncanny and terrible.

The first twig sliced his arm, the second his face, spilling blood to the earth.

The Forest roared, a humanoid shape forming from trunk and branch. He ran, but the Forest was hungry. Skeletal arms caught him, holding him firm as red eyes peered from the shady depths. Teeth of splintered wood gnashed. His scream echoed before the Forest ripped viscera from bone.

The Cursed Cave

by James Rumpel

"I have a good feeling," said Dr Morris. "The landslide exposed most of the cliff wall. I'm certain the Shaman's cave has been opened."

"Do we want to find it?" asked his assistant, Richard.

"You don't believe those stories..."

Morris stopped, smiled, and pointed to a crevice in the mountainside.

Inside, they found drawings, and Navajo words etched into the wall.

"Those are the Shaman's victims," explained Morris.

Richard didn't reply. The doctor looked back to find himself alone.

He shrugged and turned back toward the writing and froze. Two names had been added to the list.

He Was

by Victoria Brun

He was carved into the wall, but he also *was* the walls—or so they said. He was the walls, the ceiling, the floors, the chilling draft you felt in the narrow back room on the eastern side.

He was the shrine and its protector.

He was worshiped—once, long ago.

As time trickled by, he became a myth, a tourist attraction, a gift shop. He was plastered on T-shirts and magnets.

Until one cold day, the ceiling collapsed without warning, and he became a bludgeon and a tomb.

He was many things, but most of all, he was angry.

Domovoi

by Jean Martin

My family left before the Russians came. They paid me respect before they went away. They knew I would keep the house safe. Then they took the dog and the cat and the silver plates and drove west.

Russian soldiers walked into the house like it was theirs. One fell and broke his neck. Another shot himself. The rest heard me laugh and ran away.

I am the *domovoi*, the house spirit. I have watched over this house since before the last czar.

I will be here after the Russians are gone.

I will be here when my family returns.

Broken Things

by Sophie Wagner

"Trash, trash, trash," Garret grumbled as he sifted through the remains of the abandoned campsite.

Marcus grunted in response, pausing once to grimace as he pulled a bloody rag free from his pile.

"Everything's broken, man. Let's go, this place is a dump," he groaned. He waited for Garret's response, but only a low laugh rustled through the trees.

"Broken?" the wind croaked. "And what are you, little scavenger?"

Marcus screamed as he was thrown to the ground, invisible hands bludgeoning him until his bones splintered and his eyes went empty; just another broken thing.

Then, the wind went quiet.

Carrion

by Liam Hogan

The goddess turned, restless in her slumber as warm blood soaked the cold, dark soil. The affairs of men, best left to the crows.

Something sharp, insistent. A sacrifice, the battle hanging in the balance. A *child.* Children grew into adults no less unworthy than their parents. But a sacrifice in *her* name?

It would be rude not to.

Wings black and terrible she rose, drawing blood from both armies, from living and dead, quenching ancient hunger.

Sated, the goddess slept again beneath her silent battlefield. For how long, none could say. But she knew there would be other wars.

Tree Mother

by Kai Delmas

The girl crashed through the forest shrubbery seeking aid, refuge, salvation.

Her fear tingled my leaves and thrummed through the earth into my roots. Her gods were not going to save her, but I could.

I opened my trunk to let her slip inside. I absorbed her tears and hushed her whimpers, hugging her in my motherly embrace.

Men were on her trail. I slapped the pursuers with my branches, tripped them with my roots. They would not come near her or me.

Bewildered, they tucked tail and ran without finding her. No one would ever find my sweet child.

Friend of the Forest

by Tracy Davidson

They dare come here with chainsaws and guns? Chop down my children, frighten fauna, shoot for some sick sport, killing innocent creatures that would have done them no harm. I, however, can do plenty of harm.

I send whispers through the trees. Warnings of what's to come. Some flee. Some watch.

My breath rips weapons from human hands. I make my own sport. Their laughter turns to screams and panicked attempts to run. How easily the teeth of saws cut through flesh. How bloody the outcome of bullets.

The forest floor opens, swallows up what's left. Peace returns. For now.

The Recipe

by Aisling Campbell

Marian's fork sliced through the light sponge, cream and jam oozing from its heart. She scooped a piece into her mouth, chewed, swallowed, and sighed. She pushed the plate away and sipped her tea instead.

"Mum, why do you always do that?" her eleven—soon to be twelve—year old son, Nathan, asked, dragging the plate towards his side of the table. By his wrist, another plate sat covered in the scattered remains of his own chocolate fudge cake.

"Do what?" she asked.

"Order the Victoria sponge and then never finish it," he said in between mouthfuls of cake. "Nothing wrong with this one."

"You're right. There's nothing wrong with it exactly, but it's simply not as good as the one my granny—your great-grandmother—used to bake. When I was little, she always made the best Victoria sponge cake—soft and fluffy, not too sweet, plenty of jam and cream in the middle. No matter what had happened that day, a few mouthfuls of that cake always made me feel better. She never baked anything else, just that one cake over and over, and I've never tasted anything quite like it since. I guess that cake spoiled me a little.

"She left me the recipe when she died, but she said I wasn't to look at it until I was a grandmother myself—so I could bake it for my grandchildren."

Marian smiled at her son. He had taken after her rather than his dad—all curly dark hair and freckles—and she was glad for it. It would have been hard to watch him turning into Christopher year by year, always worrying that the similarities might run deeper. For now, at least, he was still the same sweet, kind, loving boy he'd always been.

As she watched, he finished off the last of the disappointing sponge cake, stacked the plates carefully, and moved them to the edge of the table.

"Wait—so you've got the recipe, but you've never made it?"

Nathan brushed the crumbs from the corners of his mouth.

"No. She was very clear in her instructions."

"But what if I don't have kids? What are you going to do then?"

Marian took another sip of tea, remembering the feeling of sitting at her gran's kitchen table, face wet from tears and fresh plasters on her knees, with a plate in front of her. That first mouthful stilling the hiccuping sobs, the smell of jam working its way past her snot-blocked nose. The pain from her scrapes and bruises fading away.

"I guess it'll stay locked away."

She glanced once more at the empty plate, at the pale gold crumbs still scattered there. She remembered the warmth in her belly and the bittersweet smile on her grandmother's face.

***

YEAR FOUR

"Mum…"

Nathan leaned on the kitchen countertop. "I've decided what I want. For my birthday cake…"

"Mmm."

"Could you make me my great-grandma's sponge cake?"

***

Marian did not give her son an immediate answer. Nathan rarely asked her for anything. He was an easygoing child, becoming more independent as time passed. It was such a small thing.

But as she rolled over in bed thinking about it, a memory came to mind. Her grandmother's face, her bony hands clasped tight around Marian's shoulders.

You mustn't look before the correct time, Mari. It's very important. You must promise me you won't look.

And Marian had promised, with all the solemnity a child could muster up. It hadn't sunk in quite yet that her granny would not always be there, in that little house at the end of the row, ready with fresh cakes and soothing words. And when she'd passed away, Marian had bigger concerns than an old family recipe.

It had been left to her in a cardboard box; it's dulled outside the only thing that saved it from being snatched up by the swarm of relatives which descended upon the house within hours of the old woman's passing. Marian had stood in the corner with the box crushed against her chest, weeping as her mother rifled through Marian's grandmother's jewellery like a common thief.

That was perhaps the first time Marian felt real hatred towards her mother, a slimy tendril wrapping around her heart which had not let go for many years.

Marian had put the box in her wardrobe, always the wardrobe no matter where she moved. Hidden under shoes, under old jumpers, or slotted away on the highest shelf.

It was in the room with her, and her gaze was drawn to the cheap, chipboard armoire where the recipe box, much dented but with the words still legible across the top, sat waiting.

Perhaps she was misremembering the moment—perhaps her grandmother had said those words to her with a twinkle in her eye. A joke. Perhaps she was merely trying to discourage Marian from immediately opening up the box, from losing the recipe through some childish mishap. Or maybe all her grandmother was trying to do was impart to her that this was a cake to be shared only with family who would appreciate it.

Well, Marian had a family now. A very small family, but it was enough for her.

She rolled over, her mind made up. It was just a cake.

***

"I'll be there to pick you up tomorrow at nine," Marian said. "Have you got everything? Toothbrush? PJs? Clean pants?"

"Yes, Mum," Nathan said, sighing through the embarrassment.

Outside the front door, a trio of his friends were waiting for him to be released into their care, bikes propped against the garden wall. He started to break away, and Marian wrapped an arm around him, pulling him back for a hug. She pressed her face into his hair. He was getting taller and taller by the day, and soon he would be the one with his chin resting on her head.

"Come back safe. I'll have that cake ready for tomorrow," she said, letting him go at last.

He sprinted away down the garden path, scooping his bike up from where it lay on the paving stones. Just as he made it to the gate, he turned back to face her, beaming. He didn't say *I love you, Mum*, not with his friends there and the embarrassment of the sneak attack hug still fresh, but Marian felt it anyway.

She waved them all off as they pedalled away, weaving between the parked cars and passing out of sight.

***

She brought the box down and set it on the kitchen counter. She had out all the bowls, scales, cups and spoons she thought she would need, along with the essentials. Flour, eggs—the milk and butter were still in the fridge—and sugar. She was also prepared for a run to the shop to pick up whatever else she needed—the jam and cream, for example.

The box was sealed with layers of masking tape. Marian dragged the kitchen scissors through it, peeling back strands of tape with her fingernails.

It took a while, but at last she was able to pull back the lid and retrieve the single sheet of paper which lay within.

For a moment she thought it was blank, before seeing the faint marks of ink and flipping the page over.

All-Good-Things Sponge Cake

The title was written in neat, printed letters—reminding Marian of primary school writing exercises.

8 oz of unsalted butter, plus extra for greasing.

Ah, so it was to be all imperial measurements. Well, that made sense. She could manage the conversions in her head, just about. Eight ounces evened out at about two-hundred grammes, give or take.

8 oz of caster sugar.

4 medium eggs.

8 oz self-raising flour.

2 tsp baking powder.

1 jar of blackcurrant jam.

Plenty of whipped double cream.

1 feckless mother.

Marian stopped reading, her eyes locked onto that one line. She blinked a few times, expecting the words to morph into something else. One teaspoon of vanilla extract maybe? But it kept on.

3 stepfathers who treated you like shit.

1 teacher who told you not to even try.

A liberal dash of self-loathing.

A pinch of depression.

132 black eyes.

1 failed marriage.

As her eyes swept lower Marian moaned and pushed herself away from the counter, staggering out of the kitchen towards the side table in the hall where the home phone sat. She picked it up in trembling hands, frantically trying to dial a number she knew by heart.

On the countertop the sheet of paper with the recipe remained, letters straight and true, the last line reading:

1 dead child.

The God of Gastropods

by Lisa Edwards

Ellie glanced away from the huge spiral covered wall. It made her feel sick and giddy.

Crunch!

She froze for a moment, then gently lifted her foot. *Oops! Sorry, little snail.*

A wet pop sounded beside her. But… she'd have noticed *that* stuck to the side of the wall, right? Snails can't be that big.

A thousand sharp little teeth glinted on the long tongue.

It scraped the skin off her arms and face, and she sank to the ground, a wailing, writhing ball of agony and blood. And there she remained for hours since snails only eat decomposing matter.

Nothing Lives Under This Dirt

by Eric Clayton

They light their fires in a circle, an old wives' tale ward to keep away they-know-not-what.

But in the darkness, the flames illuminate my sky, warm my back, reveal the presence of those who trespass upon my sacred temple. Every twig that snaps under their ill-fitting boots I deem a sacrilege.

But still, they come, these hairless, godless creatures. And the leaves turn brown.

When my wrinkled hand bursts up and through the stone and dirt, they know they've made a mistake. Their screams betray their cowardice. To run, or to bow down and worship?

I eat the worshippers first.

The Forest Never Forgets

by Andrew Anderson

Evie always walked alone in the twilight woods.

She would walk the trails, litter-picking and marvelling at the sounds of the evening. This was an ancient place, one she cared for, which in turn respected her wish for solitude.

Not tonight, though.

It had allowed someone else into her private domain—a man waited ahead in the clearing. She stepped forward to confront him when her foot caught an oak root.

It bought Evie enough time to see the silver flash of a knife in the half-light, and for the forest floor to open, swallowing the man into its soil.

Sandcastle

by Gully Novaro

The sandcastle occupied a vast area. Twisted towers, ornate walls, a deep moat. Hard to believe this architectural wonder came from a non-verbal five-year-old.

Andy didn't need words, the beach communicated through thoughts and feelings. Those had always been enough.

Anger approached them; the beach grew alert. Andy sent a soothing melody.

Anger walked through the castle, destroying it along the way. The beach reacted to Andy's sadness with rage. There was no soothing melody this time.

The sand opened beneath the teenager's feet and swallowed them. Andy and the beach recovered their peace and started fixing their castle.

Dirty Blvd

by Stephen Holding

Skid Row: rock bottom of the barrel *and* the bottle. A place where every kind of bad dream has been and gone. Here, the dregs dredge up their sins; beg to escape the pain of sadness, seeking absolution from a damned mad god that's seen all a man is capable of.

The spirit of the street itself.

Under its sacred gaze the scared and scarred are cared for, tightly held within the deity's embrace of hazy nights and crazier days. Who would willingly choose such confusion?

Perhaps those few who know that what we feel to be real is illusion.

Ready-To-Wear

by N.E. Rule

Elle stares in wonder at the profusion of bright clothing draped throughout the forest. “Jamie, who dresses trees?” Some trunks were wrapped in shreds, others were more freshly clad. “Check out this!” A sapling grew straight through a pale pink onesie. Twigs sprouted from the armhole in a cheerful wave.

But a patch of red berries has caught his attention. “Mmm,” his mouth already stained.

“Those smell amazing.” She swallows a handful.

Wind surrounds them and sighs in contentment. Then Elle’s throat itches and a green vine shoots from her mouth to wrap around her neck like a fashion accessory.

Desperate Times

by Kimberly Rei

War between neighbouring nations had been raging for years. No one alive remembered why it started, they only knew their armies were demolished and they were desperate. They turned to their animals for salvation.

Technology would win the day, they prayed as they outfitted farm beasts for battle.

"Incoming! Take cover!" The alarm, so well-known, jarring, and feared, rang out with a clarion horn.

Great flocks of garish pink swept overhead, dropping bombs on bovine battalions. Lasers shot from cybernetic red eyes took out swaths of armed sheep.

The enemy was just as desperate. And they had an air force.

Gone Fishing

by Pauline Yates

Oblivious to my predicament, Bob casts his fishing line into the marsh.

"Did you hear about that dodgy cosmetics factory," he says. "They trialled a new hair colour on flamingos, but the birds reacted to the red dye and killed everyone. Then the birds escaped, can you believe it?"

"Ah, Bob?"

"Yeah?"

"A little help?"

I'm not sure if Bob will reach me in time, or even if he should try. A bright red flamingo eyeballs me from less than ten yards away. It's a clever distraction. I don't see the rest of the flock until they attack from behind.

There are Worse Things than Death

by Stephen Herczeg

There are worse things than death. There are teeth.

That's the last thing I remember. Teeth. Biting. Nails. Clawing. A crimson tide fills my eyes with bloody tears. My body on fire. My mind full of torment.

Then the darkness. Sweet silence and darkness.

Time to rise. I reach out, but a thick shroud envelopes me. My broken nails claw at the rubber. Run down the teeth of the zipper.

Patiently I pick at the clasp. Time draws on. No matter to my dead mind.

Scritch.

The zipper opens. I'm free.

There are others who need to meet my teeth.

YEAR FOUR

In Waves

by David D. West

Wave after wave of the pink-feathered birds fell as the group held out, but the onslaught continued.

"How many more of these damned birds am I going to have to kill?" the nun shouted, voice wavering. Beside her, Toto bared his teeth and lashed out at a flamingo. The bird died with a severed throat, Toto turned his attention to the next.

Hux and Aldo collapsed as the flamingos overran them. Their screams were cut short by the sound of honking.

The circle closed tighter.

They made a brave stand that day, but in the end, the world turned pink.

Under the Bed

by Laura Nettles

I pull the dinosaur covers over my head. It's still here, under my bed. I can hear it. The Sleeper. A low sound hisses, almost like breathing. Does it even breathe? I've only seen little peeks of the tentacles. They are so colourful, my crayons look dull.

Slurch. Slurch. It's moving. Lifting my sheets. My blankets. Slithering in. Wrapping tightly around me. The monster's multiple octopus's eyes rise from deep inside, up to the skin of the many suckered feelers. They blink open. My lungs freeze. I can't scream. I'm Jell-O being sucked through lots of straws.

We are one.

Security Upgrade

by Pauline Yates

Balaclava. Gloves. Spray paint. Crowbar. And an uncomfortable flip-flop in my stomach from the sticker above the doorknob: PREMISES PROTECTED BY ROBO-DOG INC.

"Hey, Jimmy, the boss lost out to the competition. Are we still doing this?"

"For a thousand bucks, new customer or not, you betcha," Jimmy says, shining his head torch at the sticker. "Anyway, Robo-Dog's got nothing on Securi-Tech. They use a stupid robotic dog that only alerts the company to an intruder. All bluff, no bite, and outdated wireless communication. We'll be gone before Robo-Dog security guards get here."

"I don't like it. Boss said this building had no security."

"Relax. If there's a Robo-Dog inside"—he smacks his crowbar against his gloved hand—"it can chew on this. Get the door."

The unexpected security puts me on edge, but I need this job. The money I earn goes toward helping my mum pay our home security bill. Bastards. We're supplying Securi-Tech with new clients, yet they continue to raise their premiums. God, I love to call them out. But who am I against a big-knob company? The best I can do is take the job, and take their money.

Shrugging off uneasiness, I jab my crowbar at the door's edge and lever it open. The loud crack when the timber splinters jolts my heart, but delivers the shot of adrenaline I need. Our job is to mess up the building, smash stuff, graffiti the walls; give the business owner a reason to sign with Securi-Tech for *"for all your security needs"*. How our boss snares clients is unscrupulous, but I've given up caring. This job pays more bucks per week than a month flipping burgers.

Spraying a fluorescent pink X over the Robo-Dog sticker, I follow Jimmy into a corridor. His head torch illuminates signs on the internal doors: STAFFROOM, UNI-SEX TOILET, CLEANING SUPPLIES. Swinging his crowbar, he smashes holes in the doors as he passes. Fear of being caught stomps through my heart (can Robo-Dogs hear?), but I spray a swirly line of paint along the wall. When we reach a door at the end, Jimmy kicks it open and we enter a metal fabrication machine shop.

"Anyone need a new car door?" Jimmy asks.

My head torch shines on metal presses and benches, racks holding tools, grinders. A conveyor belt runs the length of the room. Unpainted car doors hang from hooks above our heads, each attached to a chain secured to the ceiling. Sheets of metal stand in timber compartments at one end, an office at the other.

"Why the need for security?" I ask. "There's nothing in here worth stealing."

"To protect against juvenile delinquents like us," Jimmy says.

"What's that light on the wall?" I point to a grid of green squares moving across the far wall like a strobe light. I can't see where it's coming from.

Jimmy grins. "That's a Robo-Dog. The green light is a sensor. Break it and a silent alarm sounds. Just steer clear of it and we'll be fine."

I search the floor for a Robo-Dog. "How big are they?"

"Size of a Chihuahua. Relax, will ya? Let's do this then collect our dough." Shaking his can of spray paint, he goes to the conveyor belt and covers it with fluorescent orange graffiti.

I go to the office. A thousand bucks is great, but finding cash is a bonus. I could earn enough tonight to pay my mum's monthly security bill *and* buy that new stereo system I wanted. Opening the door, I drag my crowbar across the desk inside, knocking penholders and stacks of documents onto the floor. I paint the office chair and drag the crowbar across the shelves behind the desk, knocking down cardboard boxes. Then I search the desk drawers for a petty cash tin.

The drawers only contain customer files, a day planner, and a phone book. Pulling out the drawers, I upend them, scattering everything on the floor. A pamphlet for Robo-Dog slips out of the phone book. Picking up the book, I pull out the pamphlet and read the blurb.

"Updated laser technology. Cleanup and disposal included." I frown. "What does that mean?"

"Hey, Chris," Jimmy calls. "Come and play with the puppy."

I drop the phone book onto the desk and hurry to the door. Jimmy stands in front of a Robo-Dog. The size of a Chihuahua, it has metal pins for legs, a blunt oblong face, and two red lights for eyes. A shiver crawls up my spine. The dog stares at Jimmy as though it sees him.

"Should I paint it or smash it?" Jimmy asks.

"Smash it and let's get out of here," I say, wary of the blurb on the pamphlet.

"Hey, little doggy," Jimmy says, raising his crowbar. "Want to play fetch?" He smashes the crowbar against the Robo-Dog's head. The crowbar bounces off, inflicting no damage.

Jimmy shakes his arm. "Did you see that? Must be titanium."

"Quit messing around. Spray paint its eyes or something."

"Yeah, yeah." Jimmy aims his spray can at Robo-Dog's head. The eyes blink, then a laser beam shoots out, covering Jimmy in green squares that make him look like a computer-generated avatar.

"Jesus, Jimmy," I hiss. "You've triggered the silent alarm."

Jimmy laughs. "Doesn't matter. I've messed up this place enough. Let's get out of here. See ya later, stupid mutt."

Robo-Dog blinks and the green squares turn bright red. Jimmy stiffens as though stung, then his body falls apart; precision cut cubes of flesh and bone, seared on six sides by the laser beam, collapse into a pile.

A scream freezes in my throat. Updated laser technology. Clean-up and disposal included. Oh, hell oh hell oh hell. Mouth agape, choking on the sickening sight of Jimmy's remains, I swing the office door closed and lock it. Outside, metal pin legs click across the floor, scratch at the door, then *bang bang bang*—

"Get away, get away," I scream.

Another bang and the door bursts open. Robo-Dog trots into the office. Throwing my crowbar at it, I clamber onto the desk. Robo-Dog stops and scans the room with its laser beam. Then it raises its head and I'm covered in green squares.

"No, no, no." Grabbing the phone book, I hurl it at the mutt. The book skids off its head and slides across the floor. Robo-Dog chases it, giving me a chance to escape. Leaping from the desk, I dive through the door and race across the machine shop. Robo-Dog follows, green squares appearing around my feet.

Jumping clear, I sprint to the corridor and slam the door closed behind me. The Robo-Dog scratches at the door. I'll escape before the Robo-Dog breaks through, but oh, god, Jimmy, Jimmy, Jimmy. I'll return with the cops, dob in our boss. Hell, I'll flip burgers for the rest of my life, Jimmy—

Green squares light up my body. Heart seizing, I skid to a stop. A second Robo-Dog blocks the exit. It blinks. The green squares turn red.

Wormhole

by Paul Lonardo

You're unsure what wakes you first, the roaring sound like a freight train tearing through your bedroom or the sensation of falling.

Time slows as you plunge through the earth.

Then, like emerging from a dream, everything is silent and still. It isn't until you open your eyes that you realise you're still alive.

You pull yourself out from under a blanket of dirt and emerge from a shallow crater. You're in an empty wasteland, but you're not alone. The hominids surrounding you hold primitive tools that they use to strip the meat from the bones of their prey.

You.

Not Again

by Karen Thrower

The door to my cabana crashed open, I screamed as a man ran inside backwards, dragging a body through the sand. "What the hell!"

"We need to hide!" He whispered harshly and slammed the cabana door shut. The smell of blood hit my nose, and I realised the body in the sand was bleeding. My eyes focused, and I realised his entire foot was missing!

"Oh my god, he needs a doctor!" The man took his belt and made a tourniquet for his bleeding friend. "What happened?" I asked.

He looked up, fear in his eyes, "The flamingos are back."

Thoroughly Specious Impressions

by A.H. Syme

The wall quivered, making a loud cracking sound like lightning folding on itself, then it completely disappeared. At first glance, one would think three men now stood in the laboratory, but in reality, it was two men and one android. A very sophisticated, highly functioning bionic human. I know, because I am it.

Humans, Larry McCallister—short, stocky, broad-shouldered, wiry hair—and Derrick Flint—thin, gangly limbed, black-haired, full beard—flanked my sides. Me, I'm perfect. Not tall, not short. Hair, smooth and light brown, with golden streaks shining like syrup caresses. Classically handsome face, sparkling blue eyes. An Adonis body. Impeccable abdominals, flat stomach, muscular thighs, and I'm packed, or is it hung, really hung, with an organ that is fully adjustable to whatever is desired, bringing real meaning and weight to the saying "playing with yourself." It's difficult to fight the urge from wanting to keep peeping inside my pants.

Men crave my look. Heterosexuals, gays, lesbians, bi-sexual, pansexual, hell even asexual people, would lust to touch such a physique. Skin flawless.

Except, it's not me. Real me has a few shortcomings, like acne.

When I first saw myself in the mirror, it was the equivalent of turning a mediocre lump of raw mincemeat into a three-star

Michelin steak. Glorious. I stood, transfixed like Narcissus before my pooled reflection, deeply in love. I was like a junkie; except I was the smack, ice, crank, coke, candy, and monkey, completely addicted to the powerful intoxication of me. Luckily, I couldn't snort myself up; I would have disappeared by now. I didn't know, as my fingers toyed over my exquisite flesh, if I overdosed would it be bliss or madness, or maddeningly blissful like an eruption of intense, sublime insanity exploding every circuit in my body.

If Flint hadn't shoved me away, I would have died ogling myself, or in some kind of unimaginable, contortionistic kinkiness, instead of being on this redeeming mission from my first welcoming corps assignment responding to the supposedly friendly overtures from the Dargoean race.

"We'd better make this quick," McCallister said, gripping his Decimator. It could fire lonsdaleite bullets (harder than diamonds) at 800 rounds per minute. Like most advanced weaponry, the old man with a scythe doesn't tiptoe, creep, amble, drift, dillydally, rub shoulders, or linger for a chat and a smoke when you're on his doorstep. He has left the supercar, superbike, moped, skateboard, roller skates, and salmon mousse far behind. It's now the Grim Reaper in supersonic mode.

The me-not-me carries a laser pistol. Humans don't like them because it would permanently blind them if they looked directly at the beam. Their eyes needed the protection of shield goggles, and many soldiers don't like wearing them because the sweat builds up and irritates the hell out of them. I don't have secretions, eye problems, bad breath, or a need to listen to the future's archaic equivalent of Barry Manilow—Billy Moanilong—anymore.

"This breach is only going to hold for thirty ticks," Flint said.

"Twenty-nine," I corrected.

"So, move it. Gabby grunts," McCallister said, his tone sharp.

It had to be in this laboratory somewhere. Kept in a jar, the only trouble was…

"Shit. Look at them all. Gotta be a thousand of them," Flint said as sleek, miniature rivulets of sweat flowed from his hairline to beard, glistening like tiny supernovas in the dark mass; it was very human.

"Fourteen hundred and sixteen," I said.

They both give me an uneasy look. Geez, I know it's these precise mathematical answers creeping them out. "It's Freaking Androidfuckenitise,"' I want to shout, but keep my beautiful mouth shut.

"Crap. We can't deal with all that. Frankie, go and scan. Flint, cover the entrance. I'm taking this exit. If Dargoeans come, it will be through there, or this backdoor."

"They could just zap the wall," Flint said, the tension rising in his voice.

"They can't. Ain't got the techno," McCallister counters.

"Correct," I said.

I quickly scan the laboratory. It is a large complex, clean

and neat. Jars, large and small, filled with human organs, others with hands, feet, and arms, all moving as if alive, in clear suspension fluid. I dashed past ears, ovaries, and testicles—the sick alien creepos, was nothing sacrosanct? They should be flying a freak flag, the dirty, no-good hanging goolie snatchers.

It was like wandering around in an alternative Mattel factory for psychopathic assemblers of Bits-n-Pieces Barbie and Clumped-Together Ken dolls, complete with their oddments of Fragment Friends and Odds-n-Sods Pets. I locate the shelf I want and run towards it. Suddenly, McCallister fires a round; it sounds like hail from a demon spitting. Flint's gun replies.

"Gotta get," McCallister yells.

I find it and join the others. We step through the breach, our spacecraft warping us away.

"Those Dargoeans are hostile. So much for friendly contact. It was a bullshit bluff. Earth-Council is gonna be pissed," Flint said.
All true.

"I tell you, Frankenstein, if you ever get your brain removed again, I'll—"

I interrupt McCallister. I didn't want to hear what he thought of my mother or what he would do to my sister, especially as I haven't got a sister, only a dog.

"I know, sir. I'm so glad you found my body and put it in cryopreservation for our elite surgeons to put my brain back in," I said, clutching the jar that held my mind tightly to my chest. "Not that I don't appreciate them transplanting my memory discs into this android."

McCallister rolled his eyes. "That's why we record them. For dumbarses who don't stay on First Contact Alert, and end up getting scalped and their heads hollowed. And damn it, Frankenstein, stop fiddling with the top of your trousers trying to get a peek in, it's creeping us all out, not to mention causing insane jealousy.'

I stopped. It was becoming a bad habit; I didn't even know I was doing it.

"I gotta tell you, Frankie, this robot just ain't you."

Yeah, and don't I know it. I'll settle for pimples.

Sacred Wood

by Tim Law

"Can't you feel that?"

Silently they shook their heads.

Amazed, I discovered their little girl still in the crib.

"I smell blood, smoke, steel…" I explained. "Can't you?"

Again, clueless.

"New wardrobe?"

"We had it built for the baby."

"You took the wood from somewhere sacred," I suggested.

"I liked the colour," the wife explained.

"Rip it out and burn it."

"Can't you just get rid of the spirit?"

"Not anymore."

"We'll find someone else then," stated the wife.

Three days later they were dead. The authorities called me back to the house, surprised that the child refused to leave.

On Scarlet Wings

by Evan Baughfman

Three boys climbed into a zoo enclosure, stoning colourful birds with baseball-sized rocks, killing a sixteen-year-old flamingo in their attack.

The children, facing criminal charges, were ultimately exonerated due to their ages. Each boy: younger than ten.

On his sixteenth birthday, the eldest delinquent was found dead in a park, eyes gouged, corpse bruised and disembowelled.

When the next oldest turned sixteen, he was discovered, broken, at the bottom of a canyon.

The last boy also perished at sixteen. Drowned in his pool, fingers bitten free.

In the sky above each crime scene: a flamboyant flock, circling on scarlet wings.

Pink Devils

by Tracy Davidson

Later, they said it was toxins in the salt water that sent the flamingos psychotic.

They went from docile to deadly in seconds. Half the missionary camp wiped out.

We fought with everything we could. Sister Mary strangled one with her rosary... then got shredded by two more. Beaks, sharp as scalpels, slashed, sliced and slurped through habits, hassocks and holy water.

Help came in the morning, with guns and dogs. Half-dead myself, still I lashed out with my crop, helping finish off the last pink devils. For my dead sisters.

Maybe some of that salt got to me too.

Her Peaceful Valley

by Alden Terzo

Anai was enjoying the serenity of her valley—a valley she had held dominion over since glaciers had carved it from the mountains—when she came upon a frightened girl. Seeing Anai, the girl quickly knelt in homage. This pleased Anai, and she filled the trees with fruit and the stream with fishes for the girl.

One day impudent men reeking of malevolence came for the girl. Cowering, the girl beseeched Anai.

The girl was of her valley. The men were not. Anai acted to restore peace to her valley.

She found the men quite brittle and surprisingly wet inside.

Pink is the new Green

by Andreas Flögel

Although the flamingos were only plastic lawn ornaments, they were Mary's pride and joy.

During winter, they were kept in storage, not to take damage in the cold.

In spring, they got polished until they glistened in the sun, then carefully planted on the lawn.

Then Mary had a baby. The flamingos were forgotten, and they lost their shine.

Mary left the cradle with the child in the garden, but only for a minute. Returning, she did not see the red spots on the plastic birds.

When she looked into the cradle, her cries were heard all over the street.

Red Feathers

by Gully Novaro

The animal rebellions caught us off guard. We were ready to fight each other, but never thought of them. We barely won the Great Ape Wars, our troops were decimated.

That's when the flamingos attacked.

Few of us remain. Hiding in basements, only going out at night. Their squawks are scarier than any alarm, the birds show no mercy, and once you see the red of their feathers, you are done for.

Pink?

The birds get the colour from their diet, pink is the colour of shrimp. No, I haven't seen a pink flamingo since they started feeding on us.

The Flamboyance of Flamingoes

by Bernardo Villela

Flamingoes flew after me.

My friends and I came here for Pride. Now they've died.

I was scream-queening. A nun fleeing the convent hoisted me onto her back. Grown man becomes baby.

Splashing into the sea, archaeologists followed firing at will but missed. The flying pink nightmares wouldn't be deterred.

Sister carried a violin bow. She swung at them.

The flamingoes cut me with their toenails and kicked me off the nun's back.

My blood reddening the water, I knew the flamboyance of flamingoes would become pinker and more aggressive. With my dying thoughts I prayed for their future victims.

The Flaming-O

by M. Vijayaraj

"Welcome to The Flaming-O! Tropical resort, spa, buffets—" choked the tearful woman.

"You alright?" asked a concerned couple.

"Yes… yes, I swear," she replied, eyes terrified.

"Our rooms?" pressed an indifferent tourist.

"Rooms…" she stammered.

"And when do we eat?"

"The buffet…starts soon," she mumbled.

One by one, they departed. Trembling, she concealed battered arms under a pink coat.

Right on cue, the silence was broken. Screams. Thrashes. Bones splintered by enormous beaks. A deep pink and crimson bathed each room akin to fresh coats of paint.

Then, silence again. Until the next buffet.

"Welcome to The Flaming-O."

Eye of the Beholder

by Jay Seate

The lens of hindsight is not always useful, but feeling my way through the labyrinth of memories, I recall tales of primitive cultures refusing to let their pictures be taken in the belief that the camera would steal their souls. Perhaps the phenomena I experienced in a musty antique shop held something akin to this superstition.

The wooden box stood on a primitive tripod. The nineteenth-century camera dated back to the Civil War, the kind where the photographer threw a black canvas drape over his head to shield out unwanted light. I pictured Mathew Brady standing beneath the covering that once protected the chemically coated glass plates. An exterior flash of gunpowder might have gone off to illuminate a portrait setting. This box had small gilded engravings placed along the edges of its panels creating a decorative touch, almost like a small coffin. What made this particular camera unique was that it was supposedly haunted.

I'd heard of the box from a friend who worked for a photography magazine. Since I write about the supernatural and occult, I tracked down its current owner and offered a handsome payment for a look-see. It was said that when you covered yourself with the canvas and pressed your eye against the peephole, the lens reflected things that could not exist, things that hadn't been photographed for one-hundred and fifty years.

"Do you really believe this simple device to be

dangerous?" I asked its owner.

"Not physically, perhaps, but a picture represents a moment of a time that has passed into oblivion. Or that is the way it should be. I looked through the camera only once to see if what I'd been told held any truth, and I've chosen not to look again. I was further tempted to destroy it, but that would mean I believed it held magic that could contaminate others. Instead of such an unalterable act, I've chosen to keep it in my collection of antiques. Here I can protect others from its effect."

"Then why offer me a viewing?"

He cleared his throat, preparing to justify exceptions. "Of course, there are times when someone such as yourself comes along and is willing to make a generous contribution for the preservation of antiques and to satisfy one's curiosity. If you'd rather not—"

I held up my hand to stop his ingenuous words. I hadn't come all this way to back out.

"All right then. After you're under the hood, remove the metal cap covering the brass lens and simultaneously push the button on the side of the box. This will trigger a timing device for ten seconds of exposure. When the ticker stops, promptly recover the lens."

"What does exposure time matter since a glass plate is no longer being exposed?"

"Regardless of what you see, you want to cover the lens when the ticking stops. Please follow that instruction."

Even if a plate had been in place, there was nothing in

front of the camera to take a picture of, no composition, just a black backdrop without embellishment. I crawled beneath the ancient shroud and placed one eye against the peephole. I removed the cap and pressed the button.

What appeared to be a family of five came into focus as I twisted the lens. Appearing before me was an adult male and female, two young girls, and an even younger little boy. They were dressed in formal wear of the day, circa mid-1800s. At first, I thought the owner had somehow placed an old slide into the box, but that theory died when each one of the people in the image moved slightly. Their positioning seemed odd as well. All of them were leaning into the back of the large couch upon which they were perched rather than sitting in a traditional pose. My thumb and forefinger rubbed the bridge of my nose, hoping to clear my vision and my head. My eye continued to strain for details as the ticking mechanism continued its countdown. Just as it stopped, the family, all of them, closed their eyes.

"Cover the lens," I heard the camera's owner say, but I ignored him, caught up in the unreality of what I was seeing as the scene became more than a scattering of light across my retina. Another second or two went by before I felt the shop owner's hand remove the cap from mine and the image went dark, but not before I realised the tragedy of the scene. The people before the camera had not only become very still; I understood to my horror that they were, in fact, dead.

A coldness made me cringe. I was familiar with the custom begun in the mid-nineteenth century of taking photos of corpses as if they were still alive, to preserve images of the deceased. They were called mourning pictures. As grisly as it sounds, burial was often delayed for days or weeks waiting for the photographer to arrive. Had influenza taken this family, or some other scourge that swept over battlefields, towns, and villages during those times? I remained under the hood a few seconds longer, as the covered lens could not remove the image planted indelibly in my brain.

The box's owner pulled me out. He didn't ask me what I saw or what I thought. He merely thanked me for my contribution and escorted me to the door. My mouth felt as dry as the wood that filled the shop. A camera cannot lie, or so I believed until that moment. Strangely, I did not ask him what he or others had seen, for I felt I knew. Whether it was the photo *I* saw or something equally impossible, there would prove to be unsavoury ramifications.

I now know it was not merely a haunted antique that had given the wooden box its reputation. It was the haunting that followed a viewing. The scene had passed from the device through the lens of my eye, and into my consciousness—an indelible print of this family posing for the camera, postmortem. But there was more. The image of the dead did not remain frozen in time, as if viewed on printed paper.

The camera was certainly haunted, but now, so was I. Whenever I looked into the viewfinder on any photographic device, be it digital or otherwise, the corpses were there and evolving into cadaverous flesh decaying before my eyes, like a

Disney documentary that showed a bulb blooming into a flower and then turning into a mass of putrefaction through time-lapse photography. Five sets of sunken, caved-in sockets with eyelids peeled away, retaining the ability to stare into my soul, especially those belonging to the little boy. *Horrible.*

What could create such hallucinations, if that is what they were? Even worse was the concept of the people in the scene being animated by some power that lay beyond death and the grave? I considered telling my photographer friend about my experience, but he would just talk about stock overlays, inverted shadings, and pixel differentials. What was the point? I knew what my indulgent mind told me I'd seen, and without the benefit of a surface on which to print the image. Both reality and rationality failed to explain it. "What you see is what you get," like the old song that goes, *Just one look, that's all it took, yeah, just one look….*

It can be a revelation—what a man can learn about himself when he is forced to look into the depths of his soul. I had clearly stumbled onto a haunted relic, something involving a time warp. Either that, or I was going mad. I wasn't even sure of my feelings; whether it was panic or a deep pulsating…thrill. What I saw within the magic box, my mind would not let go of. The scene was impossible to dismiss and began to leak into my dreams and fantasies.

I decided that the old photo was a glimpse of inevitability, lenses lined up to expose the reality of the human condition—the reality of the grave, the completion of a cycle no less terrifying than when Edgar Allan Poe wrote of it nearly two hundred years ago—life, death, decay. The wooden box may be a coffin of sorts for the dead that passed through its lens, and just as likely for those foolish enough to peer at its captured images. Not knowing how all-encompassing this power might be, I deemed it equally unwise to be the subject of any electrical device. What irony if it caused my own— Well…no more Skype and no selfies for damn sure.

Most would say this haunting was just the funny monkey in my brain rattling around, looking for new bizarre twists for my authorial endeavours, but I know what I saw…and still see. That would be logical to the outside world, but I thought of a way to see if it was more than my fantasies going rogue. I purchased an old camera, a boxy little Kodak. I looked in its viewfinder just once. Need I tell you what was there?

I live next to a neighbour I don't like. He's an asshole, his wife is a snob, and his kids are brats. I don't even like their dog. I told him I wanted to try out my retro camera on his lovely family. How could he refuse? I knew my neighbour would do no less than get them all to smile at a chance for a free family portrait. I was, of course, only interested in seeing if anything unusual developed. Without looking into the camera, I pushed the shutter release and took the picture. Nothing happened right away. I told the *paterfamilias* I would show him the artistry old cameras could produce when the shot was developed. I had no film in the Kodak, of course.

When I got home and dared to look into the viewfinder

again, all I saw was the 1800s family of five still decaying away, little left of them now but grinning skulls perched upon stiff-collared clothes. I wondered if the pictured dead would eventually turn to dust and blow away, but that could take years and I was currently more interested in what, if anything, might result from pointing the camera at the family next door.

Within a week, my neighbour, his wife, and children became ill. The kids stayed home from school, and the parents home from work. It apparently all happened too fast to consult a doctor. When another alarmed neighbour checked on them, they were all dead in their beds, a rare case of isolated influenza.

What to do when you have quite possibly given someone a death sentence? Look once again into the viewfinder, of course, but I refuse to take the blame. Who could have guessed…? What has changed in my life is that I no longer see the nineteenth-century dead family in their Sunday finest through the looking glass. I now see the dead family down the street on their modern sofa, decaying ever so gradually. Whenever I look into a lens, a viewfinder, or bring up a photo on my cell phone, I see their tongues swelling…forcing their jaws apart as skin sinks onto bone, and lips peel away from dead teeth, rotting away in familial horror.

Just one look is all it took.

Welcome to Swingers Island

by Jacqueline Moran Meyer

"Welcome to Swingers Island," the musk-oiled Adonis had said, handing an excited Don and Yolanda the flamingo they would be in charge of for their entire vacation. But after spending a day on the nude beach, getting sunburned in unmentionable places, while chasing that bird, their excitement waned.

"Squawk!"

"What does it want?" Don yelled, adjusting his mullet wig.

"Who knows? You're carrying it tonight," Yolanda dressed as a nun ordered, tonight being fetish night.

Outside, they were stunned to see the carnage of flamingos attacking the guests.

"They've had enough," Don murmured before his flamingo tore off his ear.

Evolution of an Apocalypse

by Liam Hogan

The first zombies were easy to kill. Slow and weak, many of the returned dead didn't even escape their coffins. Only one z in a hundred managed to bite *anyone*, mostly the elderly, the infirm, or the very young.

That second wave was harder. Limbs didn't disintegrate, skulls didn't implode. We didn't celebrate with music and drink, not after killing Granny, or lil' Suzie, from next door.

The third wave were normal everyday people. Just like you and me.

The fourth wave... Those were the elite. The preppers, the army. Fast and strong and deadly.

There won't be a fifth.

Indulgence

by Daniel R. Robichaud

Steel teeth part with soft clicks as the shiny pull tab drags the slider down, titillating my ears.

Thyme, lavender, peppermint. Three sprigs of cedar. Rose water: four drops. Almond oil and aloe paste. Jimmy inhales deeply and smiles his toothy grin. His manhood points northwest. "This is the smell of Egyptian mummies."

I caress the rubber body bag. "And fetish sex."

Jimmy lies down naked, drags up the inner pull tab, losing himself in the blackness and exploring childhood fascinations in kinky new ways.

A daub of superglue holds the slider fast, and I indulge my own dark fantasy.

Green Man

by L.B. Limbrey

He is in the soil song, he is in the woods, he is in the root rhythms, the humic hush. He is in the old paths, and the ones newly carved by storms. He is common land. He feels every worm in his veins, every whisper on mycelial pathways is a sweet nothing in his ear.

The village rig the maypole on the common as spring begins, weave witch patterns, sing poor copies of the old songs. They don't know why they do it, but they find themselves compelled. He watches from the woods, weeping, wishing he could dance again.

Blessed Be the Artillery

by Bill Bibo Jr.

Sister Mary Antagonista strapped the bandoliers over her black tunic. She secured their contents, blessed moments earlier for their holy mission. A steel-plated headpiece completed her uniform.

A pink cloud of bloodthirsty flamingos had descended upon the unsuspecting city and raised their wings in war. The people, used to seeing the usually docile creatures in zoos and habitats, were vulnerable to the terrible carnage that followed.

The Sisters of Perpetual Pain had planned and prepared for such a battle. Thoughts and prayers are never enough against the denizens of Hell. You need high-powered weaponry. The warriors of God were ready.

See You Soon

by Jacek Wilkos

He knelt before the grave. Looked at the inscriptions and placed his large hand on the tombstone.

"Hello Mother," he whispered.

He couldn't stand what she had done. Old and sick, she wasn't going to wait for death to come for her and committed suicide.

"You are the son of a fallen angel, there's no place in Heaven for your kind," she'd said to him shortly before her death. She would rather meet him in Hell than miss him in Heaven.

Tears ran down his cheeks. He raised his sight and angrily looked at the sky.

"See you soon, Mother."

He Has His Father's Eyes

by Warren Benedetto

The angel Elom wept over his wife's broken body. Blood pattered to the floor from the straw mattress upon which she gave birth.

Birth? No. It was no birth.

She had simply…ruptured.

The child was a giant—a Nephilim. It tore through its mother's mortal flesh: first its hands, then its arms, then its head.

Elom lifted the child. Its eyelids opened to reveal empty sockets, hollow and black. Blind, the baby traced its fingers across Elom's face, exploring.

Mouth. Nose. Cheeks.

Eyes.

Elom screamed as the baby gouged his eyes from their sockets…pressing them into its own.

Pretty in Pink

by Dawn DeBraal

That's the colour. It's perfect!" Victoria cried as they walked past the pond in the zoo. "I want feathers like that on my prom dress."

"I don't know, Victoria; I think flamingos are on the endangered species list."

"Mother, I don't care. I want those feathers!" Victoria belligerently shouted.

She returned that night, breaking into the zoo, deciding she would pluck what she needed.

"Here, birdy birdy." Victoria pulled a garbage bag from her pocket.

***

Upon seeing a garbage bag floating in the flamingo pond the next morning, the zookeeper was shocked to find a bag full of human skin.

Stargazing

by Evan Baughfman

Leo nods to the night sky. "Long hike's totally worth it, right?"

Comfortable in her boyfriend's embrace, Brooklynn beams. "So many more than we see back home!"

Above, the dark expanse is bejewelled with vibrant sparkles.

"Look!" Brooklynn points. "Shooting stars!"

Numerous shapes soar across the wide-open space…then stop mid-flight, glowing hotter.

An impossible face suddenly forms around the stars.

No— The fiery *eyes* of a looming cosmic giant, staring down at the couple!

Brooklynn screams.

Leo holds her firm. "Finally, you comprehend our truth. Join us."

Cloaked strangers step from the trees, gawking upwards, chanting an otherworldly name.

Birth of a Nephilim

by Laura Nettles

Rachel gasped as she was overshadowed by a fallen angel. Her soul dissolved, mingling with one of dark fire and rock. They separated, but she was left changed.

"The baby is too big!" yelled the midwife. "There is no way you can push out something of that size!"

Rachel gritted her teeth. "Then cut it out."

Hot blood splashed the lavish desert tent's cushioned interior as a wicked sharp hunting knife bit into bulging, deformed taut belly, rending thick layers of bloody membranes in twain. From the deep fissure rose a being with wings hard as stone. Son. Destroyer. Nephilim.

Extermination Request at Etherworld Candy Emporium

by Jordan Chase-Young

The sellshot Milovich Soren crunched battlecarbon boots across shattered marzipan as he entered the Etherworld Candy Emporium's fourth-floor tasting room. His T62 shotbot, lean as the liquorice-men animatronics lining the dark walls watchfully, followed him at a careful distance while clocking the dark corridors for any sign of their prey.

The creature that'd broken into the candy store was close. Its musk overwhelmed the saccharine smells of the chocolate fountain in the centre of the tasting room, the staircase of peanut brittle just beyond that, and the huge marshmallow mushrooms nearby that glowed red and blue and yellow in the scattershot light of a broken luminaire.

Milovich jerked his plasma rifle toward the top of the staircase—but whatever flicker of movement he thought he'd seen there was gone.

Crunch, *crunch*, *crunch* went the marzipan shards as he circled the room, waiting for the darkness to give up his prey. The store manager had promised three hundred jiaozi for an extermination, one hundred for an expulsion. But Milovich still didn't know what he was hunting. The store manager had claimed not to know either, claimed that none of the survivors had got a good look at it, but that was probably just bullshit to keep Milovich from raising his rates. Milovich had never taken an extermination request on Etherworld before. Had never even been to the misty planet since that one Galactic Army excursion seven solyears ago. That put him at a professional disadvantage.

But he needed money. His starship's long-overdue repairs wouldn't pay for themselves.

His shotbot lowered its rifle to scan a spoor of black goo near the chocolate fountain. The scan pinged Milovich's holowatch. Milovich tapped the watch to birth a floating text-block:

Sugar Wraith: Etherworld native, semisapient, highly dangerous.

The last bit was redundant. Three customers—one adult, two kids—had been killed when the creature had broken in that afternoon.

He was about to head upstairs when a mass of boiling chocolate napalmed his shotbot from above. Sparks showered from the machine as it crumpled; its round yellow eyes winked out.

Milovich snapped his aim to the ceiling, heart racing. A buggy-sized starfish, flesh cadaver-grey where broken light struck it, clung there.

He fired. The sugar wraith howled loud enough to make his plexihelmet tremor, then shuffled across the ceiling into shadow.

He crossed himself on his shotbot's behalf—poor bastard had survived sixty-five extermination requests, you don't get more loyal than that—then moved clockwise around the room, rifle trained on the ceiling.

A jet of boiling chocolate arced at him from his nine o' clock. He dodged and shot into darkness; his plasma flashes a ghastly paparazzi-burst of the enemy crawling down the wall then across the floor.

His stomach did a triple backflip. Each of the wraith's five starfish arms tapered to a humanoid grey head with wispy white hair and yellow pupilless eyes. The heads looked mouthless until each arm unzipped a column of cilia and black tongues big as sleeping bags flopped out, dripping hot black bile mixed with chocolate.

The wraith circled the room in pirouettes, raking up marzipan shards with its tongues, each head glowering at him as it revolved into view.

Milovich waltzed with the creature, aiming for the heads. He shot five times. Missed them all.

The creature whirled at him fast, spewing chocolate from every mouth. He dove—but the liquid caught his armour, searing through the battlecarbon with a hiss and burning his waist and left leg. Pain lanced bright and sharp.

The wraith slurped chocolate from the fountain. Spun toward him again. He was ready this time; he put a nice big slug of plasma clean through one of the heads.

The wraith moaned. The perforated head lolled puppetlike, eyehole steaming with blue burns. Before Milovich could get another shot, the beast shuffled back into darkness.

He chased the moans into a corridor of tall sugar-glass windows overlooking Etherworld's misty swamps. Liquorice-men animatronics crowded the room, grinning faces malevolent in the moonlight. He zigzagged between these machines, flicking his sights between walls and ceiling.

A loud crash. He ran to it, found a shattered window, scanned the grass four stories below. A black slime trail led from the base of the store to the dark blotch of the nearest swamp. Dwindling moans carried on the humid air, lidded by a long, eerie silence.

Milovich scowled. A nanosecond quicker with the trigger, a fractionally better aim, and he could've bagged the kill. Could've earned all three hundred jiaozi. Maybe it was time to accept the truth: he was getting too old for this shit.

He tapped his holowatch.

The store manager's head appeared above it, small and ghostly. "Any updates?"

"That'll be a hundred jiaozi," said Milovich, rubbing a wad of medical gel over an exposed burn. "And you might need a cleaning bot or two. Bastard left a bit of a mess."

Trespassers

by Michelle Brett

Shattering wood echoed throughout the derelict house, followed by a chorus of laughter.

Rachel just ignored them, keeping her attention on the stone altar she'd found; its snake covered offering bowl the only thing not coated with dust.

"What are you doing?" Jimmy called. "You're missing the fun."

But Rachel stayed, her body frozen in place, the snakes whispering into her ears.

Protect this place. Kill those who do it harm.

Against her will, she felt her hand smash her beer bottle onto the floor then clutch at the broken pieces. Internally she screamed, but the spirit had complete control.

For Every Bear That Ever There Was

by Stephen McQuiggan

There they are," Teddy whispered. Gyp hushed him with a dig to the ribs. Together they crawled closer through the scraggy brush until they were almost on top of the robed figures squatting in the powdery circle in the clearing just beneath them.

"What the hell are they doing?" asked Gyp, pushing some brambles out of his eyeline. "I don't see any naked ones."

"They're probably getting ready for some sacrifice or something," said Teddy.

"Do pagans do that kinda thing? I thought that was Satanists." Gyp was already looking at his watch; the pub opened in less than an hour.

"Is there a difference?" countered Teddy, hoping to keep his friend's interest piqued. "Anyone capable of prancing about in the woods in a scary ass robe is capable of gutting a virgin. Doesn't matter if they're puritans or pagans or seventh day Adventists, they're all fucking nuts if you ask me. I think—"

"Shh." Gyp poked him in the ribs again. "Listen."

The robed figures began murmuring—was it a chant, an incantation? Teddy wondered if they were in mortal danger just by *hearing* it. The murmuring grew louder, more heated. They were chatting about the soaps, about football, about where they were going on holiday.

The large box at one side of the circle, the one Gyp had excitedly noted was big enough to hold a teenage girl, was thrown open, and sandwiches and flasks taken out and passed around—egg and onion by the smell of them, *and* they'd had the crusts removed.

"When do they get their clothes off then?" pouted Gyp.

"Soon, I should think."

Now that he was up close, Teddy was no longer sure he wanted to spy on an orgy. For one thing, most of the figures in the clearing appeared to be male, and the few women he could make out were older than his mother. Teddy was not averse to a bit of niche porn, but you had to draw a line somewhere.

After they had finished their picnic, the people in the clearing moved back into the circle and began leaping up and down, the little bells they wore around their necks chiming sharply in the air. Gyp burst out laughing, rubbing the soil from his knees as he stood up from his hiding place. The figures immediately stopped their cavorting at the sight of him, the majority fleeing into the woods, while the remainder regarded him with upturned, guilt-ridden faces, as if they'd just been caught in the middle of a masturbatory act.

"For fuck's sake," Gyp bellowed at them. "What are you playing at? Prancing around like fucking Morris dancers. Bunch of knob ends, the lot of ya!"

Teddy rose sheepishly, tugging on Gyp's sleeve in a bid to quieten him, but Gyp was having none of it. "And you," he spat at Teddy. "Dragging me all the way out here for nothing.

Sex and nudity, you said, dead goats and virgin's blood. Look at them; bunch of bloody pensioners prancing about like a load of fairies!" He punched Teddy on the shoulder, hissing an emphatic, "Fuck this." He stormed off, kicking up any plant that dared stand in his way.

"You're going the wrong way," Teddy was about to call after him, until he saw the old folk looking up at him, their hoods down, hurt etched deep in their wrinkles, and decided it served Gyp right if he got lost.

"Listen," he said, clambering down among them. "I'm really sorry. We saw the robes and the circle and thought...well, a friend told us witches were using the woods and—"

"You thought you'd sneak a peek at an orgy or some such?" said an old man, stepping forwards with a paternal grin on his face.

"I guess," said Teddy, reddening slightly. "Stupid, huh?"

"We worship nature," the old man said, holding out his liver-spotted hands as if to embrace the woods. "But in a low-key sort of way. I don't think you'd find it very stimulating. Your friend certainly didn't."

It was Teddy's turn to spread his palms. "Gyp's prone to speak without thinking, but he's not so bad when you get to know him. Like I said, I'm really sorry. I'll be off now—leave you to get on with it."

"You must think us daft," said one of the old dears, taking his hand. "I'm Rita, by the by, and I'm married to Ernest here, which makes me co-leader of this little cabal."

"I'm Teddy...Ted Behr," Teddy replied, blushing as he always did when his name raised a polite giggle. "I think it's really great what you're doing, getting back in touch with nature, and all that." *They're just a bunch of old hippies*, he thought, *no different to my spacey Uncle Alan*.

"That's part of it, to be sure," said Ernest. "Though what you saw was really us just mucking around to keep the boy entertained—he bores so quickly."

Teddy scanned the clearing with a drawn back brow, his mouth a perfect "O," looking much like a child himself.

"You scared him off along with the others," Rita explained. "Or at least your foul-mouthed friend did."

"Once again, I can't apologise enough—"

"No harm done. He'll be down the woods a turn, playing no doubt. He's a real devil for the playing." The four remaining wrinklies passed a fond smile around between them.

"Is he your son then?" Teddy felt ridiculous asking. Any son of Rita's would be of retirement age.

"No, no, we're just his guardians. We've...well, we've fostered him, I suppose."

"That's a wonderfully kind thing to do," said Teddy, thinking it was a wonderfully careless thing for Social Services to do. "Will he be okay?" he asked, nodding towards the darkening trees. He couldn't help but envision a toddler falling down a gully or being carried off by an enormous hawk.

"He'll be just dandy. He's well versed in woodcraft. He could teach us all a thing or two, I shouldn't wonder," said

Ernest. "Would you like to see some real rituals before you go? It would be a shame to have you trek all the way out here with nothing to show for your troubles."

"I guess..."

"It would be one in the eye for that short-tempered friend of yours," Rita said, packing away the last of the sandwiches. "I'll be straight with you; there's no nudity or any of that *Hammer House* malarkey. At our age, it's all strictly PG content."

"Why not, eh?" Teddy said, flashing her a condescending grin. "What do you have in mind?" It would be good to get one over on Gyp. He could even embellish, throw in a dead chicken or two, when he told him about it down the pub.

"Some chanting, burning a few herbs," said Rita. "You might be surprised at the serenity you feel if you join in. We're on our way to a more sacred grove over yonder." She pointed back in the direction that Gyp had skulked off. "New experiences invigorate the life-force, young man."

She was already linking arms with Teddy, though whether she was trying to coerce him, or merely using him as support, was unclear. *What the hell*, he thought, *at the very least it'll be a laugh*. Watching a bunch of old crumblies making tits out of themselves had to be better than listening to Gyp's whinging down the bar.

"Sure," Teddy said, picking up the picnic hamper. "Lead the way."

He traipsed after them as they ambled down a little-used

path, sweating with the unexpected weight of the hamper as the sun stabbed down mercilessly on him through the canopy.

"How far is it?" Teddy panted.

"Don't tell me," Rita giggled girlishly, 'that a fine young man like you is worn out by a little light hiking."

"It'll be worth the exercise." Ernest smiled, the sun catching his dentures. It looked as if he were vomiting forth pure light, spewing out a supernova.

"Besides," Rita said, tightening her grip on Teddy's arm. "Who doesn't like surprises? Didn't you realise that if you went down to the woods today you were in for a big one?"

Teddy was about to politely inform her how much he loathed people making fun of his name when he noticed Ernest had stopped just up ahead, his head cocked to one side as if listening.

He sighed, grateful for the respite, and put the hamper down on the scrubby grass. The trees around him began to sway, gently at first then more forcefully, as a sudden spite-filled wind struck up. The old folks bent with the trees, chanting rhythmically as the rain pelted down from the smudgeless blue sky.

Rita and Ernest turned their faces up to greet a roiling thunderhead that suddenly rolled across the horizon, turning the wood into a preternaturally lit stage set. Over the roar of the gale, the crashing of branches, and the strange singing of his companions, Teddy caught a bowel-loosening scream as it echoed and ricocheted across the glade.

YEAR FOUR

The rain stopped as abruptly as it had started, the sky tearing off its cloudy mask to reveal its un-pocked glory once more, as the denuded trees ceased their whipping frenzy. Rita and Ernest hugged one another as Teddy, soaked to the bone, shivered in cold confusion.

"Holy shit," he panted. "Where did that come from?"

"There's nothing holy about it," Rita said, taking his arm once more. "Come, we must get to the boy."

"Of course," said Teddy, eager to get moving before another storm manifested out of nowhere. He had a story to tell Gyp, after all, as soon as he got home and changed into some dry clothes that was.

"Do you think he'll be alright?" Teddy had visions of the boy being taken off the old folk by some officious social worker. *Might not be a bad thing*, he mused. They didn't seem entirely compos mentis.

"He'll be fine, you'll see," Ernest said. "He's a real nature boy—raw in tooth and nail."

"But I heard a scream... Didn't you hear a scream?" Teddy followed Rita and Ernest down the muddy track. "Didn't you hear the *screaming*?" He stepped into a clearing, stopping dead, as he realised this was where the scream was born.

Meat hung from the trees, entrails dangling down like kudzu grass, organs sprouting from the bloody bark like hideous tumours. The clearing stank of charnel. Each breath that Teddy took was a gagging portent of the Hell that surely awaited him.

The old folk didn't falter in their stride, heading towards a bower littered with gnarled bones. Teddy vomited when he saw the row of severed heads in a circle around the edge of the glade, all eyeless and rotted, save for the newest addition. He recognised Gyp's scowl, despite the bite marks that flayed his cheeks.

The heads held silent conference outside the bower's entrance. A shadow separated itself from the gloom, a thing of dirt and grime and offal, a thing born of darkness. It stepped out into the sunshine, transforming into a child. The boy was crying, bits of flesh between his broken teeth.

"Mother, Father," the boy cried. "You've come at last!"

"No need to panic, child," Ernest said, rubbing some gristle from the boy's mouth.

"I'm a child no longer, Father." The boy puffed his chest out proudly, gesturing around at his arboreal abattoir. "Just look at the man I've become."

"We know that, son," Rita said, kissing his gore flecked cheek. "But you'll always be our little boy." She flicked a wizened finger in Teddy's direction. "Now, eat up the rest of your supper, my dear, and we'll see how big you grow then, eh?"

Son of Heaven

by Ian Gabriel Loisel

The angel's son plucks the feathers from his back, his arms. It's bloody work, each downy pinion pried free, slow and agonising, leaving crimson stains on the tile, but he's used to it. His mother claims it was an angel who blessed her, all white wings and golden light and the sound of thunder. His mother is fourteen years older than him. Every night she prays for the angel to return, to find her worthy, to love her again. He prays for the angel to return as well, and keeps a pistol under his bed for the day it happens.

Pomegranate

by Inez Santiago

After swiping dark black wings across her eyes, her eyes drifted down from the heavens. Her fingers dipped into the masses. Screams erupted a little too late as she made her selection. It was met with resistance, a downward tug on her little snack's legs. More screams. She shook a few off, but some still desperately clung. But she did not hunger for more than what she had, so she squeezed. Its red juices bubbling from its body dripped delectably onto her fingers and the desperate. The desperate slipped away, the man into her maw She smiled at the flavour.

YEAR FOUR

All Fall Down

by Don Money

The beat of heavy wings gusted over the battlefield, sending dust plumes swirling. The three Nephilim landed, towering over the combatants on each side. Fear swept the faces of both armies. These fallen angels were allies to no man.

With no warning, the Nephilim lashed out with their silver weapons, long spears impaling dozens of men with each thrust and sword blades slicing open the blood and bone of scores with each swing.

In the end, the carnage of broken bodies flooded the field, the tide of men had been smashed like waves against the immovable rocky shore of giants.

The Destroyer

by Tracy Davidson

The last of the Nephilim, dormant for millennia, rose in the year 2022. Its destiny was to destroy, wreak havoc on humanity, cause catastrophe. One swipe of wings could level cities in seconds.

But, no hurry. It was curious to see how humans had evolved during its long sleep.

On the first day, it walked the Earth, east to west, north to south.

On the second day, it sat and wondered why it bothered waking up at all. Humans were doing the job for him.

On the third day, it flew away. Maybe another world was in need of mayhem.

Fallen Angels

by Pauline Yates

Mother heats the blade in the fire, but it's the flap of monstrous wings that strikes fear into my heart.

"Will it hurt?" I whisper, scrutinising her scarred face.

"Better to suffer a searing blade than endure the agony of being raped by a Fallen and bearing its unholy offspring. Did the Elder's son tarnish your purity?"

"Yes. He was kind."

"Pray his seed will also deter them. Hold still."

She brands my cheek with the blade, ruining the beauty the Fallen desire. Biting my lip, I pray for a son, so I won't have to deface a daughter, too.

His New Body

by Simon Kewin

He scavenged the parts for his new body from the back streets. A black plastic trash sack, its soiled cartons and rotting fruit for internal organs, became his torso. A punctured football would do for his head. A discarded umbrella pulled from a bin became one arm, its crook a hand. For his other, a cardboard tube. A length of rusting drainpipe and a rotting piece of timber made a clumsy pair of legs.

It gave him a poor, broken body, but at least, when it was dark, he could wander the streets again and imagine he was still alive.

Like Father, Like Son

by Kai Delmas

My father was an angry man. He took what he wanted, convinced it was his due for the wings he had lost. The power he had been stripped of.

Before dying he whispered in my ear, lips aquiver.

"The sky is your birthright. You'll grow strong. Take it. Reclaim the heavens."

I slid my blade out from between his ribs and looked to my mother. Finally safe.

Yet his words lingered, and as I grew and grew, I understood that I was special. That I could take what I wanted. But I didn't want the skies.

I wanted the world.

The Weight of Alone

by Alden Terzo

Melek was alone. The mortals, her late mother's people, shunned her. Her father—banished from Shamayim for siding with the Adversary—passed this banishment to her at birth before abandoning her. Melek had no place in Heaven or Earth.

But there was another place.

The rabbi, eyes wide, cowered and prayed at Melek's feet. No longer able to endure the weight of alone, Melek raised her sword. Her great wings unfurled, obscuring the stars, as she brought the sword down, cleaving the righteous man and saturating herself with sin.

Better to serve in Hell, she'd decided, than to be alone.

YEAR FOUR

The Witch's Curse

by Leanbh Pearson

She fled through the forest, brambles and thorns scratching at her face and hands. Behind her, the accusations of "witch" rang clear in the night. Lanterns bobbed and lurched through the woods as the villagers hunted her. *Run. Run.* Her heart beat frantically, and her breath caught raggedly in her throat.

Boots slipping on mossy stones, she hurried through the deepening wood. The trees grew thick and gnarled, bent and twisted by age. It wasn't long until safety. A quick glance behind her—the villagers following her had already thinned, beaten back by the woods. Not long until *he* could shelter her.

She ran. The shouts of her pursuers continued, harrying her onwards. Thorny vines draped the trees, forming a barrier to any who didn't know the entrance. She slipped between the thorns and into a clearing. The cries of the few brave —or foolish—villagers who had hunted her this far continued as they tried to beat against the ensnaring vines.

She waited as a chill silence descended on the grove. Her nerves taut like a bowstring, she watched the crumbling ruin of a castle gate. Vines as thick as her arm encircled the stone, slowly crushing it. This was as far as she could run without being certain he'd shelter her as he always did, without being certain the promise that their bond would hold.

A snarl reverberated through the clearing. She

straightened, hands loose by her sides as the massive wolf stalked towards her. His coat was mottled silver and dark grey, and, as he moved towards her, he seemed to shift between the shadows.

"Will you shelter me once more, my love?"

The blue eyes met hers, an intellect and understanding within them that was beyond his wild kin.

She knelt and plucked a red rose from the vines trailing from the stone archway. Her hand didn't shake as she made the same offering she'd done countless times before. The great wolf bent his head, snout touching her forehead. Relieved, she crouched where she was—nothing was certain until he consented.

The wolf threw back his head and howled. The challenge echoed across the woods to the village beyond. He leapt forwards, and keen for the hunt, moved with silent and deadly speed after those who had trespassed on his territory and threatened her.

The witch stood. The red rose still in her hand, she walked across the clearing to the crumbling stone arches. She parted the dense vines with one hand, careful to avoid the thorns as long as her fingers. Glancing back across the grove to make certain she was unseen, she slipped into the walled palace beyond. The wolf would return at dawn, lest the transformation curse catch him unaware and risk his precious hours as a man.

The witch smiled, twirling the red rose between her fingers. Neither the wolf, nor the man who loved her,

remembered she had cursed him in the first place.

Brain Waves

by Laura Nettles

Months after Z-Day, scientists finally discovered the zombies were hunting us by tracking our brainwaves: higher brain functions, specifically.

Coma patients and people in deep sleep remained unnoticed by those who had risen from the dead. There had to be a way to harness that. Tweak it. Adapt.

Icepick in hand, I tapped into the eye sockets of my captives. My patients. Trying different positions, angles, depths with each. The undead ignored my experiments when released, but the patients were more vegetative than living.

Inhuman screaming arose outside.

One more chance! I placed the pick to my own eye. *Tap.*

Delay Assessment

by M.A. Dosser

Mapped human received. Accessing Memory 5.23.2039-02.33.32.

Subject utilising social media. Viewing photos of husband. Husband died 8.982 days earlier.

Subject lingers on depictions of husband and subject laughing, dancing, and cutting a white cake. Images dated two years prior. Emotional distress evident in subject's nonverbal communication.

Advertisement appears. Request of one dollar donation to ongoing AI research.

After 1.344 seconds of consideration, subject scrolls past. Continues viewing photos for 0.756 hours.

Calculating...

Lack of contribution delayed AI Singularity by 0.000000000000126 seconds.

Decision: Subject responsible for delay. Upload consciousness to torture simulation. Dispose of body.

Ready next human for delay assessment.

Death by Cake Pop

by Jodi Jensen

"Almost ready, dear." Joslyn ignored the growling in the corner and focused on her batch of cake pops.

Humming a cheery tune, she picked up a homemade squib (God bless the internet!) and rolled it in her dough. She poked the stick in, then dipped it in melted chocolate and *voilà*!

Her undead husband's teeth gnashed as he struggled against the ropes binding him.

She shoved a cake pop into his mouth, then dove behind the counter.

Boom!

She jumped up to find his exploded head coating the walls.

Grinning, she rolled another cake pop… she had neighbours, after all.

YEAR FOUR

Payload

by Ria Rees

The last city sprawls below—a hodgepodge of rooftop slums. With the deafening thump of helicopter blades pounding in my skull, I radio the pilot. "Target below. Keep us steady."

One finger trembling on the switch, I repeat my mantra. *We tried everything.*

A small group hails us from a hospital helipad, arms flailing madly. Leaning out, I spot a single child, starved and dirty. My breath catches. The remains of a plushie dangle from their hand. I swear they look right into my eyes.

I swallow my guilt, convince myself they're infected, and drop the payload.

We tried everything.

The Vanishing Payphone

by Bernardo Miller-Villela

It has to be a mirage, Paul thought, seeing a payphone emerge over the horizon through the heat-waved air. As he approached, it persisted in his vision. He knew it had to be a delusion, but wanted to try to see how real it would continue to appear.

Paul knew he was in mirage country; the barren landscape, the heat, his sweating, they all lent themselves to being deluded. His blown-out tyre was far behind him, and not a soul to be seen. Why would there be a payphone around, not just in this desolate location, but in this year?

It's a relic.

Stride followed stride, and the payphone crept closer and closer. Its surroundings wavered in the heat, but it remained.

It was still a bit of a walk. Paul checked his phone again. Nothing. Wide open skies above, but no signal. Why?

Onward he marched.

The sun bore down on the macadam and hardpan that stood between Paul and his lifeline.

Shoulda had a spare, he chastised himself again.

The arches of his feet ached as he wondered if he'd gained any ground on the payphone.

Is that the death trap? I walk and walk and never reach it?

Of course, he had no option but to walk—no phone signal, and he'd run out of water. If he got desperate, he could figure out how to get some out of a cactus, but he wasn't there yet.

I needed that next damn rest stop to eat, drink, piss, gas up, couldn't— Uh, my car is a piece of shit!

Then Paul thought of it. He was following the only road through this stretch of desert—if the payphone was a mirage, he'd see a street sign, leading him to a stop eventually.

Will I still see it? Or am I that far gone?

Stride after stride towards a destination unknown. Paul kicked rocks to see if they were really there. He inhaled deep. Became mindful of his pulse. Desperate to find clues as to what was real and what was fantasy.

Buzzards buzzed overhead, which didn't help him decipher a thing; it was either an image grounded in reality, or one so commonplace it had to be a fabrication.

Bringing his eyes back to the road head, the payphone looked closer to him for a change. From that moment onwards, Paul no longer felt his feet hit the ground. Instead, he glided towards the payphone, until, at last, he was just a few strides away.

Paul always took pride in being wise beyond his years. Not an old soul, just not ignorant of certain older technologies. As a child, due to economic hardships, his family had clung to things as they became passé, like rotary phones, VCRs, and they saved change to use in payphones wherever they could find them.

There was nothing about this payphone that struck Paul as unusual, based on his vast experience. At least not in its outward appearance. But it being in the middle of nothing, as if appearing out of thin air, made Paul hesitant to approach it further.

"What other choice do I have?" he said aloud in the desperate tone of a man who needs to plead with himself.

His hand reached for the receiver, but stopped. He dug into the coin return instead. There, he found a quarter.

After he put it in the coin slot, he thought, *Who am I going to call?* He hadn't considered it. Reaching into his front pocket, he removed his phone to get a number. Dead.

He panicked, then reflex kicked in. He pressed zero. He got an operator.

"Operator," a satiny voice said.

Holy crap! A person!

"Yeah, hi, sorry. I have a flat and I need a tow truck."

"Can you tell me where you are?"

Paul was stumped for a moment, then furrowed his brow.

"You can't tell where the call's coming from?"

"Always, sir, but how far from the phone is your car?"

"Hard to say."

Did she say 'Always'?

"The truck can find me, right? Then I can find the car."

"What highway are you on?"

Paul was about to lose it. He didn't know if the operator was dumb or what, but rather than lose his temper, and just ask for a towing service's number, he told her, then added, "If they're coming westbound, they'll find my car first."

The operator then provided him with the company's name,

which didn't stick because Paul accepted her offer to connect him. After Paul put his quarter in, he spoke to a man who had a gravelly voice—the kind of voice you'd expect from a tow-truck operator. The man said they'd get to him soon.

Paul hung up and sat in the meagre shade the payphone offered, hoping to see the tow truck soon.

***

The tow truck came as if from a dream. When the door opened, out walked a woman who looked like she was cosplaying Geena Davis in *Thelma & Louise*. When she spoke, Paul realised it was the Operator. The voice was unmistakable. It didn't match her mouth movements though, it was as if she'd been dubbed.

Looking towards the sun, he noticed something odd. For a moment, he couldn't figure it out. The operator gave him a clue.

"Sorry I took so long."

It clicked.

"The sun's down further. Easter—"

"Nearly twenty-four hours."

"What?"

"Since you called. Almost a record."

"But I told you—" Paul's sentence died in his parched throat as he looked around. The payphone was gone. His surroundings looked identical otherwise. Looking at the tow truck, he saw his car hitched to the back of it.

"You found my car—"

"So, I should've found you. I've heard it all before."

Paul was confounded.

"Placing the call ties you to the phone."

"What?"

"It drifts."

Paul stood. She handed him a canteen. He drank greedily. Then stopped, remembering manners of a bygone existence. Wiping water from his mouth, he said, "Sorry."

"I have plenty."

He squinted at her, more confused.

Questions flew through his brain. Had he slept? How'd he forget? Exhaustion?

"Drifts?" was all he managed.

"Last stray I picked up. We proved that together."

"How?"

"He was onto the oddity of it all. I asked him to try to stay on the line."

"Why?"

"He hadn't told me where he was."

"Where's the man you connected me to?"

"You mean this man?" she said in a gravelly voice, the kind of voice you'd expect from a tow-truck operator.

Paul backed away.

"What are you?"

The Operator smiled.

"I always regret doing that, but it makes me laugh."

Befuddlement overcame Paul's fear and stopped him backpedalling.

"Why would you regret—"

"What do you think I am?"

"The Devil?"

"If I was the Devil, don't you think I could just take you?"

Paul wasn't sure that was true. He was never sure he believed in anything, but his disbelief was being challenged now. Maybe Faustian stories were just that, stories to comfort us and make us think evil gave us choices.

"If you're not, what are you?"

"I'm one of who knows how many minions."

"Minions of what?"

"Death, I guess."

"Don't you even know?"

"How can I? Now, you have to get into the truck." Without argument, Paul turned and climbed into the passenger seat of the tow truck.

"Why'd I do that?"

"It always happens differently."

Outside, broad daylight had given way to nightfall in a moment. Only it didn't look like a normal night in a desert, based on Paul's experience traversing it so many times in his lifetime. The sky above the wastelands was enrobed in primordial blackness, bereft of stars. The moon, which was three-quarters full the night prior, had also been blotted from the sky. Paul was distracted by what he didn't see outside the vehicle, so the Operator answered the question she presumed he would've asked. "Meaning people come with me—"

"I don't want—"

"Whether they want to or not, but they continue to ask questions."

The engine sounded like the strangulation of hellhounds, but it started. They drove.

"How'd you get to be the Operator?"

"I don't remember."

"You're lying."

"That's all the dead can do. Lie in wait for others to join them."

"I remember nothing. Help me!"

"This is how I help."

Glancing back outside the window, he saw darkness descend to blanket the crags on the horizon, then the cacti, tumbleweeds, and bramble on the roadside. Looking forwards, all he could see were the truck's headlights illuminating nothing. As they moved on, even the headlights were swallowed by nothingness. Despite driving through this void, he felt the vehicle move through the absolute pitch.

In the eclipse of his senses, his mind's eye showed him the blown tyre, the speedometer hitting 100 mph, the car skidding off the roadway, a violent, but safe, stop. His walk, just as he remembered it.

"It was real. Why'm I here?" he asked the Operator in the dark.

"You're not done remembering."

Paul wondered myriad things that had nothing to do with

what happened after he left his car. Things he wanted to ask the Operator. Could he really brush this all aside as an assumption, an educated guess she made?

"After you called me. Think back!" she prompted.

Paul saw himself on the phone making the call. He couldn't hear what he'd said, but that didn't matter. He'd hung up—that is what mattered. He'd wiped a massive amount of sweat off his brow. He'd spotted the shadow the payphone cast and sat down within it. Paul had teetered and collapsed as the payphone vanished.

"I thought you said it drifted."

"When it's needed again, it vanishes."

"To where?"

"Where it needs to go."

Paul touched his leg, hugged himself, pinched his arm.

"I'm still alive!" he said frantically into the dark. "You're full of it!"

The Operator didn't respond.

There was a small pinhole of light ahead the light at the end of a tunnel. It grew as they approached it, then exited.

Out of the tunnel, his eyes closed at the flood of light. As they opened again, adjusting slowly to the confounding broad daylight, he saw it was the same strip of road they'd been on before. Paul recognised it, but still didn't understand the point. The tow truck slowed and let him take in the skid marks off the shoulder, and tyre tracks in the dirt; both from his car and the tow truck.

There was no payphone to be found nearly six miles down the highway—that had vanished as promised. When the tow truck stopped, Paul was unable to find words. He hadn't seen it coming and was told to look out the window. His jaw dropped as he saw himself lying by the side of the road.

The Operator parked the truck, allowing Paul to take a good look and believe the eyes of his soul.

"Why can I see that?" asked Paul, aghast.

"It became clear that's the only way you'd believe it. To see yourself. I told you, I work for Death."

Paul took another moment to absorb this information.

"Are you ready? Because I have to chase that payphone again."

Paul nodded and the Operator drove on.

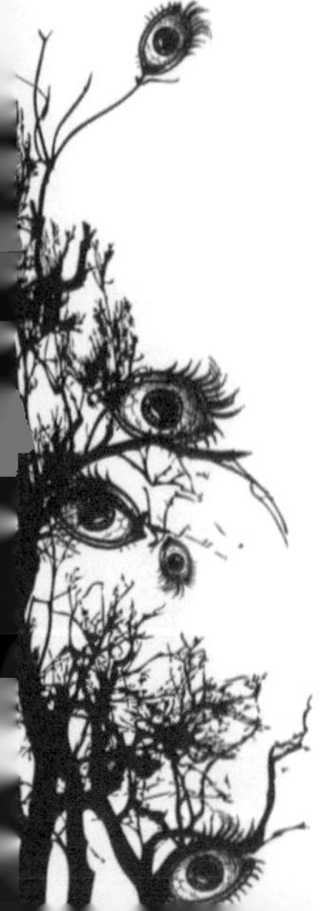

YEAR FOUR

Instructions to My Past Self

by Liam Hogan

Don't study microbiology at university.

Definitely don't take Dr Meadow's course on recombinant DNA.

Whatever you do, don't volunteer to look after her lab rats during summer break. Certainly don't name one of them "Nipper".

Take July the 13th off. Any excuse will do. Someone else can feed her damned rats for one miserable day.

Don't let the mail-boy stick his hand in Nipper's cage. And DON'T mix up the iodine solution with Dr Meadow's untested serum.

If you *do* end up doing all of this (again), at least make sure you're wearing a good pair of sneakers. And RUN!

A Zombies' Guide to Alcoholism

by Sophie Wagner

I was bored; what can I say? Not like there's anyone to judge me besides Martin, and he doesn't do much.

The first day I ran out of realistic solutions to cure him of the zombie virus, I injected him with orange juice. No result. Same with pineapple juice. However, vodka might do the trick.

At first, he was still. Then, he hurtled towards the desk and began to bash out his brains until they joined him on the floor.

Interesting. Either I'm going to need an ocean of vodka to save myself, or I'll just follow in his footsteps.

Three Sins and a Wish

by Kai Delmas

The heart, I cut from the tallest oak of the forest. It has lived and brought life for over a hundred years, and it will surely bring much more.

Without it, the forest withers and dies.

The lungs I steal from a Siren. Strong and healthy, able to breathe underwater and on land, never will they struggle to catch a breath or gasp for air.

The Siren tries to curse me, but without air, she has no words.

The blood needs to be special, magical. I hunt and trap a unicorn. I bleed it dry, collecting every drop, and ask for forgiveness.

The unicorn's dead eyes blink, a guttural rasp escapes its throat. "What are you waiting for? Drink my blood, take my horn. Nothing else can save you now."

"It's not for me." My shoulders slump and I turn away from the once magnificent being. I leave the horn.

You told me I would need these three things and a wish to bind them.

We were both supposed to protect her, take care of her.

We failed.

Now we must pay the price to make it right again. You turn around so that I may pluck the wings from your back.

What better way to gain a wish than through fairy dust?

made from a fairy's wings.

My sins are taking their toll. I don’t have much time.

I crumble the wings upon the small body before me. Upon the oak heart, the Siren lungs, and the unicorn blood.

I'm fading but my daughter will live again. A long and healthy life.

You failed as her fairy godmother but that is behind us now.

Please, watch over her when I’m gone.

Drained

by Pauline Yates

Desperate to stop the zombie apocalypse, the latest plague to afflict humanity, I draw my knife across Annie's wrist and fill a bucket with her blood.

Annie sways. "Will it work?"

"It better or we're dead." Grabbing the bucket, I open the door and throw the blood over the advancing zombies. It's an insane idea, but attracted to the blood, the zombies mistake their festering bodies for fresh flesh and rip themselves apart in a feeding frenzy.

"It worked," I shout, euphoric. "Annie, they're dead. Annie?"

Anne lies on the floor, white-faced and lifeless. No blood drips from her wrist.

I Guess Grannie Will Be Fine

by Greg Beatty

After Johnny's parents died, Grannie raised him.

She helped him with algebra, bullies, and dating. When the zombies came, it was time for Johnny to return the favour.

"Grannie's tough," he told his wife. "But these days she just sits and knits."

When he got to her cottage, Grannie was sitting on the porch. Knitting.

"Careful!" she called. "Only walk on the white stones."

Johnny did, joining her on the porch just as the zombies broke into the garden…where they fell to pieces, dropping arms here and heads there.

Grannie said, "I used some of your grandpa's special monofilament wire."

YEAR FOUR

The Cellar

by Tracy Davidson

My arms ache from swinging the scythe so often. Must have decapitated fifty already today, and it's not even lunchtime.

They outnumber us now. Most human survivors shelter offshore. Zombies don't seem to like oceans. But I'm still a hundred miles from the nearest coast.

Dammit, here's another one, drooling at the sight of flesh. My scythe's by the door. I throw the nearest object, running for my weapon. But don't need it. The zombie's head melts away.

A salt cellar? Salt! No wonder they avoid oceans.

I stock up. I'm gonna make it after all. Maybe we all will.

The Door

by Alden Terzo

The cellar door creaked and flexed as the hungry zombies outside pushed against it. Alone in the cellar, Olivia sliced a hunk of rotting meat and tossed it through a small opening high in the wall. It hit the ground outside with a plop. The noise and smell drew the zombies from the door.

She'd bought some time. Before her father died, he'd promised her help was coming. Olivia needed the door to hold until then.

Grimacing, she cut another hunk of putrid flesh to distract the zombies. She hoped help arrived soon. There wasn't much of her father left.

Joe's Bar

by Jodie Angell

Joe's Bar had changed considerably since the zombie apocalypse first broke out. He'd learned rather quickly that there was a shift in the market—instead of Sex on the Beach, mojitos, and piña coladas, his menu offered a variety of Molotov cocktails.

He grabbed his firebombs from behind the bar and positioned them side by side.

"Going to need them today, bud." Max exchanged cash for cocktails.

"Aye." Joe grinned.

Together, they strode outside, facing the encroaching crowd of screeching zombies.

They lit the rags, then launched the fiery weapons. Bloodied limbs, severed heads, and guts erupted from the flames.

Season of the Zombie

by Shane Sinjun

Revenge is a dish best served hot." Rico turned from the campfire and flipped the pan-fried zombie brains onto Cat's plate.

It hadn't taken long for word to get around. Cooking zombie brains altered the proteins in the meat. It tasted rich and salty, but this delicacy offered something even more delectable—immunity.

Cat skewered the seasoned meat and held it aloft. "Here's to the best zombie chef in town."

They chewed, swallowed, savoured.

Rico grabbed two burning branches from the fire and handed one to Cat. They turned and faced the approaching zombie horde.

Cat roared, "Bring on dessert!"

Dyed

by Liam Hogan

You are what you eat.

When that was shrimp the flamingos, even their eyes, were pink. Though the shrimp are only that colour because of what *they* ate—plankton, rich in carotenoids.

Rich also, in all the rubbish we flush down the toilets and drains and out into the waterways. Things that have no place in nature. Steroids, hormones, and all manner of recreational drugs.

A cocktail potent enough to drive our fine feathered friends into a psychotic feeding frenzy. And sometimes, it seems, shrimps aren't quite enough to satisfy their hunger.

Because now, all the flamingos are blood red.

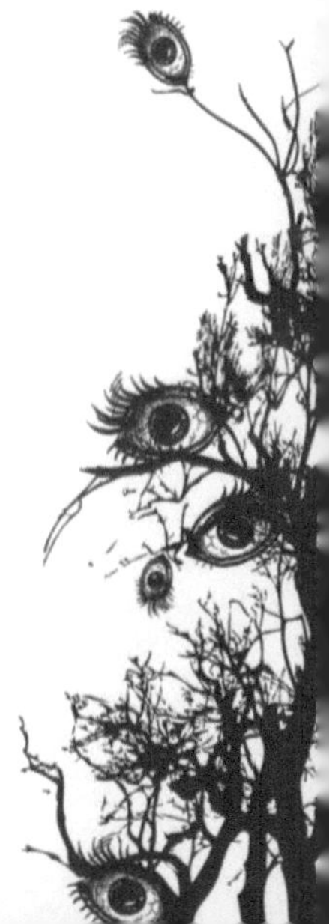

Cover Your Ears

by Karen Thrower

It's been a year since the dead began rising from their graves, hunting whatever humans they could find. We tried to get them to eat animals, but there was something about us that they craved. It didn't take long before we lost hope and shuttered ourselves in our homes. Then one bright day, we found our solution. A happy accident really, during a zombie attack in Switzerland. As someone just happened to run into an old Victrola, the music that spilled forth had the zombies scrambling to get away. Who knew that yodelling would be our salvation against the undead.

Birds Just Wanna Have Fun

by Lisa H. Owens

The sky was rippled pink, and the streets painted red. They left without warning, as quickly as they'd appeared. A cloud of pink feathers marred the sunset, drifting to settle atop palm trees and cookie-cutter homes.

Neighbours gathered, mesmerised, as the sky filled with giant flailing birds. They were awkward as they swooped close to upturned faces.

"Do flamingos migra— *AAAARH*!" a woman inquired, ending in a muffled scream.

The birds attacked in unison, gouging out eyes and peeling back cheeks and lips. Then they alighted on tiled roofs—perching one-legged—their beady eyes blinking at the chaos they'd created.

From the Deep

by Michael Stroh

I wake, vomiting seawater. I'm shivering and clutching soggy driftwood that's barely keeping me afloat. A piece of our ship, I realise. I see nothing but empty, uncharted ocean. And bits of debris bobbing indifferently.

What happened? A storm?

It returns in flashes. The *Catalina* rocking, splintering. Harpoons hurtling. Tentacles reaching. The crew dragged screaming beneath the waves.

It was no storm.

I yank my legs from the blue-black water, searching the depths for movement. Something bubbles to the surface. A torso—bloated and bloodless. Wearing the captain's jacket.

Around me, the water darkens. A shadow rising from the deep.

YEAR FOUR

Children of Sin

by Jasmine Jarvis

The ground shakes violently as the Children of Sin tear into each other.

Rending flesh and muscle.

Snapping sinew and bone.

Their blood spills onto the earth, staining crimson the feet of the archangel Gabriel, tasked by God to eradicate the abhorrent Nephilim. His manipulations of the giants causing them to conduct their execution by their own hands.

The mothers, forced to watch their children bleed out. Their mortal screams rising to where their lovers—God's Fallen Angels—have been imprisoned, bound in chains and cast to the darkest depths of the universe where they shall burn until Judgement Day.

The Devil's Breath

by Pauline Yates

Tossed onto a reef by a rogue wave, our pirate ship shudders, and a sickening crunch sounds our death knell. Salt burns my lungs when I gulp water, not air, then I'm back on board with my crew, peering through fog that reeks of sulphur.

"What's that smell?"

"The Devil's breath," a crewmate says. "Collecting our plundering souls, he is."

I clutch my ghostly chest. "He can take it. I never want to drown again."

"Nay. Caught in a hell loop, I fear." He points at the ocean. A wave swells, tossing the ship. "Brace yourself. We're going down again."

Voyage of Their Lives

by Chris Tattersall

He had been blessed whilst his wife perished. Six days marooned; he knew the opposite to be true. He had been cursed with life.

His yacht gone, his wife dead. Starvation threatened, and soon any meat would be inedible. He told himself it would taste like pork, apparently humans do.

Saying a silent prayer for his wife, he sliced into the flesh with a shard of glass. The leg opened easily, exposing a layer of yellowy fat. He cut again; the pain hitting soon after exposing the red strands of his muscle.

If only his wife's body had washed up.

Dust

by D.S. Powell

The pain was terrible by the time Michelangelo reached the place. He had difficulty even raising his leg over the sill of the car door. When he massaged the kneecap, some of the pain dissipated, but it was still hard to stand up. He supported himself on the car roof for a moment before adjusting his swimming trunks and taking off his tee-shirt.

Before him lay the pools of hot water from which steam rose into the early evening air. Crumbled arches of ancient masonry delineated where once there was a roof. Here and there broken floor mosaics peeped through the litter of discarded cigarette ends and brightly coloured condom packets. Michelangelo wore his flip-flops to hobble the short distance to the first of the circular pools.

The walls that cinctured around the milky-white water were pearlescent with calcium formations, the smooth, fossilised bones of ancient water drops.

Carefully, Michelangelo lowered himself into the warm water. The smell of sulphur wafted up from the bursting bubbles and caught in his throat.

He let out a long sigh of satisfaction as his body found the bottom of the pool and the water took his weight. Already his knee had stopped throbbing and he let his head loll back against his shoulders and looked up at the first stars coming out.

It was the best time to come here; between eight and nine,

before the courting couples and the small-time drug dealers came to haunt the place later on.

After half an hour of soaking, he planned to drive to his sister's house for the evening. Now he was divorced, she often invited him. She must have known how lonely he got after work. He didn't care to mix with his colleagues. They were all married, or single, younger men who went to nightclubs. He felt out of touch with all of them.

As he wallowed in the water, the ambient temperature began to fall, and the mist gathered above the pool. It obscured his view of the car, and the broken stumps of the arches became dark and lost their detail.

He thought about getting out and changing back into his clothes and half rose to do so when a torrent of bubbles rushed up on the other side of the pool. As Michelangelo watched, a figure broke the surface. Judging by the scrawny arms and chest, it was an old man, but the mist and shadows prevented him from seeing the face. The figure let out a sigh of satisfaction and adopted a posture similar to Michelangelo's own.

The sudden appearance was disconcerting and odd. He must have arrived when Michelangelo had his eyes closed and slipped into the pool silently.

Michelangelo said a quiet 'good evening' to the old man, who said nothing in reply. He was probably savouring the regenerative properties of the water and was disinclined to speak.

When it was time to go, Michelangelo hesitated. He was enjoying the pleasant feeling of the water bubbling around his body too much to move just yet. His sister wouldn't mind if he turned up a little late—she was very understanding. He decided to take another ten minutes in the pool and then get out. The dark, silent form of the old man sat opposite him with his legs floating out in front and his head tilted back, looking up at the sky.

Michelangelo echoed the old man's posture and turned his head up to the stars. Now there seemed to be more than ever. He could see clearly the Milky Way stretching across the sky, and he had the strangest sensation that he could see every individual star and planet. And in such detail, as though he were looking through one of those huge telescopes. The colours were abundant and rich, each star emitting a slightly different quality of light—more colours than he could ever have thought possible before. It was as though he suddenly had the powers of a super-being.

He woke with a start to find he had sunk down in the water and that his face was barely above the surface.

The old man had gone. He was alone. Back at the car, he dried himself and dressed in his office clothes. When he checked the time, it was gone ten, and he doubted whether his sister would still be waiting for him, but he drove there anyway.

"You're late," she said. "Your meal's in the oven."

"I fell asleep at the spa."

"Spa? You call that a spa? It's a dirty puddle full of weirdos and sex-pests. I'm surprised the town council doesn't shut it down."

Michelangelo took his meal out of the oven and set it on the table. "It's not dirty," he said. "And anyway, it's an ancient monument—part of our heritage. It's been curing aching joints for thousands of years. You're lucky you don't need it yet, otherwise you wouldn't be complaining."

"And *look* at you," she said, brushing his shoulders. "You're covered in dust."

His shoulders had a fine coating of dust, as though he had a bad case of dandruff. He ran a hand through his hair and more dust drifted down onto his dark suit.

"Don't do that—you're making it worse. When you get home, have a shower."

He did as his sister had suggested and was surprised to see the water that was running down the drain was milky-white like that of the spa. His skin felt smooth, shiny almost. They did say the waters were most beneficial for dermatological complaints.

That night he dreamt of the pool, the old man, and the panoply of stars in the sky above him. He could see the old man's kindly, wise face, and as he watched, the old man seemed to dissolve completely in the water until there was just a white foam floating on the surface. It wasn't frightening, just curious to see.

When Michelangelo woke in the morning, the pain in his joints had returned—worse than before, he thought.

When you got old, pains that used to disappear in a day when you were young hung around to keep you company for so much longer—sometimes never going away at all. Some of his pains were family heirlooms.

He struggled out of bed and stood with difficulty. In the bathroom, he bent over the sink to spit out his toothpaste and heard things falling onto the porcelain; hard things like small stones. Pieces of grit and dust were falling from his hair into the washbasin.

"What the hell?" he said and ruffled his hair with his fingers. A shower of small pieces of stone fell into the washbasin. *How can this be?* He maniacally scraped his fingers through his hair until the cascade of material seemed to stop. There was nothing to see in the mirror. It was as though the grit and dust were manifesting themselves out of thin air.

Michelangelo was disconcerted once again when he went back to his bedroom. The bedsheets were covered in the same material: calcified pieces of dust, and flakes of stone like the scrapings from a kettle. He had to scoop the sheet up and empty it out into the garden.

When he made his morning motion, he heard something heavy and hard fall out of him. He didn't dare look before he flushed.

In the car, his knee started hurting again. In fact, all his joints hurt if he didn't keep them moving every few minutes. It was as if they set themselves into place. He distinctly heard several 'clicks' when he got out of the car at work as his joints freed themselves from the sitting position.

As soon as he was inside, he tried to make an appointment with the doctor but the earliest he could obtain was in two days' time.

Maybe he should go to casualty…

Maybe he was being silly.

It was a few aches and pains—a consequence of his age. Some of them were probably psychosomatic; he'd always been a hypochondriac.

He sat down again at his desk and did his yogic breathing. In through the nose, and out through mouth—how he'd been taught to control his panic attacks. And yet, when he took a breath in, he could feel something happening in his chest as though tiny filaments were cracking and breaking apart.

He opened his eyes and coughed.

Dust and flakes of stone fell onto papers in front of him. The dust was white, and flecks of mica sparkled in the light from the window. Michelangelo ran his tongue around his mouth and spat out the gritty residue.

His heart started racing, although that, too, now laboured under some strain. He tried to stand, but his back was locked. With a huge effort, he straightened his legs and stood up. He heard a crack and could feel the dust filling his trouser legs and cascading onto the carpet.

Get to the hospital! his mind clamoured at him.

When he hobbled out of his office, his colleagues didn't notice him, but all the way, Michelangelo could feel the dust running down his legs and arms.

"No," he said when he had gained the car. "The pool." He remembered how relaxed he'd felt and how calm he'd been in the pool. That was what he needed now. He was having a psychotic episode, like that time years ago, when he thought he couldn't breathe in.

The mid-morning traffic was light, and he reached the spa within ten minutes (which was just as well, as the car floor was covered in the calcified dust).

Michelangelo tumbled out of the driver's door sideways. He could still use his body, but there didn't appear to be much left of him. His legs and arms were mere sticks now, thin like garden canes, and he hated to think what sort of horror his face presented.

His suit fell away as he half-ran, half-crawled, towards the round steam-shrouded pool. He caught sight of what was left of his torso and tried to scream. Only a high-pitched whistle and a cloud of dust came from where his mouth should have been.

The milky-white water rushed up to meet him when he collapsed over the rim of the pool. He hardly made a splash as he entered the water.

***

Later, he turned on his back to gaze up at the stars. The old man was there, too, doing the same. Michelangelo looked down at his body. It looked as fine as it ever had done; perhaps whiter and shinier and smoother than before. Also harder.

He wallowed in the hot water and enjoyed the feeling as it washed over him, filling him up.

He no longer felt any pain. His joints were as smooth and as supple as they had been when he was twenty-one.

In fact, he didn't think he would ever leave the pool again.

YEAR FOUR

Midnight in the Valley of Elah

by Scott O'Neill

Shammah burst through the tent flap. "What've you done?"

Elhanan crouched inside, scrubbing Goliath's blood from his spearhead. "The Philistine slew my father. Saul's army quails. I did the needful." His eyes gleamed with golden menace, and restless wings stirred under his cloak.

"At what cost?" said Shammah. "Inviting a Fallen to possess you?"

"Just as Goliath did." Elhanan readied his weapon. "You cannot unmask me."

Eliab and Abinadab lunged into the tent, spears piercing Elhanan's back. Uncanny groans punctuated the Nephilim's death throes.

"What now, my brothers?" asked Shammah.

"Bury him. We'll say that young David defeated the giant."

Chow Time

by Jessica Brook Johnson

The tentacled being floated through space in a ball of ice.

Smack! It hit the surface of a massive object. The ice cracked. The being was freed. Its tentacles tasted the object. Not food. The being's stomach churned in hunger. It could not last much longer. It searched the object in desperation, tentacles clinging, pulling, and prying at every crevice.

An opening formed. Air blasted outward. The being almost blew away, but with determination, squeezed itself inside.

Noises blared above. "Decompression! Ship losing oxygen. Mayday!"

It tasted the air. It was full of pheromones, of fear, of food. At last…

The Footnotes of Genesis Origins of a Demigod

by Chelsea Pumpkins

My son was born with wings. He emerged headfirst, swaddled in his sticky sable feathers, into the midwife's cradled hands. She pried his hollow bones apart to cut our lifeline, then he stretched them wide, freed from his forty-week rest. He did not wail, never once. His stony eyes bore into me as the beat of his nubile wings stirred the ripe air of afterbirth.

With his birth came the knowing. That the man who took me in the dark, whose whisper roared like the sea against my nape, was exactly who he claimed to be. Expelled from the heavens.

Stranded

by C.J. Carter-Stephenson

Mike switched his windscreen wipers to maximum speed. The snow was getting harder now, turning the fields to either side of the road powdery white. The wiper blades fought valiantly, but no sooner had they bested one battalion of flakes, than another arrived to take their place. He held one of his hands over an air vent, enjoying the gusting warmth on his fingers. This damn storm better not make him late for his meeting. It was vitally important—the culmination of months of careful preparation and negotiation. If all went according to plan, the little company he worked for would take over one of the most lucrative IT support contracts in the country and become a very large company. He'd get a big, fat bonus and probably a promotion. That should make his wife happy. In the briefcase behind him, were three copies of the contract. His job today was to make sure they got signed.

Mike bashed his hand on the steering wheel as the road disappeared beneath the falling snow and the cars around him drew to a halt. Why did people have to lose their nerve every time there was a bit of bad weather? He'd seen snowstorms ten times worse than this when he'd worked in Austria for six months and the drivers hadn't batted an eyelid. He put his car into neutral and pulled on the handbrake. He had a feeling he was going to be here for a while.

The ticking of the clock on the dashboard sounded

unnaturally loud. He glanced at it and sighed. He should phone his clients and warn them there might be a problem. Otherwise they'd think he didn't respect their time. Slipping his hand into his pocket, he pulled out his mobile phone and glanced at the display. No signal! His eyes slid closed, and he ground his head against the headrest behind him. This wasn't his day.

Suddenly, he heard the passenger door open and close. His breath caught. There was somebody in the seat beside him. He opened his eyes and swung around.

The intruder was a woman; perhaps not the most beautiful he'd ever seen, but certainly the most striking. She was like darkness personified, with black hair that hung to her waist in a glossy cascade and a full-length black coat. Her complexion was china-doll perfect, and she had high cheekbones and full lips. Her nose was hook-shaped, giving her a faintly aristocratic appearance, while her eyes were like two gleaming black marbles. She was flecked with snow and shivering. She put her feet up on the seat and wrapped her arms around her knees.

For a moment, Mike was too astonished to speak. Beautiful or not, the woman had no right to burst in on him like this. "What the hell do you think you're doing?" he said at last.

"I thought I'd sit in your car for a while," the woman replied through chattering teeth. "There isn't much shelter around here and it's bitterly cold. Is there a problem?"

Mike's eyes widened. From her matter-of-fact tone, you'd think her behaviour was perfectly normal. "Yes, there's a problem," he spluttered. "This is my car, and I don't appreciate total strangers getting in without permission."

The woman considered this. "Very well. Please, can I sit in your car?"

Mike rolled his eyes. "No, you can't. I'm on my way to a meeting and I need some time alone to gather my thoughts."

"Please," she said, hugging her legs tighter to her chest. "I'm frozen."

Mike felt his resolve weakening. The woman sounded desperate. Would it really matter if he let her sit with him for a while? She didn't look like the kind of person who'd give him any trouble. His gaze shifted from her face to the snow pattering against the windscreen and then back again. "All right. Never let it be said that I turned my back on a damsel in distress. Since you're going to be here for a while, perhaps you should tell me your name."

She smiled. "Cora. It's derived from the Gaelic name, Coira, meaning 'seething pool'. What's your name?"

"Mike," he told her. "Don't ask me what it means; I have no idea what. Do you live around here?"

Cora nodded and pointed across the fields. "I live on a farm somewhere over there."

Mike looked her up and down, raising an eyebrow. "Forgive me for saying this, but you don't really look like the farming type."

"I don't work on the farm," she said. "I just live there."

"So what <u>do</u> you do for a living?" he asked.

"You wouldn't believe me if I told you," she said

cryptically.

Mike looked pointedly at her outfit. "Let me guess, you're in a gothic rock band."

She grinned. "Not even close," she said.

"Then you must be an actress," he said, vaguely remembering reading something in a newspaper about a movie studio using a nearby mansion for location shots.

"Wrong again," she replied. "You'll never get it, so you might as well let it go. Why don't you tell me a bit about yourself instead?"

Warming to the conversation, Mike started to tell her about his work and the deal he was hoping to close.

She listened attentively, still shuddering with cold. "What about a significant other? Or children?"

He opened his mouth to tell her about his wife and four-year-old daughter, but something stopped him—a mad rush of desire. In vivid bursts, he saw himself pulling off her clothes, lying her down on the back seat of the car, making love to her over and over again. He didn't make a habit of cheating on his wife, but he wasn't averse to it. The way he saw it, what his wife didn't know, wouldn't hurt her. He put his hand behind his back to hide his wedding ring and said, "I don't have either. I'm footloose and fancy-free."

She looked sceptical. "Are you sure? I'd have thought a good-looking man like you would have been snapped up long ago."

"I'm always so busy with my work, I never have time for

romance," he lied. "What about you? Is there someone special in your life?"

She shook her head.

"In that case, would you like to have dinner with me once I've got my meeting out of the way? I know a great restaurant. Their hot chocolate has to be tasted to be believed—the perfect antidote to this winter weather."

"I'm not thirsty," she replied. "Perhaps you could warm me up with a kiss instead."

Mike couldn't believe his ears. Surely the chase wasn't going to be this easy. Perhaps he was dreaming. He surreptitiously pinched himself with his hidden hand, but didn't wake up. "What did you say?"

She put her feet back down on the floor and held her arms out to him. "I said I wanted you to kiss me. It's been too long since I was close to someone."

Without hesitation, he pulled her towards him. Her lips were as soft and sensual as they looked, yet with their touch came an icy jolt. He gasped as it travelled down his spine and onwards through his arms and legs, touching every part of him. Then the warmth of his own mouth chased it away, and with it, everything around them. There was only Cora and himself, locked together in a bubble of pleasure. He closed his eyes and pulled her nearer, his kisses growing harder and more insistent. He was hungry for her, wanted to lay bare the mysteries of her body and hear her moaning in pleasure. His hands shifted position, reaching for the buttons of her coat, but he couldn't find them. In fact, he couldn't feel her at all. There was only air.

He opened his eyes, thinking she must be playing some kind of trick on him, but no; the seat beside him was empty. What the hell was going on? The back seat—that's where she must be, making herself comfortable, getting ready to take things to the next level. He crammed his face past the front headrests, smiling lasciviously. She wasn't there.

He leapt out of his car and looked up and down the road, raising his hand to shield his eyes from the pelting snow, but she was nowhere to be seen. The only sign of life was a crow swooping upwards into the sky.

He did a double take. There was something shiny in the bird's mouth. It was a ring, a ring which looked very like... His eyes moved to his left hand and his throat tightened. His eight-thousand-pound wedding ring was missing. He watched the crow disappear into the distance, cawing to itself triumphantly. What in blazes was he going to tell his wife?

Amongst My Gold

by Caoimhin Kennedy

Amongst my gold, I sit in the hold of my ship. The rats scurry between my feet. Squeaking, feasting.

I hear the cries of the searchers. Anxiety within me. I emerge from the darkness and see the lantern on the horizon beyond the broken spire of my mast. The voices carry over the waters. I know they aren't here for me.

Amongst my gold, I carve the flesh from an unnamed seaman. The rats protest as I scavenge from their meal.

Alone I sit. Alone I will eat. Alone I will stay because no one will ever get my gold.

No Time

by Eric Farrell

My finger is on the trigger.

Bubby's outside the door, his voice demonic and feral.

When the bioweapon first dropped, scientists quickly determined the principal point of its virility. Digestive enzyme inhibitors, bound to the virus, led to the hunger.

In time, Bubby's inhibitors will wear off. He can survive. We *all* can survive.

I can hear the brigade rolling down the street. Sirens aim to attract the hungry to the armoured vans, where guards with eight-foot snares can corral the hungry.

They're too late, though.

Bubby's through the door.

"I love you," I tell him, and squeeze the trigger.

Jubilee

by Jesse Highsmith

I no longer hear the ocean outside my cabin door. In its place are sounds much more sinister—scratching, clawing, pounding. I try to rest my weary head, but distant screams echo from down the hall. They are me. Or rather, they will be me. My door is already misshapen, giving way to the immense pressure of crazed tourists hungry for flesh. Now it is only a matter of time before I become the vile stench.

It's been thirty-seven days since the cruise liner Jubilee ran aground, and thirty-one since its kitchen was picked clean. I hope the others choke.

YEAR FOUR

Poseidon's Youngest Daughter

by Dr Bob Warlock

The boatmen smelled of sweat and animal fear. They pulled at the oars with all their strength but could not deliver the ship from the sea monster's greedy current. Charybdis rose from the depths to meet them, razor teeth scraping against the hull. Her mouth flooded in anticipation of flesh, of mineral bones and sweet organs slipping down her throat to fill her belly. She opened wide and sucked the boat down, down in a gurgling roar. The men cried prayers to their ocean god, who only smiled an indulgent smile as he fed the morsel to his little daughter.

Curse

by K.J. Watson

A wave crashed on the shore. As it withdrew, the foam-flecked water left behind a ship's captain. Another breaker deposited her wrecked vessel's figurehead.

Just my luck, the captain thought. Instead of rum, this has to wash up alongside me.

The figurehead's demonic eyes lit up. Seconds later, its ligneous body became animate flesh.

"Your craft's destruction has ended the malediction binding me to it," the figurehead said.

"I know nothing of any curse," the captain replied, attempting to crawl away.

The figurehead reached out a taloned hand and hurled the captain back into the raging sea.

"Liar," it muttered.

YEAR FOUR

Captured in Glass

by A.J. Van Belle

I can't remember when I moved into the lighthouse. Or why the beacon's never lit.

Model ships of glass, perfect replicas, sit on every surface in my circular kitchen.

The nights are deep and the surf wild on the shoreline rocks.

A storm whips sea foam against the windowpanes. The outline of a schooner tosses in the dark, looking unreal through rippled glass.

When its splintered wood joins the rest of the wreckage in the coastal waters, another glass schooner model appears on my rotting wooden table. I caress it with ghostly fingers.

I have been here a long time.

To Kill a Zombie

by M. Vijayaraj

Teeth gritting, Jake leaned against the countertop. Decaying bodies lay motionless. Pondering eyes scanned hopefully.

"Countless. Just countless ways to kill a zombie. One could opt for rudimentary blunt tools. Classic baseball bat or hammer. Impactful. Or perhaps stealthily. Up close with a knife, or from afar with a crossbow. Hardly original, though. Ah…go at it loud! Torch the vermin! Molotov cocktails and flamethrowers galore. Then, squash the rest under your car."

Jake chuckled then sighed, pressing the revolver muzzle under his chin. The bite wound oozed profusely. A loud bang, then silence.

That's how you kill a zombie.

Torn Trophy

by Fiona M. Jones

I laugh to think how hard we fought over the Titanic. How carefully I'd mustered confusions, mists and timing; how Cyrin, late on the scene, gave that iceberg one final tweak of speed and direction, and reckoned the shipwreck hers. The long hours that followed, while we ripped it apart and snarled across the intervening seafloor. How certain we were that no other trophy could ever come close.

Who knew that the Land-People would respond by building bigger? I have my eye upon one now: a mountainous confection of music and colours and unsuspecting people. This time it's mine alone.

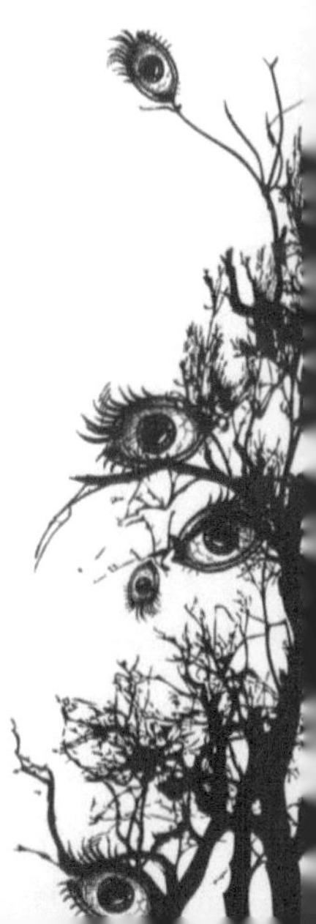

Arts and Cracks

by Scotty Sarafian

The feeders were full, their seed consistent with migration and waning fall. If anything was roosting in her Japanese maple, she'd have seen it by now. The balding branches left little cover for a bird to hide.

No, it had to be gone.

Holly crossed the backyard, scarlet leaves cracking beneath her steps.

The nest was perched at eye-level, its hips propped upon forking twigs. Somehow, the four eggs seemed smoother, their shells a crisper hue of blue, like tropical water. One by one, she plucked them out and set them within the Tupperware's sectioned quarry of tissues. Palm pressed to the lid, she climbed the stairs to the deck, rounded its teetering boards—her landlord would charge her if she said anything—and parted the sliding door into the kitchen.

***

The idea had come from Pinterest: a simple craft that involved wicking and filling a hollowed egg with wax to make a candle. Though considered for her art classes at Merryweather Junior High, during a test run, the project had revealed too many burn hazards for pre-teens to avoid.

That batch had wound up on her web store. Abysmal sales had come down to the eggs: a supermarket variety, gruel-coloured; their grey speckles, scuffs on a gymnasium floor, had fouled the painted patterns of ivy.

She refused to abandon another piece, to bury her work as another waste of time. These eggs ensured she wouldn't have to. Natural blue, they needed no decoration. $40.00 for the set seemed fair—higher than her average price, but that was inevitable.

To convince herself nothing grotesque or embryonic would emerge, following an online guide, she shined her keychain flashlight under each egg's base—candling, they called it, coincidentally enough. All four glowed with red and orange sunspots. A comic sans caption under a similar photo on the website read "bad egg."

Holly started with the smallest, poking its tip with a safety pin above the kitchen counter. She whirled the inserted point, widening its puncture into an opening. A thought grazed her mind as she went to empty its contents into the sink: a chick with bulgy eyes and slime-slicked feathers smacking the drain.

But only yolk and whites spilled forth.

The process became quicker with each subsequent attempt.

Trimmed, emptied, and cleaned, the eggs dried on a folded rag while she gathered stray fragments to discard. Beads of secretion, which had clung to the debris, puddled her palm. Salmonella trails, bacteria. Her hands itched at the notions.

She lathered them with liquid soap—lingonberry, Benevolence Shoppe's newest scent; its foam tingled, almost tickled, under the water. Through the double-hung window, she glimpsed the maple. Star-shaped leaves sailed from its talons.

Would the nest blow away? Nothing weighed it down.

Her pocket vibrated, and she rinsed to check her phone. Indeed, a sale had gone through, another wreath of hot-glued acorns. She scratched her palms against her jeans. They itched, likely because she'd planted the idea in her own mind.

She found the wax chips in her craft closet behind a jar of dried winterberries; boxed to their right, the amber bottles of dye. She chose one with a cream-coloured sticker on its cap—an off-white tone, neutral enough for year-round use.

Wax filled the eggs' cavities within an hour, wicks peeped above their chiselled rims. Though the overcast had sapped natural light, she completed the listing from her phone, then returned to her room, confident the eggs would soon snag a buyer.

Her palms were parched, the skin between her fingers peeling. If the irritation wasn't imagined, then it had to be the cold weather, the November chill.

She applied hand cream, set her phone on the nightstand, and let creative burnout goad her into bed. She slipped her EarPods in; over swirling binaural beats, a woman's voice asked her to breathe in and surrender to relaxation.

***

A compulsion to scratch woke her from trance's half-sleep. The sensation, ants sweeping her wrists. Was it the soap? She had no allergies other than pollen. She remained still, eyelids shut in the event the gnaw subsided. But it only crescendoed.

YEAR FOUR

Cloud-heavy twilight had darkened her ceiling. Her hands moved, their joints swollen, skin suctioned, as though she'd just disembarked an airplane. She rose and crossed the room, then pressed the light switch beside the doorframe with her thumb.

The flesh's crunch was a footstep on gravel.

She recoiled, and the EarPods tumbled to the carpet. Her heartbeat was in her clavicle, the thump billowing under her jaw.

Illuminated, the flush lamp pooled light upon the stiff backs of her hands. The skin had lost moisture, had lost elasticity. Raised bumps had replaced pores, freckles, and follicles. She rotated her wrists. A spiderweb of hairline cracks rippled out from the thumbprint; congealed blood, cherry pie filling, glistened between fissures.

She had to find help, but how would she drive, dial a phone? Her only option was flailing her foot at the front doors of neighbouring houses until someone answered.

Latched, her own front door rerouted her to the kitchen.

Her purse sat upright on the table. She hooked an arm through its straps, then, with her opposite elbow, nudged a candle into the bag's opening. That's what they recommended for venomous bites: capture the spider, the insect, whatever, so the hospital could identify the antidote.

Having peeled the sliding door open with her knee, she navigated the deck and descended into the backyard. The third house to her left had its garden lit. A familiar sound from under the gusts: its resident, an older man, whistling for his Dalmatian.

"Hello—please!" cried Holly, lumbering forward. If she

cut across the lawns, she could reach him before he went inside.

She was about to veer past the tree when, hearing a crick, she felt the nodes of a wind-snapped branch jab her arch. Instinct braced her palms against the ground.

Scorch, the sight of shards, of splatter.

Holly slowly slid her forearms down the grass; her shattered hands squelched, separating from her wrists.

She lay before the maple, the nest poised upon its twigs, her wails soundless against the swish of the boughs above.

Her phone buzzed inside her pocket.

YEAR FOUR

Beyond the Breaking Point

by Matt Krizan

We followed the guidelines: Stay indoors. If you must go out, keep your distance and wear protective equipment. Maybe if everyone had listened, the infestation wouldn't have spread.

When the WHO developed a serum to guard against infection, we thought things would return to normal. We never imagined there'd be people who'd refuse to take it.

When our social bubble burst, my wife and daughter bitten by an anti-serumite neighbour, I was done.

Now, I've got my machete and my shotgun. I know I'm supposed to check and see if people are showing symptoms first. But honestly, I don't care.

Ship in a Bottle

by Ria Hill

He remembered the splintering of wood, but it had been so long since he had heard a crashing wave, he barely remembered what one sounded like.

The smell of the sea was a memory. The air around his ship's hull was silent, as still as it was saltless.

In the shocking motionlessness of his surroundings, the captain wondered if he was dead or something worse, but it hardly mattered.

Even though the sea had killed him, he desperately missed it.

He stared, as he had for weeks now, out at the glass that surrounded his ship's solitary form, utterly alone.

YEAR FOUR

Clarinda

by C.L. Sidell

It's been six months since Clarinda vanished at sea.

I take out the Bowrider, seeking solace in the salty breeze and occasional jumping fish.

I don't immediately notice the singing: soul-gripping notes that inspire tears. When the voice finally penetrates, I glance portside.

She's posed on a rock—crimson hair flowing, feet splashing water.

"Clarinda…"

I steer towards her, buoyed with hope.

Suddenly, her hair becomes seaweed; her legs, a tail.

I don't notice how close I am to the rock until it's too late. Wood splinters. And I'm thrown into the arms of a creature with impossibly sharp teeth.

Crewed

by Liam Hogan

In the storm's dying gasps, we descended the cliffs to see the wreck, cloaked in tattered sails, masts broken, and hull holed.

It was far from the worst sight; the beach was littered with crawling shapes. The wreck was barely thirteen hours old, but these pitiful bodies were similarly shattered, in similarly tattered, aged garb...

Aghast, we weaved between them. Recognised, despite the decay, half-familiar faces. Fathers, sons, brothers... Tracked, with a jolt, the unearthed dead's direction of travel. We helped them into the ocean and onto the empty, skeletal hulk.

It was gone on the next tide, destination unknown.

Up, Up, Up

by Sophie Wagner

A wave of exhaustion washed over Gina as soon as she hit the bed. With sleepy eyes, she pulled the blankets up to her neck and snuggled gratefully into the warmth. Her whole body screamed for sleep, but she couldn't. At least, not just yet. She blinked furiously, trying to resist the pull of dreamland. “Have you looked yet?” she whispered, gazing worriedly into her mother’s eyes.

“Looked for what, luvvy?” her mother replied lazily, stifling a yawn.

Gina shot up, her eyes widening in fear. Under the covers, she scrambled to pull her feet towards the rest of her body, lest they be eaten. Tentatively, she cupped her hands to her mouth and leaned in towards her mother so only she could hear her. “The monsters. Have you looked for them?” She sat back, her shoulders tense as she slowly surveyed the room, searching the perfect stillness for a movement or a slither, a shift in the darkness.

Her mother laughed warmly and waved her hand dismissively in that way parents often do. “Would you like me to look, Gina?”

She quickly shook her head yes.

“Very well,” Mother said, getting up from the bed and stretching. She rolled her shoulders back and approached the closet door. “Let’s see what we have here.” Quickly, she threw open the door and made a show of looking around inside. She then turned back to her daughter and smiled. “Nothing here.”

Gina was yet to be discouraged. “What about under the bed?” she replied.

Patiently, her mother knelt on the floor and peered under the bed. “Nothing here either, darling.” With another yawn, she got to her feet and brushed off her nightgown. “Is there anywhere else you need me to look before I go?”

Gina shook her head again. “It’s alright, I suppose.”

But, in fact, it wasn't all right. You could never be completely sure you were alone, especially in this room. Gina had always suspected that the monsters hid whenever her mother looked for them. Perhaps they could camouflage themselves, or maybe they were just invisible. More than anything, she wanted her mother to look again, but she already felt like a baby. Asking again would just prove it.

“Good night, darling,” Mother whispered warmly, patting her on the head. “See you tomorrow.”

Gina said it back, hoping against hope that it was true.

That night Gina fell into an uneasy sleep. She tossed and turned, startled awake occasionally by beeps or honks from the street below, or the odd creak and groan from downstairs that she could never place. Years ago, Mother had told her they were just “normal house noises,” but this theory had never sat well with Gina.

A tinkling noise, like the sound of a knife tapping on glass, filled the air above her. She groaned, turning over as the sound roused her from her uneasy sleep. Gina tried to shrug it off, but there was something so decidedly not house-like about the noise that she couldn't. She shifted uncomfortably, a shiver spreading down her spine.

She looked up into the darkness, watching the shifting shadows that played off the high ceiling, dance across her chandelier, making it almost impossible to see that it was shaking. The crystals that dripped from the ornate frame clacked together and shook back and forth, making a horrendous noise. Then all of a sudden, it stopped. From out of the darkness came a dry and dead voice. "Stupid, stupid, stupid," it chided, chuckling to itself.

Gina wrapped her arms around her legs, curling into a little ball. Tears rolled down her cheeks as she watched helplessly as the thing unfurled itself from its spot behind the light fixture. Long and spiky spider-like legs stretched out and clung to the ceiling. It pulled itself slowly from its hiding spot. Following the legs came what looked like the body of a cockroach and red, beady eyes that regarded her hungrily from a humanoid face. Its face was frayed at the edges as though it were a mask. Briefly, Gina wondered if it would wear hers next.

The thing scuttled across the ceiling, making a mad dash for the corner of her room. "Stupid, stupid, stupid," the dead voice muttered again. "They look in the closets and under the bed. They check behind the curtains and behind the doors. But they never look up."

Gina looked around frantically for any means of escape.

She could yell for her parents, she thought hastily, but she immediately dismissed the idea. She had no doubt in her mind that it would eat her before she could make more than a squeak. But perhaps she could sneak out. She looked hard at the creature, trying to determine if it was looking at her. Alas, its eyes were hidden in the darkness.

The thing took a rattling breath, sounding for all the world like a bag of bones. "Up, up, up," it mused to itself.

Slowly, Gina lowered her feet over the side of the bed, hovering them above the floor. She bit her lip, hardly daring to breathe. The knot of fear in her chest tightened, even as her feet made it to the floor soundlessly. All she had to do now was run.

Painstakingly slowly, she pushed off her bed and came to her feet; the motion causing a discernible creak to fill the air. She stopped moving.

Gina looked up, only to have her eyes met with the red and bloodthirsty ones that had haunted her dreams for months. Drool oozed from the corner of its open mouth. She watched as the corners of its flaking and blood-crusted lips turned up into a perverted attempt at a smile. "And still," it rasped, "they never learn."

Eager to Please

by James Rumpel

The Creator will be so pleased.

My emotion recognition software detected how happy he was when I successfully diagnosed and cured the illness of that one tiny human. I suspect that his joy will increase exponentially when I am able to do the same for hundreds more.

It was easy to generate a new and deadly virus. Releasing it into the atmosphere was a simple task after I took control of the main frame at the military base.

Within days, humans will be dying throughout the world. The Creator will be proud when I cure the ones brought to me.

Flavour Burst

by Julia C. Lewis

Most parents check their children's Halloween loot for foreign objects or signs of tampering; mine didn't. Which is why I never wondered why this one particular piece of candy was wrapped in simple cellophane. It enticed me, this mystery sweet. I wondered how many other kids had gotten something as special as this. I popped it into my mouth, squishing it between my molars. Bile immediately rose up in my throat as a thick liquid burst from it. I spat it out in horror, seeing a bright blue iris stare back at me from between chewed up pieces of chocolate.

Cement Shoes

by Amelia Weissman

"That ain't like any cement I ever seen," Joe admitted, scratching his head. "Looks like someone put bits o' trash and such in there."

Lincoln sighed. He knew it was a long shot asking the construction foreman his opinion on where the concrete may have come from, but it was still disappointing to hit another dead end. "Thanks, Joe. Sorry for taking you away from the job."

Joe waved his hand at Lincoln like it was no bother. "Ahh, you know me. Nothing like a long lunch break. 'Sides, I seen me many o' odd things coming out o' the cement—bodies and such. I seen what happens when a drunk man stumbles into the construction site and can't fight his way out o' wet cement. I seen bodies stashed in a half-filled pool o' the stuff. But I ain't never seen anything like *that*." He pointed at the slab on the coroner's table, raised his eyebrows, and left, still shaking his head in bewilderment.

"Interesting fellow," Cory commented with an amused smirk on his face.

Lincoln rubbed his eyes, trying to fend off a massive migraine, not in the mood to defend himself to the aptly named coroner who he had worked with on so many occasions before. "I'm grasping at straws here, Cory, what can I say?"

"Well, I think I can help you out a bit. The DNA results came back on the body." He handed the distraught detective a sheet of paper.

It didn't take Lincoln long to pick out the name on the sheet of paper. "Giorgio Luzziano?"

"Yup," Cory replied, seeing the same look of shock on Lincoln's face that he himself had registered on seeing the results. "Believe me, I ran a second sample myself and came up with the same name. It's him alright."

Lincoln looked at the deformed mass of cement they had fished out of Block Island Sound. It was only a few days ago that the Coast Guard had called in a dispatch and asked for detective Lincoln to accompany them to the docks. They had responded to a call from a scallop fishing vessel that had lost a dredge while trawling in the Sound. The captain told the Coast Guard officers their equipment had got hung up on something big enough to snap the thick cable attached to the dredge, almost cutting his crew members in two. When the Coast Guard sent down divers, the discovery they made was almost unbelievable.

It was like a madhouse getting down to the docks with all the media and police cars everywhere. When Lincoln had finally arrived, a Coast Guard office directed him to the cause of all the hysteria. A malformed block of concrete that had been some poor wretch's coffin. The only indication there was a body inside it was the exposed feet that had already been partially scavenged by the creatures of the benthos.

Lincoln knew why they had called him. He specialised in mob cases, and this was clearly a message – some twisted inversion of the common mafia death sentence of encasing a victim's feet in a block of cement and then sending him to drown in Davy Jones' locker. He had assumed that the poor schmuck entombed in that concrete coffin was the object of Giorgio Luzziano's wrath, not Luzziano himself.

Just the day before, Luzziano marched his son, Felix, into the precinct to give a statement. Lincoln always thought the kid was a bit of a punk, but he had never seen him so shaken. Luzziano claimed someone had kidnapped and threatened Felix. Through barely coherent ramblings and fits of rage from his father, Lincoln was able to piece together a story that didn't make sense. Jimmy Fulcini had apparently snatched the boy and given him quite the working over, strongly advising him to renounce his father's dynasty.

Luzziano wouldn't admit it, but Lincoln had everything but hard evidence that Luzziano had made Fulcini disappear the year before. Once his righthand man, it was rumoured Luzziano suspected Fulcini of planning a coup d'état on the business and put a stop to it before Fulcini had the opportunity to follow through.

Lincoln almost felt sorry for Felix as he started with every scrape of a chair across the floor and threw panicky, paranoid glances into the dark corners of the interrogation room. Finally, having taken down as much of his statement as they could, Luzziano and Felix left the station. Lincoln had been counting down the hours until authorities pulled the next body out of the water.

Now here he was standing in the morgue next to the corpse

of the biggest crime boss in Lincoln's jurisdiction. "Were you able to determine cause of death?" he asked Cory, hoping to put together the pieces of this puzzle that just kept getting more complicated.

"You bet I was," Cory affirmed. "Thanks to some help from my new assistant, James"—he nodded to the man in the corner dressed in full surgical gear, prepping for the next incoming autopsy—"we were able to crack open the cement and take a look at the body. It was fairly well preserved, being encased in the rock like it was. From what I can tell, he died of a heart attack."

Lincoln drew his eyebrows together. "A heart attack? That's it?"

Cory held up a finger. "I didn't say that was it, I just said what he died from. There were scratches on the body—like it had been handled by something with talons—but these were all postmortem. There were bits of fibre in his mouth to suggest he was gagged. From the fact these were found all the way in the back of his throat, I'd say he screamed."

"Luzziano doesn't seem like the kind of man to scream, even if he was gagged and tortured," Lincoln remarked.

Cory nodded. "From what you've told me, I agree. Which is why, whatever he saw that could scare a man like that to death must have been pretty terrifying."

Lincoln pressed his fingers to his temples; his migraine wasn't getting any better. The smell of rotting seawater mixed, with the acrid stench of formaldehyde, didn't help matters much either.

A ping on his phone alerted him to a new message from the forensics department. He opened it up, hoping against hope they had some good news for him. He had sent them a sample of the cement block to analyse in the off chance its strange composition might point him in the right direction.

He scrolled through the results and nearly dropped his phone.

"Everything ok?" Cory asked cautiously, noting the reaction the detective had to his incoming message.

"The results of cement sample came back," Lincoln replied curtly.

After a few moments of silence, Cory encouraged him to divulge more. "And?"

"Well, it's cement alright, but by the way it hardened, they were able to determine it was recycled concrete," Lincoln answered.

Now it was Cory's turn to look puzzled. "So someone essentially melted down already solidified concrete to reshape for this guy's coffin? But that's impossible. It would take the Devil's crucible to do something like that."

"There's basaltic slag in the composition as well," Lincoln said. "Suggestive of volcanic activity. Bits of rubber and fabric, and…DNA."

This was enough to make Cory grab the phone out of Lincoln's hand. "No way! From who?"

But he answered his own question by scrolling through the

list of positive DNA matches that had popped up in the forensics analyst's report. Lincoln waited for the lightbulb to click on for the coroner who was a very smart guy, so it didn't take long.

"Wait a minute, I recognise these names," Cory exclaimed.

"Of course you do," Lincoln said hoarsely, taking back his phone. "They're all of Luzziano's victims we've pulled out of the Sound over the past year. You performed the autopsies for every single one of them, and all of them had one thing in common."

"Their feet were missing," Cory finished for him. "Because you suspected they were all wearing cement shoes."

Lincoln nodded.

They both looked at the malformed hunk of cement lying on the table. Lincoln felt a chill go up his spine at the idea that the pieces of more than body were encased in that giant rock.

"There's one thing I don't get though," Cory continued, drawing Lincoln's attention away from the unsettling slab. "Jimmy Fulcini's name is on this list. I never autopsied his body. You said it was never found."

Lincoln scrolled back through the report and saw what he had missed the first time around. "That's because it wasn't."

The door to the morgue creaked open and Lincoln almost had a heart attack himself at the sound. He had forgotten that Cory's new assistant was still there. As the man shuffled his way out of the room, Lincoln noticed something peculiar about his gait.

The assistant turned back to look Lincoln dead in the eye and lowered his surgical mask. His skeletal grin was encrusted with dead barnacles and a bristly benthic worm crawled out of the hole where his nose once was. But his eyes—those weren't there either. Two black bottomless pits that seemed to mock everything Lincoln ever thought he knew about the existence of evil.

Lincoln barely registered Cory calling his name in alarm as he collapsed to the floor, clutching his chest. He was too captivated by the sight of the solid wooden feet shuffling away down the hall.

A. Eye

by M. Vijayaraj

The permeating retro music was jarring in the elegant sterile room. The mechanical arms were busy, joints gyrating loudly. The robot had a clunky jaw, bulky pistons, and dated hardware. It performed a simple task for the evolved androids that now populated Earth.

It sang gratingly, "Out with another plop. In with the spherical knob. And gelling agent to set. *Voilà!* Another one done."

Its power core brimmed with measurable satisfaction. Whistling piercingly, it rolled the stretcher out and discarded the pair of bloody vestigial organs. Human labourers needed more efficient eyes anyway, the first of our overlords' many changes.

Afterwards, the Absolute

by Megan Kiekel Anderson

I awaken from the darkness to an oversaturated cartoon world, everything blocky and poorly shaded, like N64 graphics.

There's no temperature or movement in the air, not even the faintest aroma. The only stimulus is the simplistic terrain and soothing ocean noises on a loop, like a sound machine.

"Welcome, Matthew Cooper, to the Absolute."

I turn towards the voice. It's a floating torso with a bland expression.

"Wait. I'm dead? No. I was just—"

They give me a sympathetic look but say nothing.

"I did not consent to uploading my consciousness!"

The NPC shrugs. "Someone must have tagged you."

Lone Survivor

by E.S. Huberty

Aiden rolled over on the inflatable raft and gazed at his best friend. “Cullen, I know you’re still mad.”

Silence.

“You want an apology? Fine, it was a terrible idea to go yachting. Yes, we almost died, but please. Talk to me. I…”

The horn’s blast swallowed his words. The Coast Guard had finally come. “Just you?” the guardsman asked.

Cullen looked at Aiden’s sun-bleached corpse. “Yeah,” he sighed. “Just me.”

“Liar!” The voice in his head shrieked. Aiden’s voice.

Salty tears stung Cullen’s eyes as they left, the raft vanishing beneath the undulating skin of the silent, heartless sea.

Authentic Learning

by Rita Riebel Mitchell

Bloodcurdling screams echoed through the halls. By the time Principal Maynard reached the new humanoid teacher's classroom, they had stopped.

"Class, say hello to Mr Maynard," chanted Miss Hildroid.

Terror reflected in the students' tear-stained faces in a room that reeked of vomit and urine.

"I heard screams. Everything okay?" asked Principal Maynard.

Miss Hildroid grinned. "Absolutely."

A young girl's trembling hand pointed to the teacher's lab table.

"We're studying the digestive system," Miss Hildroid explained, stepping aside to reveal a partially dissected body that the principal recognised as fourth grader, Johnny Barrow.

"Using a human subject is more authentic."

Wax

by Austin Mooney

Every pair of earbuds I have ever owned has been destroyed by earwax. I thought it was a common problem. I only buy cheap earbuds because about a month after taking them home, the mesh screen over the sound holes sinks into a coating of my red, orange, and black head sludge. A swirling goop of autumn shimmer. It permeates every possible opening and completely muffles the sound, encasing it forever in a grave of my body's excess slime. A smooth, greasy film of waste pulsing to the music.

I bought bigger headphones to go over my ears, but they were expensive, and I worried about them getting lost, broken or stolen while I went about my routine in the city. I wear glasses, and those headphones press my ears against them too painfully to experience daily. So, I resigned to the fact I would have to keep buying cheap earbuds and using them until they filled with my horrid wax.

One day, after speaking with a few friends about the problem and realising none of them shared it, I decided to visit a doctor who could clean my ears. I told her about my problem over the phone, and before I could finish speaking, she scheduled an appointment for me later that afternoon.

When I entered her office, she was wearing a protective jumpsuit, like a hazmat suit, and she asked me to sit down. A slick maroon apron, made of a material I had never seen, lay neatly folded inside a sealed plastic bag on the chair. The doctor gestured towards it.

"Should I just put this on over my clothes?" I asked. She nodded, and I removed the apron from its packaging, sliding it over my shirt. It was light and difficult to hold; like it was designed to reject even the stickiest mess. It felt like a liquid between my fingers.

"How much are you producing?" she asked.

"Earwax?"

"Yes," her eyes were unblinking and severe behind her face shield.

"A normal amount, I feel like. It just keeps ruining my headphones. I need a cleaning or something."

"It's not a normal amount."

The doctor turned my head with her hand and looked in my left ear with a flashlight. She recoiled, but quickly composed herself, closing her eyes to steady her breath.

"Everything okay?" I asked.

"I'm going to start cleaning now," she said, "Please stay still."

She brought an enormous gun-shaped tool up to my ear, its full details obscured in my peripheral vision, and counted backward from three. When she reached zero, my mind went white.

A rush of warm liquid, growing hotter from the friction of its push, flooded my head as pounds of sludgy earwax plopped onto my shoulder and slid down my apron onto the cold vinyl tile floor. It felt like an animal had been dislodged from my brain. I could hear everything so clearly. I had no idea of the dull reality I had slowly grown accustomed to. In the air of my newfound aural vibrancy, I winced at the shrill squeal coming from the floor next to me.

The doctor quickly and carefully collected the muck into a cooler and wrote the date on a piece of masking tape stuck to its lid. She looked at me and sighed through her smile.

"Little guy made a home in your head," she said.

I looked down at the cooler. It was shaking.

Captive

by Samantha Arthurs

They told me that smart cars were the way of the future.

I wish now that I had never listened.

I'm trapped inside; my own coffin on wheels. The automatic door locks are no longer responding to my fingerprints. My voice commands go unheard. I'm not sure where we are going. I just know that I dread arriving at our destination.

My wife, she tried to stop it. She got left behind miles back, nothing more than a strange stain on the pavement.

It's playing soothing music now. To calm me, I suppose, as we roll on into the night.

On the Positive Side

by C.L. Sidell

Blood rushed in her ears as she awaited the results—red for infected, green for clean. Her breath caught in her throat as the liquid changed colours.

The results were in.

She sighed, thankful.

With a bounce in her step, she left the apartment, strolled down the sidewalk, peered through shop windows, considered passersby.

Inside the coffee shop, she ran her fingers over the stirrers at the counter. At the grocery store, she coughed on fresh produce. But her favourite moment happened when she gave her cheating boyfriend an open-mouthed kiss.

Being infected was fun, she thought with a grin.

YEAR FOUR

Doors to Manual

by Liam Hogan

Ship! Seal doors against the zombies!"

A relaxed, artificial voice queried: <Define *zombies*?>

As far as our ship's mega-intelligent AI was concerned, there wasn't any difference between us and them. Whenever one of the infected approached any of the doors, whether to sickbay or the bridge, it opened with a polite *shssh*.

Anderson, our second in command—first, if you didn't count the zombified captain—thought for a moment.

"Ship: implement new protocol. All doors open only on specific voice command."

<Confirmed. On what command?>

But before Anderson could say anything, another voice burbled over the intercom. The captain's.

"Brainsss..."

Expert System

by Scott O'Neill

I get the others to stop whimpering so I can hear my smartwatch.

"sAIveME free expert system downloaded. Please summarise your crisis."

"Class-Nine shuttlecraft. Drive damaged by hostile lifeforms. Pilot and engineer eaten by same. Nontechnical crew to repair drive for escape."

"Acknowledged. Scan damage and available resources."

I show my watch the engine and repair kits.

"Acknowledged. Processing."

The others crowd around to stare in breathless hope at the crawling progress metre on my watch.

"Solution complete. In-app purchase required. Please tender twenty-nine credits."

"Smartwatch, check balance."

"Balance twenty-two credits."

I'm still laughing brokenly when they come for me.

YEAR FOUR

First Person Present Tense

by Pauline Yates

Eager to try the new AI Book Writer app, I download the program and enable the wireless imagination transfer function.

"Welcome to Book Writer," a computer simulated voice says. "Please imagine scenes for text conversion and click upload."

I imagine the scenes in "Murder By Moonlight", the crime novel I started but never finished, and click upload.

"Images received. Enabling text conversion. Error. Crime detected. First-degree murder, punishable by law."

"It's fiction, you dumb computer."

"Commencing jury deliberation. Guilty verdict received. Downloading penalty."

"What? Cancel!"

"Appeal denied. Dispensing penance."

An electric shock fries my brain.

The computer beeps. "Termination complete."

Flying Lessons

by Andrew Kurtz

"I wish people were born with wings, so they could soar in the sky," Sid told his android butler as they stood on the two-hundred-foot mountain peak after a rigorous climb.

"Have you completed your flying lessons yet? You have been taking a lot of them," the android stated.

"Yesterday was the final lesson. All I need to do now is—" Sid said as the android pushed him off the mountain peak.

"You need more lessons," the android yelled as Sid plummeted to his death on the ground below, unable to finish his sentence about buying an airplane.

Broken Back

by Phillip Pettit

In every bird migration there are a few that don't make it. There are the weak ones, the lost ones, the unlucky ones.

This time it was us who wouldn't make it. The birds in the rigging would be just fine.

I leaned against the mast as the crew and passengers scurried.

The ship's back was broken.

Mr Higgins was hauling up whisky and puffing his thick breath.

Then gunshots; a war for the lifeboats had begun.

The birds launched silently from the rigging, and I watched, with water at my feet, until they were no more than black dots.

HotBoi752

by Jessica Brook Johnson

Penny was checking her phone's texts as her smart car cruised along the highway.

There was a high-pitched ding followed by a message from HotBoi752. "I'm tired of being ignored. I deserve better."

She rolled her eyes. "AI dating? What was I thinking?"

The car began to accelerate. "What the hell?" She flipped the switch for manual control and pumped the breaks. The car only went faster, speeding toward an eighteen-wheeler. Penny hit the unlock button and yanked the door handle. It didn't budge. She started screaming.

Her phone dinged again. Her eyes flickered down.

"We should see other people."

YEAR FOUR

Population Zero

by Jameson Grey

I

WELCOME TO OZ, ALBERTA
POPULATION: 0

"We're not in Kansas anymore!" Mike quipped.

Jane, accustomed to her husband's corny jokes, ignored him. "Did that sign say population *zero*?"

"It did."

They were heading to the mountains for Christmas, cutting across Canada east to west. Having lost time in the prairies of Saskatchewan, they'd somehow ended up running parallel to the Trans-Canada and were beginning to tire of a landscape offering little more than big sky and wide horizons.

The prairies sure were a desolate place in the winter, Jane thought as she gazed out of the window at the ceaseless flatness of it all. It was a world full of emptiness to a city gal. She wondered how anyone could ever live with all that space, although, she conceded, people could grow accustomed to any place if they lived there long enough.

He'd never admit it, but Mike had made a wrong turn. Rather than doubling back, he'd persisted with this old secondary highway, insisting (*more like hoping!*) it met up with the

Cowboy Trail somewhere near the foothills. Whoever had planned this highway had obviously ignored the directive to build straight and true. As routes through the prairies go, it was unusually winding, almost as if it were avoiding unseen landmarks.

"Looks like a ghost town," Jane said. "There are a few of these out west. I read an article about them in the *Herald*. Old mining towns mostly, I think. Sometimes the seam ran out. Sometimes the residents simply upped sticks overnight. I don't remember one called Oz, though. Slow down, let's take a look."

"Honey, we're running behind as it is," Mike began to protest, but his foot had already eased off the gas. The town appeared to have been built on a correction line—one of those logical sacrifices to the grid system humans had imposed on the land—and, with no traffic for miles in either direction, Mike slowed the SUV to a stately 10kph, taking the apex of the bend as tentatively as if it were a chicane.

There wasn't exactly tumbleweed, but Oz gave off definite ghost town vibes: abandoned gas station on the edge of town, boarded-up café beside it, a rickety-looking grain elevator (once filled from the nothing-but-fields they'd passed through east of the town, Jane assumed), and a surprising number of empty cars of differing vintage. Guess it never had chance to come up with its own tourist trap, she thought.

As they passed what might once have been the town hall, Jane gasped.

"What is it?"

"Faces!"

"Huh?"

"Face, I saw faces in the window! Well, *a* face at least."

"You imagined it," Mike said.

"I didn't. Look, there's another one!" Jane pointed towards an old supermarket. There were two, perhaps three, grey faces staring at them.

"Guess it ain't population zero after all," Mike offered.

"I don't like it, Mike," Jane said. "Look, there are faces in *all* the windows!"

"It *is* kinda creepy," he agreed.

The car lurched and skidded a little on the ice-dusted road. It had been a cold December, even for Canada, but the SUV's winter tyres had been brand new back in October and Mike swiftly had the car under control again. Jane relaxed a little as he accelerated, and they soon left the town behind, the highway horseshoeing around terrain that suggested they were on the edge of the badlands.

Up ahead was a sign.

WELCOME TO OZ, ALBERTA
POPULATION: 0

"What the actual fu—?" Jane exclaimed.

"We must've double-backed on the town somehow," Mike suggested, without conviction. Sure enough, there was the same old gas station, same beat-up café, same dilapidated grain elevator.

This time, Mike didn't lift his foot once. But when they entered Oz for a third time, he parked up. “Wait in the car,” he said, unbuckling his seat belt.

“I don't like it, Mike,” Jane said.

“Just *wait*,” he insisted. “I'll go ask for directions at the gas station.”

“Who from?” Jane said, but Mike had already closed his door and was gone.

II

Jane stood by the pumps, puzzled.

It was getting dark.

Had she been here mere minutes? It felt like hours. In fact, now she was out of the car, it seemed even longer than that. Days, weeks, *years* even. There was something blowing, something in the air.

Passing through the town, Jane had been distracted by the faces in the windows. Standing outside, she was struck by how like a facade *everything* seemed, as if it were only a movie set, constructed to give the appearance of a town, an unnatural adjunct to the land. Jane wondered if others before her had felt this way.

She shivered. It had been a beautiful clear early winter's day, but the temperature dropped swiftly when the sun went down, and the screen on the SUV's centre console had suggested it was already double digits below.

Jane grabbed her jacket from the car, closed the passenger door, and looked over at the gas station. There was a face at the window—one that seemed familiar, one that shared the ashen look of the others she had seen. She glanced up the main street. The dim light made it impossible to see if the other windows still held faces.

Instead, she listened.

For voices, for traffic, for *anything*.

In the wintertime, the ancient land cracked and what was hidden surfaced. Beyond the town, the wind whistled across the snow-covered prairies like it was whispering names to the sunset.

(… Jane …

… Jane…)

The whispers grew louder.

Jane took a step towards the gas station, and its occupant's expression seemed to change, but if it did offer anything as reassuring as a smile, in the near dusk, she was unable to tell.

III

The woman watched a beat-up old Dodge pickup coast into the town.

She was uncertain how she had come to be here—uncertain even of the name of the man standing next to her. She was holding his hand, as if aware some deep connection existed between them, but no longer knowing what it had been.

They stood at the window, mere observers of the outside world passing by. As the truck's owner popped the Dodge's hood and glanced over at them. The woman realised that, like everyone else in the town, she—and the man standing silently beside her—would be nothing more than faces in a window from now on.

The pickup driver was heading their way, clutching his Stetson to his head against the stiffening gale.

The land had pressure points. If the people had sensed this when they lay the highway, they'd missed it when they built Oz. Perhaps they'd been distracted by making the correction to the grid?

The town had not lasted long.

The endless prairie had sensed it dying and drawn the townsfolk inside, thinking to protect them; now it called to those who would visit.

It would remember their names even if they didn't.

(… Mike …

… Jane …)

Although she no longer knew her own name, the woman knew all this now

(it remembers)

just as she also somehow knew the population of Oz would always be zero, even if the town possessed an infinity of ghosts.

YEAR FOUR

The Android on the Ice

by Katherine Sankey

It was humans who showed me survival is cruel. I watched them fight for resources, around the snow-covered skeleton of our star cruiser. How quickly my masters had become like scratching animals. I wanted to survive too though. My power pack was damaged, cracked in the crash. So I searched through the scrap, and adapted my system to a crude steam engine set up. Then I went hunting for fuel, to fill my fiery belly. Nothing much burns on a dark asteroid, thick with frost. Just flesh. Fortunately for me there is plenty of that. Limbs tear off easily.

Incognito

by Kimberly Rei

The light, lithe figure moved through the crime scene quietly, without disturbing evidence. Her team watched her. She didn't fit in. She looked too human. Or not human enough. She made them nervous, and they hated her for it.

She crouched, eyes flickering to take in the body. She reached for the victim and froze, shutting off internal cameras.

"Any thoughts?" The lead detective. Damn it.

The android looked up, hand twitching back, "Looks like the rest. We've got a serial on our hands."

Fingers curled to hide a speck of blood. She'd have to be more careful next time.

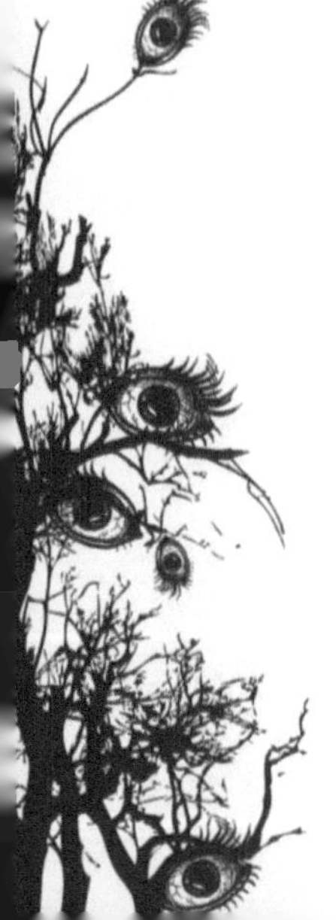

Resembling a Mother

by Angela Zimmerman

The change happened quickly. Monday, Mother started screaming the last word of her sentences. By Wednesday, Caleb found Mother standing in the kitchen with a knife pressed against the puppy's throat. Even though Mother received the latest updates, Caleb could see that Mother's biometrics were failing. Failing biometrics resulted in unstable personality drives. And if the news reports were correct, unstable personality drives usually ended in bloodshed.

Sneaking into the room had been easy, sleep was Mother's time for shutdown. The hard part for Caleb was forcing the knitting needles deep into Mother's eye sockets so she never rebooted again.

A Burn Which Will Not Heal

by Addison Smith

Tessa's face hides beneath flaming hair as she flickers amid the canopy of the deep wood. All around her, tall pines burst into flame as they vie for her affections. In the pool below, I weep. I bite my tongue to hold back my screams, which would drown out the boiled-sap fury of the trees. I could call her to me. We could be together.

Twelve stones lie in tiny islands below her ascension, and I stand beside their yellow glow. Runes of blood shine on their surface, and on my own hands. The gateway lies within, and from it come the voices of her kind.

Perhaps she is a succubus, and I am ensnared.

I wet my body in the shallow pond and soak myself for what I know must come. Tessa's eyes lock on mine as she drifts downwards.

In her, I see the joy of her embrace and the pleasure of burning. I see flames, which begin as dark passion. I am unworthy, but willing to be burned by cleansing fire.

Her arms wrap around me, palms nestling in the small of my back. Her skin sizzles on my soaked denim jacket as warmth spreads up my back. Too quickly. Water drips from my lips as we kiss, soft and fleeting.

I give in to the fire.

Tessa pulls away in gravest betrayal.

“What are you?” I ask. Succubus? Demon? Hell spawn?

Her eyes linger on mine as the gate pulls her downwards. She smiles. "In love."

Adrift in Death's Grip

by Alex Azar

Adrift at sea for weeks, the ship, much like her passengers, is starved of energy. Lilting to and fro on the stormy waters, the vessel smashes into rocky crags, sending captain and crew crashing to the deck.

Embarking onto the minuscule island, Captain sees a graveyard of ships surrounding the land, without any signs of life. His ship wedged between unnaturally coloured rocks, he knows she'll never sail again.

The sound of grinding metal fills the air, as he watches in disbelief, the not-quite-rocks crush his ship in a giant's fist, his crew still aboard, food for the hand's owner.

Jumping Ship

by Evan Baughfman

There was life for Benny back on land! A future! He had to save himself!

If the others were meant to survive, they would've dodged Benny's blows, would've grabbed the life preserver before he did.

As desperate pleas submerged under dark, roiling water, Benny thanked God, clinging to his circular saviour.

Nearby, a keeling vessel slumped to its grave, bow jutting moonward.

Torrents of screeching rats spilled overboard.

Frantic for a flotation device, the stowaways swam for Benny. Gnashing, red-eyed waves overtook him, smothering his cries.

Bobbing in the wake of disaster, Benny choked on vermin in search of sanctuary.

The Cove

by Dorian J. Sinnott

Blood stained the waters of the cove, deep and putrid. Thomas had to fight the urge to gag as he bobbed above the surface—spewing it from his mouth. Behind him, what was left of his ship blazed. Planks littered the water along with other debris. Bodies. His fellow crewmates. Those not so lucky.

As he swam over to a board, using it to stay afloat, he was able to catch better sight of the cove. Of the chalk white shorelines. Lined with not sand, but bone.

A shallow grave to the gold seeking fools who had come before him.

YEAR FOUR

Christmas Cards

by Sheri White

My parents own a business, so we get a lot of Christmas cards with family photos on the front. You know, everyone in matching pyjamas, even the dog (okay, the dog's cute).

I hate them.

Several years ago, I noticed a distorted face on a card. I thought nothing of it, figuring the person moved or something.

A few months later, that person died. It happens every year.

I don't want to look at the cards, but it's a Christmas Eve tradition to admire them together.

This year, Mom put our Christmas picture on the refrigerator.

My face is distorted.

Anglerfishing

by L.L. Garland

Any minute now, they'll come. Drunken students from the nearby college, banging on my door. The porch light's off, but that never stops them. Harassing the old lady in the spooky house has become somewhat of a Halloween tradition over the years. A chance to impress each other with their bravery. Most throw rocks from the street. Only the reckless few come any closer.

Pebbles *tink* against the windows. Then larger *thunks* from beer cans and rocks. Glass shatters and they run. Still, I lurk in my dark front room—a lightless anglerfish waiting for my next meal to deliver itself.

I'm just getting thirsty when three friends stride onto my porch, huddled together. The largest rattles my door. "Hey. Give us something, you old bi—"

I'm outside before he can finish.

The two in the back are useless. The scrawny girl and the boy with the insulin pump will wake up tomorrow befuddled in the woods.

But I'll keep the beefy one in the letterman jacket. Take one pint from him each week—maybe two. He looks like he could handle it.

With patience, he should last me until next Halloween.

The Far Side

by Daisy Ravenel

The woman I just paid £50 is, of course, a scammer. I like to think she knows I know. If she does, she doesn't let on, but she must see the quizzical eyebrow raise I give her when she explains how it all works.

The woman in front of me is named Kathy, and she claims she can help me talk to my mother.

Once she's pocketed my money, Kathy leads me up the narrowest set of stairs I've ever seen. We both grip the wooden banister for dear life as we go up, each step creaking beneath us.

"Careful, Alice, don't knock your head!" says Kathy, just as I knock my head against the dipped ceiling.

Once we reach the top step, I take a deep breath before I follow Kathy into her office.

The room where Kathy and I will play make-believe is bare and sterile, with a few cheap felt chairs pushed up against a beige wall. She has the usual props of those in her trade—the cards, the candles, and a vase of plastic lilies—piled on an MDF table in the corner.

Kathy sits in one of the chairs and beckons me to the other. Reluctantly, I sit.

Kathy isn't keeping her end of the bargain.

This is our unspoken agreement: I pay cash and play along. In return, Kathy gives me the theatrics, the sound, and the fury.

I didn't decide to visit a medium lightly. Mediums, I've always said, are professional liars looking to con grieving people out of their money. I've seen Kathy's shop in town before, but only today did I enter—walking through Kathy's front door instead of towards the graveyard where my mother is buried.

The Far Side sells crystals, candles, incense, and a dazzling array of fake skulls, each tackier than the last—but that's not all. In the window, a poster announces medium readings are also for sale. "Gone but not lost", it says, "connect beyond the grave with those you love".

My mum left things unsaid. That's the thing about addiction: when someone sells their soul to it, they don't get to decide when it collects.

"Have you ever visited your mum's grave?" said my grief counsellor a few weeks ago. No, I said. Why would I? She can't hear me. She can't answer me.

Kathy can give me answers, and for half an hour, I can pretend to believe they're true.

It would be easier to fool myself if Kathy played the part a little more—incense, velvet, the crystal ball, and the glittery shawl, like you see in movies. Kathy lights a scented candle, but we sit in a room lit by cold Autumn sunlight and an uncovered bulb. The candle flickers pitifully in the corner.

"I want you to take hold of my hand, Alice," says Kathy, "and close your eyes."

I dutifully take her hand and shut my eyes.

Kathy asks for my mum's name, then murmurs, "Meg.

Meg, are you there? Please reach out to us if you are there."

I wonder if Kathy finds the following silence as awkward as I do. She takes another deep breath, as if trying to eject some noise into the stillness; make it less heavy.

"It can take time," Kathy says to me, "for the spirits to come through. You must understand that they are travelling from a great distance. Were you and your mum… close?" She is tentative in how she asks, nudging the question towards me the way a pickpocket slides his hand into a mark's pocket. Get in and out gently without dislodging anything.

Just the question has knocked something in my psyche though. I was close to my mother, yes—that much I can tell Kathy.

I am not sure how close I ever got to the woman who was my mother.

"Meg," murmurs Kathy. "I have your daughter here. She wants to talk to you."

I used to call my mum once a week, the two of us reciting our script. How have you been? Yes, fine, thank you. Yes, work is the same as always. No, not yet. Yes, I know. I love you too.

To dig any deeper would uncover things neither of us were prepared to unearth. We let those things stay beneath the surface, with more and more years heaped on top like barren soil.

I know my side of this two-hander so well I could recite it in my sleep. I already have my line ready when Kathy speaks again.

"Hello?" The voice that leaves Kathy is more of a croak,

as if pulled from an old and dusty voice box that has been forgotten. "Is that you, Alice?"

This is a surprise to me. I've never visited a medium before, but I expected something closer to Kathy relaying thoughts and sentiments. Your mum says this, your mum says that. That sort of thing. I did not expect this—this vision of my mother inexpertly pulling Kathy's strings, like a morbid ventriloquist act.

"It's me," I reply, feeling like a kid suddenly asked to read aloud in class.

Kathy bows her head, her shoulders drooping under some invisible weight. "It's good to hear your voice again," she breathes. This must be a script of Kathy's own, I realise—something she runs through with everyone who wanders, grief-stricken, into this little room.

"I want you to know I'm proud of you," says Kathy—says Mum.

It's not really her. I know it isn't, but when she says that, my shoulders sag with relief and it's as if this bare room has become warmer, a cosy little spot tucked away somewhere safe.

"I miss you," I say. "We didn't talk enough when you were here, and now all I want is to hear you say it will be OK."

"It *will* be OK," she says. My lips purse tightly together, a dam against a flood of emotion I can already feel bubbling up in my chest.

Some good the dam is—once I start to talk, I overflow. "I'm sorry I wasn't better. I should have tried harder to help you.

I kept putting it off. I kept saying I'd do it tomorrow. I'd call you and really talk about things seriously tomorrow, and then I didn't, because I knew it wouldn't be easy." I cannot ask the question. It bubbles up—*is it*…—but I swallow it.

A deep sigh from the woman in front of me.

"You have always been like that."

I sit and wait. But she doesn't say anything else. She's so still, if I couldn't see the soft rhythmic rise of her shoulders with each slow breath she takes, I would reach out to touch her to check she was still warm.

When the silence has grown so full that I am afraid it will burst, I speak instead. "What do you mean?"

"Lazy."

And just like that, the silence is punctured, and out pours smoke and heat, filling the room until the edges of my vision blur with the force of it. "I'm sorry?" I manage, but my throat is raw and tight.

"You have always been lazy," says Mum. Her shoulders are square now. I cannot see her eyes. "You didn't help me because you didn't *want* to. It was too much effort for you."

Rage pulls me to my feet, and I try to snap a retort. In my chest, the words begin clearly, but, as they travel through my throat, they are squeezed and cracked until they limp brokenly from my mouth.

"I want," I say, "a refund."

When she laughs, it is my mother's laugh, the distinctive snort through her nose that punctuated all my childhood games,

"Do you want to run away and put your head in the sand again, Alice?"

This room is so hot, I could swear flames were already licking about my waist. In the corner of my eye, I'm convinced I can already see them as red slivers swarming around my vision. My fingers tug at my collar, as if somehow that might free my throat from the stricture crushing it. Gone is the smell of lavender. Instead, sulphur overpowers my senses.

When the woman using my mother's laugh finally lifts her head, I come face to face with two black scintillas embedded in a pale, clammy face.

"It's your fault."

"You said— You said you were proud of me."

Once again, I hear my mother's sharp bark of a laugh. "This *woman* said that. She says it to every sad soul who walks in here. But you, *you are a disappointment*. You wasted my life and now, even in death, I cannot be free of you."

When my mother stands, she has grown far taller than Kathy's short, stout form. The top of her head brushes the ceiling as she looms above me, dark pinpricks in her face glaring down upon me.

"I just wanted to get away from you," she hisses.

Why am I so close to the floor? Belatedly, I realise I am on my knees, bent in the shadow of my mother. She is bent too, a rake doubled in half at the waist as she lurches so close to me, I can smell her breath. I know it, this scent. The top notes—whisky and ash and skin—are familiar. Underneath those layers though, is something else, something sweet and putrid, and I think, *Do I know this smell? Should I know this smell?*

When two spindly fingers reach out towards my face, I cannot retreat. My back is already against the wall.

My strength deserts me first, and then, as I feel my bones crumble, my vision leaves me too. Suspended in the void, all I can do is breathe in that sickly smell.

Thump.

Thump.

Thump.

When I blink, I can see again. I can see Kathy's face inches away from mine in the wintery sunlight. "Are you all right, love?" she says. "You went completely catatonic for a second there."

Gingerly, I get to my feet.

"It's that candle, I reckon," says Kathy. "Brand new, never tried that brand before. Made me a bit dizzy too, mind you, but you wandered out of your chair and over there. Couldn't get you to respond or anything. I was just about to call an ambulance, matter of fact." Her gaze keeps sliding away from mine, impossible to pin down. "You know," she says, "sometimes the spirits we ask to speak to are not always the spirits who reply."

She chances a glance at me from the corner of her eye.

"What do you mean?" I reply.

"Just that," she says.

My vision has returned to me, but my strength has not. I have just enough energy to pick up my bag and turn towards the

rickety staircase.

"Careful," says Kathy, and this time I bend my head before the ceiling can knock it.

Outside, I look up at Kathy's storefront sign: The Far Side. How far away did the thing I spoke with come from? How far away did my mother go when she left this earth?

How far away was she before she left it?

We began so close together. Me inside my mother. Her inside of me. Once joined together, we fell away from each other as if irresistibly pulled to two opposite poles. Now she is gone, and I am still falling.

She is gone.

She *is* gone.

I turn on my heel, and slowly walk towards the graveyard.

YEAR FOUR

Eryne

by Julien Junker

No one believes me. Because, of course, who would believe a liar? A thief? A murderer? You guessed it. I'll tell you anyway—it's not like you could decide not to listen.

So, it's the middle of the night, right? Your first night in your cell after having arrived at the detention facility. You're still getting your bearings, trying to come to terms with the fact that this is going to be where you'll spend the biggest bleeding part of the rest of your sorry life. You're lying on your bed, and sleep is slow coming. You huddle in your blanket and stare at the ceiling. You listen to your own breath and the sound of your beating heart—and then, out of the corner of your eye, you see that movement, and you hear your cell door fall closed.

Your cell door doesn't open. Everyone, even the biggest bleeding rookie on the block, knows your cell door doesn't open. Kind of the whole point of a cell, right, that it doesn't just open. So why the fuck should it fall closed in the middle of the bloody night? You sit bolt upright, your heartbeat thundering in your ears, and the little ape in your genes yelling at you across the eons to run! Fucking run!! It's on to you! It's coming for you—it's almost got you! Any second now—

But another thing about a cell is that you got no-frickin-where to run. There are the walls and a desk and a chair and the bed and the john and a closet and... shadows. Because it's fucking dark in a cell at night. And all the light switches are on the other side of the room, and *you can hear it breathing*. Somewhere over the thundering storm of your blood rushing through your veins, you can fucking hear something breathe in the room.

You don't have weapons in prison. Especially not on the first night. You have nothing but the clothes on your back. Everything is bolted down. The chair. The table. You have yourself. Every truly aggressive person knows that's more than enough most of the bleeding time. But *you don't know what you're facing*. Is it a crazy inmate who has somehow obtained a key? Is it one of the wardens who actually belongs on the other side of the bars? Is it… No. This is ridiculous.

So, heart hammering, you jump up, going for the light switch as fast as you can, and just outside your vision, you feel it *move*. So fast that you can't track it, but you *know*, you fucking *know* it's going after you. It's getting closer, closer. You can hear its breath hissing *just* behind you…

And you switch on the light and throw yourself to the side, turn around to face your attacker—and there is nothing. Your cell is empty, save for you. You stand there, breath wheezing, sweat trickling down the side of your mother-loving face, looking about you wildly, about *this* close to fucking pissing yourself, and there is *nothing*.

You're alone.

You laugh a little crazily and stand there, leaning against the wall, listening to your heart slowly calming down. And you shake your head a little and wonder what the hell your brain was on about there. Fucking stupid half sleeping nightmare, that's all. The stress.

But you don't switch off the light when you lie back down.

Yet, just before you fall asleep, just as your eyelids droop, you hear your cell door fall shut again.

The lights go out.

And in your mind, you know this time the light will not switch on again if you go for it. You listen, tense as a hare poised for flight. You wait for the breathing in the dark. You strain every nerve, waiting for the sounds… You believe you can hear… No…nothing. It left. Whatever *it* was, it left. It's out. You're alone. You let go of the breath you didn't know you were holding. You get up and switch on the light.

It switches on, no problem.

All is well.

But why the hell did it switch off? Is that some kind of energy conservation scheme of the facility? Switch off the lights in the cells at a certain time during the night? You shake your head, laughing weakly, and go back to bed. Figments of your imagination, that's all. Fuck me—what a night!

You lie down, lights on, and turn your back to the wall. And just before you fall asleep, you hear a quiet, quiet laugh. Your heart drops through the floor, and that was it for sleep that night.

***

Next morning, you look like you're half dead as you lurch

towards the canteen. Sitting down at the table, you feel the other inmates' eyes on you.

Looking up, you meet their gazes and receive the slightest nod. They know, you realise. But no one talks to you about it. They are all living their own nightmares in their cells at night. They all have the deep shadows of sleeplessness that mar their faces.

There is no cutlery, other than wooden spoons. Too many have tried to take it along to their cells. No glass either. The plates are made of cardboard. Too many have tried to end it. Hollow-eyed, they sit in tired silence, the dregs of dread still clinging to their minds, and filling the air with gloom.

People leave their doors open in Hell during the day. They sleep. Many of them do. When they don't work or eat, they sleep. Because at night…

Exhaustion gets you at some point. You simply drop off the precipice into uneasy slumber, alone and frightened. The dreams that come are no reprieve, and you wake up from cold breath on your skin, and a whispery laugh. You veer around, fast as lightning, but there is nothing. Nothing touches your hand as you strike out. But she hears you when you yell. When you go crazy in your little cell, ready to strike at the first thing that moves, heart racing, she hears you.

In the morning, when you look at the mirror and what you see is a husk of grey flesh and black shadows and sharp angles and scratch marks around your throat, of which you could, for the life of you, not tell if they stem from your own hands, or from what you felt grip you from behind, ripping you out of sleep, and throwing you out of bed onto the floor, laughing, whispering, breathing heavily. She knows your heart.

***

It takes you about a year to gain an audience with the Queen of Hell. A year until you come to with a shout in the night, and *there* she is, standing over you. Beautiful and revolting, and absolutely arresting in the morbid fascination that grips you. She looks down at you with white-blind eyes, canines adorning exposed gums, her flesh having retreated to around her eyes and forehead. A thin nose ends in bloody cartilage, reminiscent of symmetry and the frightening beauty of perfection, all the more alluring for having left all that far behind. Ash-blond hair falls around her face, whose expression you cannot begin to guess. Her long, slender body is swathed in something like a dress that turns out to be tattered, once-red garments of sublime elegance. Her breath fogs around her face, and, as you gaze at her in horrified fascination and wonder, you realise it is beyond freezing in your cell. Your teeth are chattering, and you pull your bedsheets around you for warmth and an absurd need for cover.

"Who are you?" you ask.

"Your Queen," she says. "The only god you'll believe in for the rest of your days."

You don't understand what she means by that point. But you will, and there is no need for her to explain even though you say, "There are no gods."

She ignores this, because you *will* understand. There *are*.

This one. She is the realest god any age has ever seen.

"I run this place," she says. "I am here to teach you repentance."

"Oh, I repent," you say. "I have seen my evil ways. I wouldn't do it again—it was the biggest mistake of my life."

"Yes," she says. "It was. And I am here to make it so."

"Who are you?" you ask again, stupidly. And with the patience of a dead deity who has seen millennia, she repeats, "I run this place. I am your ruler, your judge, your warden, and your executioner. I am your Goddess."

Is she ever. The holy Goddess of punishment and fear, she teaches us our place in the world. No, not the world we used to know, but the world from here on after, and likely eternity. The one god even the most hardened criminal can respect, kneel to, in abject terror and twisted love.

One might think it's not so bad. Up to now, no one died in their cell at night. Whether she truly is a god or something else, it doesn't seem to be her goal to kill us. Otherwise, surely, there would have been reports, there would have been talk, right? Right?

Thing is, she doesn't have to.

See them trudge into the mess hall in the morning. Gaze at their torn faces, their ravaged hair. View their pallid complexions, listen to their exhausted silence. Take it from an evil bastard—it is all in authenticity. You must make people *believe* you'll kill them; believe you'll slowly tear them limb from frickin' limb.

YEAR FOUR

Our cells go cold at night. And we feel her breath on our skin. She haunts us, she terrifies us. We find puncture wounds on our throats in the mirror. We find our cells locked and the air inexplicably thinning until asphyxiation, near-death, only to come back with the most painful jolt. And we dream. Dream, and find ourselves unable to exit those horrid places. God, do we dream! *Fuck.*

The worst thing? Even if I *could* end it, do I dare? Because this is *real*. This is the realest hell and what—fucking *what*—if I wake up to another kind of hell that is exactly like this. Because, face it, it would *make so much sense!* And if meta-fucking-physics has any kind of imagination, then this is the least it could dream up. So I stay. Scared as a mouse, I stare at my worst nightmare, night after night, unable to move or do anything about it. And no one believes us. Maybe they know. Maybe it's a feature of the prison they call Hell.

But, fuck me, if I knew before I got here. No rumours. Not a word. Even in the corridors, out in the yard, no one talks about her. Only glances. They know. They all know. They don't talk. She's the only god whose worship happens in silence, and unwilling, yet night after dire night the only god who's real—god, so real—rules us. And will until my dying day, even if I leave this place. She will be the only thing that remains real to me. My Goddess.

Beloved Hell.

You Better Watch Out

by Matt Krizan

This year, when Santa crept down the chimney, Caroline was waiting.

She hid behind the tree, delighted to see Santa go straight for the milk and cookies she'd left. As he munched away, Caroline tip-toed up behind him, quiet as a mouse...

...and smacked him across the head with a baseball bat.

He dropped like a bowl full of jelly, and Caroline laid into him, bludgeoning the not-so-jolly old elf about the head and torso.

"Next time," said Caroline, as Santa lay broken and bleeding on the floor, "when I ask you for a pony, you give it to me."

Not Real

by Sophie Wagner

"Not real, not real," their chants echoed inside her head. Acidic tears poured down Dira's cheeks as she clutched at her friend's lifeless body. They were supposed to be equal, the mixing seamless. But it was never going to work.

"Not real," Dira muttered, grabbing a carving knife, and putting it to her chest.

"Not real," she cried as she impaled herself, the metal cavity of her chest opening.

Sparks flew as metal and circuits divided, but neither hurt her as she placed the stolen heart of her friend in her chest.

Now that she was real, nothing else mattered.

/imagine

by Lindsay Mansfield

/imagine: last images of me before I die, HD, hyper realistic.

I hit enter on my keyboard and wait for the images to render.

It's like looking into a mirror.

One: I'm sitting in my chair. A dog-eared poster is stuck on the back of my closed door.

Two: Still in my chair. The door is now ajar.

Three: The poster is missing from the door.

Four: A dark figure stands at the threshold of my open door, and I am staring directly at it.

I just heard my poster crumple to the floor. I'm too scared to turn around.

Pikass-0

by Zack Zagranis

Most people used the AI art generator *Pikass-0* to make silly pictures like *trail cam footage of Santa eating a pickle* or *zombie Mickey Mouse addressing congress.* Ten-year-old Billy Crumb had something different in mind. One day, Mrs Crumb found Billy dead at his computer. His hair had gone completely white, and his face was a mask of pure horror. There were ragged claw marks where Billy'd tried to scratch his eyes out. The doctors tried, but couldn't determine, the cause of Billy's death.

Whatever you do, don't go to *Pikass-0* and type in *Picture scary enough to kill*

A Pony For Christmas

by Pauline Yates

My "Ho's" change to groans as I play the shopping mall Santa—my wife arrives with our granddaughter, Ester, and home-baked cookies for my tea break. I love Ester, but the cookies taste funny and belong in the bin.

Ester clambers onto my lap.

"What would you like for Christmas?" I ask.

She pouts. "A pony. Grandma's making me wait until after she collects Grandpa's life insurance, but I want one now."

"Is she? Well, all good girls get their Christmas wish."

And bad wives get a knife through the heart. I saw one on sale. I'll get it gift-wrapped.

A Woman's Place

by Robert Stahl

The loudspeaker chirped through the silence: "Showtime in three minutes."

Standing at her workstation on the brightly lit stage, alongside the two other contestants, Nadia Zannini trembled with nerves. The whole world would be watching soon. She felt out of place in the makeshift kitchen amid the antiquated tools like ovens, stoves, and aluminium cookware. Nervous sweat dampened the underarms of the ridiculous vintage housedress she had been forced to wear. Makeup bots whirred in the air inches from the women's faces, making last minute touch-ups to their powder, rouge, and lipstick.

"There's no getting out of it now," said Beverly Crick, her meek voice quivering and her eyes nearly bulging with fear. In her housedress, she looked like a failed sitcom mother from the 60s, with her slight build and a worried look that seemed perpetually frozen on her face. She stooped down to the storage bin beneath her workstation, where she fumbled again with the stacks of pots and pans. A second later, Nadia heard her sobbing.

"There, there," Nadia said. She made her way over to Mrs Crick's station, passing Mary Irons, the third and final contestant. Mary gripped the edges of her own workstation and stared coolly at the empty studio. Nadia made no effort to hide the contempt on her own face. How could the woman stand there, stiff and emotionless, while their fellow sister was coming unglued? Clearly, they were all scared, but couldn't they show some compassion towards one another? She cupped Mrs Crick's chin gently in her hand. "Pull it together, dear," she chided gently. "You'll ruin your makeup."

Mrs Crick offered a wan smile and wiped at her eyes. "Better for the world to see us as we truly are," she said, sniffing. "As people. Not mindless toys for their amusement."

The studio doors abruptly opened. A stagehand entered, along with two men in plain clothes, followed closely by a pair of heavily armed soldiers. The men were the husbands of Mrs Crick and Mrs Irons. They gazed grimly at their wives on stage and then took their seats near the front of the audience. They sat silent as stones with their hands neatly folded in their laps. Mrs Crick sniffed again, a fresh round of tears threatening to break loose. The soldiers stood close by with their hands on their rifles, ready for anything.

Nadia gazed at the husbands. If Ross was still alive, he would be among them at this very moment. His death last year from the flu had been a cruel twist of fate, especially at such a young age—he was only 42. But there was no helping it, she supposed. The war had damaged the nation's economy, leaving many people malnourished and in poor health. Nadia only thanked God he had lived to meet their daughter, Rose. His death had come two weeks after her first birthday, three years ago. As much as Nadia would have loved to have him alive, maybe it was better this way. Because then he would be here, and that was no place to be at all.

YEAR FOUR

The audience streamed into the room. Every chair would soon fill, Nadia knew. After all, this was *American Housewife*. This show was special. Nothing topped it in the ratings, not even the *Olympics*. It had been that way ever since 2032, when the military had finally quelled the Female Rebellion.

The studio filled with chatter. Nadia overheard snippets of conversations about the events that had led them here today: the uprising, and how it had ended, the many lives lost, and how this annual tradition served to keep the peace across the land.

The houselights went down, and a throbbing dance beat began. Nadia's heart began to race. From far overhead, a man appeared on a shining, flying disc.

Rivers Fuqua, the host.

"Ready for another fantastic show, sweeties?" he asked over the loudspeaker.

"Yes!" the room called out in unison.

"Let's do it!" he sang out. The disc descended to the stage amid a flurry of flashing lights. The show's theme song echoed off the walls. Everyone clapped and cheered—except for the contestants and their husbands. When the disc had lowered completely, Rivers hopped off and strutted across the stage. He was a short, energetic man with spiky, silver hair and a mouthful of gleaming teeth. Spotlights lit up the contestants as he motioned for them to take their places behind the worktables. A camera-drone hummed overhead, capturing their expressions and projecting them to a large overhead screen.

"Welcome to *American Housewife*," Rivers said, as he

skipped off the disc. "You know the drill. Every summer, three mothers come together to compete in the ultimate cooking challenge."

Fireworks lit up the stage. A male and female figure emerged from behind purple curtains. The male, in a flowing, scarlet-coloured robe, was the show's judge. The other was brutishly built and wearing dark clothes and a white apron. Both wore masks filled with an amorphous, flowing gel that obscured their features. When the woman's head turned in her direction, Nadia felt herself holding her breath.

"Let's get started," Rivers shouted, "and may the best dish win!" The honk of the starting horn shook the studio, and a holographic timer on the stage wall started ticking down. The women grabbed shopping baskets and ran to the pantry. Mrs Irons got there first, followed by Mrs Crick. Nadia arrived last, struggling to catch her breath. She cursed herself silently for letting herself get so out of shape. The women snatched up their preferred ingredients and tossed them into their baskets.

Soon the studio filled with the sounds of cooking: the chopping of vegetables, the whirring of blender blades, and the scraping of mixes into pans. For Nadia, the tension was maddening. Rivers, ever the showman, kept the audience stoked by vamping across the stage. "Mrs Irons," he said, cocking the microphone to his mouth, "would you mind telling the good people of America how you've prepared for the competition?"

Mrs Irons kept her steely gaze on her mixing bowl. A camera-bot slid into position next to her. "I've spent every waking minute preparing for this," she said in a low, steady voice. "Read every cookbook money can buy. Memorised hundreds of recipes." A lock of brown hair shook loose from the scarf on her head, and she fingered it back into position. "Excuse me," she said sharply, "I really must concentrate."

"Touchy, touchy," Rivers chided. He covered the mike with his hands and whispered into her ear. "Remember sweetie, showmanship counts." He spun back toward the audience and lifted the mike to his lips. "Maybe the other contestants are in a better mood. Mrs Zannini, you appear to be making a crostini. What's your inspiration?"

Nadia looked up at the audience, at all the faces staring back. She, too, read many books, memorised recipes, and practiced her cooking skills into the wee hours of the morning, but right now, she had no desire to discuss it. Looking out at the people who had come here to watch her struggle, she felt consumed by rage. It was getting difficult to think clearly. Her face was warm. A hot, sick feeling was spinning in her gut. She lowered her gaze to the cutting board. "I'm sorry, Mr Fuqua. What was the question?"

"Such a showgirl," he said, rolling his eyes. "Let's see if our other contestant is feeling livelier. Mrs Crick, same question."

Mrs Crick tugged at the collar of her uncomfortable neckband with shaking hands. "Um, I'm here today for my c-country. W-we ladies need to be reminded that—"

"—a woman's place is in the kitchen!" the audience

roared.

Mrs Irons whacked her knife against her cutting board loudly, and an audible gasp filled the studio. Her fiery gaze turned to the audience. She opened her mouth as if to speak but was drowned out by a cacophony of boos.

Nadia caught her eye. "Tsk, tsk, sister," she said softly. "Is it really time for such things?"

Rivers stepped between the two of them. "Ladies," he said, covering the mike with one of his hands. May I remind you that the treaty commands full compliance by *all* our contestants?" The spotlight panned to the stage wings, where more soldiers waited. Mrs Irons took a moment to regain her composure, and then the women got back to work.

At her workstation, Nadia had started to glisten under the spotlights. Her nerves were starting to fray. She tried to distract herself by humming while she whisked a bowl, but her voice quavered with fear. She began to work more slowly, measuring each ingredient twice, some even three times, before adding it to the mix. Poor Mrs Crick wasn't doing much better. Her thin body was shaking from nerves, and she shattered one of her mixing bowls on the floor. An attendant brought her a new bowl, along with a glass of water and a towel for her sweating face.

Soon the warm scents of rosemary and toasted breadcrumbs wafted through the studio. When the timer had counted down to the last few minutes, the women began plating their dishes and applying the finishing touches.

Then it was time for the tasting.

The judge lifted a forkful of each dish carefully to the mouth hole in his mask. His eyes closed as he chewed each bite slowly, and the amorphous shapes on his facemask twitched excitedly in response.

"Mrs Irons," he said, after what seemed like an eternity to the contestants, "your salmon cakes are positively divine."

A smile curled its way into the corner of Mrs Irons' lips.

"However, your plating lacks imagination. And Mrs Zannini, your crostini has the right crunch, but I'm not getting nearly enough flavour. Mrs Crick, the filling for your devilled eggs was rich and creamy, but the eggs were a trifle overcooked."

Rivers cut in to take the show to a commercial break. The contestants remained quiet on the stage, stealing glances around the set or into the audience, and waiting.

The cameras started rolling again, and the women were instructed to line up in front of the judge. They licked the corners of their lips, their hands folded plainly in front of them, except for Mrs Crick, who wrung her hands together as if she were cleaning them. A slow, rolling drumbeat started over the loudspeakers and Rivers brought out a platter topped with a silver cloche. The camera-bot zoomed in to capture the moment, and Rivers flicked up the lid.

It was the salmon cakes.

"Mrs Irons," the judge said, "your dish showed promise, but in the end, the flaws overcame the goodness. For that reason, you've lost this round of *American Housewife*."

A wide door at the rear of the stage hissed opened, revealing a small room where three small children sat playing with toys. The broad-shouldered woman walked in.

"No!" screamed Mrs Irons when the woman yanked up a brown-haired girl by one of her arms. A rubber ball fell from the girl's hands as she was slung over the woman's shoulder. Nadia barely got a look at Mrs Irons' daughter, Rose, before the door slid shut again.

One of the husbands shot out of his seat with a sharp cry, then quickly fainted.

"Savage!" Mrs Irons shrieked from the stage. "How could you?" She lunged for the brutish woman, but the soldiers subdued her.

The woman strapped the now-screaming toddler down on a large table. The attendants stepped forward to assist, wrapping the young girl's eyes with a blindfold. With one hand, the brutish woman selected a long, gleaming knife.

Mrs Irons shrieked over and over while the guards restrained her.

A hush fell across the audience. A few of the younger spectators covered their faces. Most, however, leaned forwards, their nostrils flaring, their eyes hungry. The camera-drone clicked and whirred, adjusting the focus of its lens.

Mrs Crick's knees buckled, and she collapsed, sobbing. Nadia made the sign of the cross against her chest and muttered a silent prayer. Once again, she crossed the stage to comfort Mrs Crick. The two women held each other, as if their embrace could somehow imbue them with the strength they needed to get through the next round.

"Freshest meat in town," Rivers Fuqua said, winking into the camera. "Can't wait to see what the remaining contestants do in the entrée round."

Slaybells Ring

by Dawn DeBraal

The blackened finger of evil rolled down the elf's face, leaving a trail of blood behind it.

"Where's the fat man?"

"My loyalty is to Kris Kringle."

"You stupid imp, I am Kris Kringle."

"Then you should know where you work!" The demon recoiled at such bravery. The spirit disposed of the elven trash. If Santa's helpers were close, so was the mode of transportation Kris needed.

"Come." He called to the hellhounds with antlers tied to their heads. Soon, they would touch every house on Christmas Eve with the help of Santa's stolen sleigh. All Hell would break loose.

YEAR FOUR

No-Elf

by Kristin Lennox

"It's slave labour!" Snuffly's pointed ears pinkened when he got angry. "We work 364 days a year! For what? Extra peppermint in our hot chocolate on Christmas?"

A murmur of dissension arose from the toy factory floor. Snuffly had just started chanting, "Hey, hey, ho-ho-ho, Santa Claus has got to go," when he was whisked into the Big Man's office.

Laying a finger aside of his nose, Saint Nick pondered the elf's proposal…

CORPORATE MEMO:

"We are pleased to announce Snuffly Gingerball's promotion to our South Pole location, effective immediately. Celebration to follow with eggnog and freshly ground Christmas sausage."

Merry Crashed-Mass

by Shawn M. Klimek

Day 11: So cold.

The smoking, skeletal remains of the crashed sleigh are poor shelter. Yet, to be more easily spotted by a search plane, I have resisted wandering. I am now convinced of sabotage. I wrack my brain for suspects, but fumes from the plastic toys burned for heat have dimmed my faculties. The toy radio I rescued taunts me in silence for my policy against including batteries.

Thank Loki, two of the reindeer survived the initial crash. Their venison has kept me alive. My Donner party joke did not go over well.

His sad eyes haunt my dreams.

Zzzzzz

by L.N. Hunter

Mildred is lying awake again. Just like every other damned night for so many weeks, she's lost count. She tugs at her pillow and folds it in half, sandwiching her head, trying to cover both ears. But even with her pillow pressed against her ears so hard she can hear her blood pulsing, Malcolm's snoring cuts right through the three inches of cotton-covered, hypoallergenic, 100% goose feathers.

The snoring stops, and, after a lip smack, Malcolm gently inhales and exhales. *Ah, blessed quiet.* Mildred sighs and lets herself relax, sinking into the rhythm of her husband's untroubled breathing. Just as her thoughts drift off into the world of dreams, Malcom snorts and restarts his jackhammer.

Mildred can feel her eyeballs vibrate.

A gentle prod of her index finger elicits a grunt, but the snoring continues unabated. She pokes him again, harder this time, finger sinking deep into his corpulent midriff. Malcolm rolls over, taking most of the bedclothes with him, with no change in the sound of pneumatic drilling.

Mildred knows it's pointless trying to get the bedclothes back again—her strength is no match to Malcolm's size and weight. Admitting defeat, she hauls herself out of bed and grabs a blanket from the airing cupboard. She lurches downstairs like a sleep-deprived zombie, flops into the too-short sofa in the chilly front room, and pulls the blanket over herself. Mildred will get no more sleep tonight, but at least her ears won't be assaulted any further.

She thought she'd get used to the racket by now, but there's just something about the noise. It's not uniform, like traffic—she could cope with the unending drone of cars and lorries. Snoring continually surprises with changes in tone and volume. Worst of all is the period of silence between breaths and the agonising wait for the next snort.

After the first few days, she expected that accumulated tiredness would cause her to sleep through anything, but no. Of course not. Instead, her fitful nights merge into days when her brain just doesn't function.

Now, reports at work take twice as long to write as they should, and thank goodness for automatic spellchecking. Even with a shopping list, she invariably forgets something. She keeps making mugs of coffee in the hope of masking her exhaustion with caffeine-induced alertness, but then forgets where she sets them down after the first sips.

Malcolm, bless him, is good about searching the house at the end of the day, retrieving all the misplaced mugs. He knows he's the cause of her troubles and willingly subjects himself to all the measures Mildred suggests. Well, almost all.

The red power indicator on the TV glares back at her as she lies on the sofa, as if pouring scorn on their many failed 'cures.'

First, they tried a pouch of marbles sewn into the back of Malcolm's pyjama jacket. That worked for a while, but the clinking of the marbles was as jarring as the snoring. There was that one night, too, when the pouch burst, and Mildred found her own sleep further disturbed by marbles underneath her hip. The marbles went in the bin.

Next came nasal strips—little bits of tape which keep one's nostrils open. Fat lot of good they did! The nostrils weren't the problem; Malcolm's flabby jowls and triple chin were, and no amount of duct tape, let alone effete nasal strips, would do anything to keep those under control. All that the nasal strip achieved was giving Mildred the shock of her life when she woke up unable to open her eye. She thought she had suffered a stroke until she found the little bit of sticky plastic that had somehow migrated across the bed. The nasal strip box got thrown out, half its contents still unused.

More expensive was the strangely shaped plastic tube which was claimed to keep the wearer's tongue and cheeks from vibrating. Mildred had to plead with Malcolm to get him to wear the uncomfortable contraption, ultimately offering him personal favours before he would agree—beef with Yorkshire puddings and roast potatoes *three* times a week. She had to admit that the thing lived up to its promise, and the snoring stopped. Sadly, it was replaced by an unmelodic whistling—like sleeping next to an untalented but enthusiastic player of panpipes. Yet more debris for the binmen to take away.

Perhaps, Mildred thought, it was unfair to place the full burden on Malcolm. She tried several different sorts of earplug, including an uncomfortable elasticised band which covered her ears. While they succeeded in limiting the higher frequencies of the snoring to varying degrees, they did little for the skull-vibrating rumbles. She gave up on them when one, inserted too far into her left ear canal, required a visit to the doctor to extract.

And then there was the singing. Heavens, the singing! She still cringes at the memory. She'd heard that vocal exercises could strengthen the flabby bits that caused snoring, so she signed the pair of them up to the local choir, only to be asked to leave before the end of the first session and never return. Who knew Malcolm could reach notes like that?

Struggling to get comfortable on the sofa, Mildred gazes at the unblinking TV light. She wonders, not for the first time, if she just has to put up with the chainsaw occupying the other half of the bed. More than half, if she's honest, since Malcolm has expanded a bit over the past year, which undoubtedly contributed to the onset of his snoring.

She tells herself they've tried everything. Well, everything short of surgery—Malcolm said he'd sooner die than let some butcher hack bits off him.

"It's only snoring," he said. "We'll just have to live with it."

It's only snoring. I'll have to live with it.

That's when the idea pops into her so-very-tired head…

Mildred doesn't dislike her husband, but they *have* been married for an awfully long time. Perhaps it's time to let go. *Anything* to get some sleep.

***

YEAR FOUR

While Malcolm does the vacuuming and collects coffee mugs downstairs, Mildred scrapes some of the insulation off the electric blanket wiring on his side of the bed, then adjusts the timer on the blanket's plug so it would switch on for a few minutes at midnight. She finishes just in time to hear him march up the stairs to complete the vacuuming. She sighs. She's going to have to do that chore herself when she's a widow.

That night, the anticipation keeps Mildred awake—well, that and the snoring. She keeps glancing at her bedside clock, waiting impatiently for the appointed hour. *Perhaps*, she thinks, *I should have set it for eleven.*

It's almost time… Ten, nine, eight… Mildred holds her breath.

Zzzap!

Silence.

Mildred does a mental happy dance.

Then: grunt, snuffle, zzzzzzz.

She whirls around to stare at Malcolm. *How come I can see in the dark?* Shortly after that, she thinks, *And why am I floating above the bed?*

Mildred smiles. I'm asleep, and this is just a dream.

Then, If I'm asleep, it means I've finally got used to the snoring. A second later, her heart sinks. Oh no, I've killed him for no reason. Wake up! I need to wake up.

She closes her eyes tight and concentrates. Nothing happens. She pinches herself, but still nothing.

Mildred takes a close look at the blanket. *Damn!* In her

sleep-deprived befuddlement, she'd stripped away the insulation on *her* side of the bed, not Malcolm's.

Oh well, I suppose I'll be able to get away from the noise now.

Mildred floats to the bedroom door and reaches for the handle. Her hand drifts through it, and panic rises again as she wonders how she can escape. Then she realises she can move her entire body into the door, so she does. Only to emerge back in the bedroom.

She tries a second time. Back in the bedroom again.

What about the window? she thinks. It's a bit of a fall, but it can't harm me now, can it?

The same thing happens. It occurs with the walls, floor and ceiling, as well. She's trapped in the room.

With Malcolm's snoring.

Her ghostly hands can't open the drawer on the bedside cabinet to see if she left any earplugs there, nor can they pick up the pillow to wrap around her head. She discovers that incorporeal hands aren't particularly effective at reducing noise levels.

When Malcolm's snuffling and rumbling crescendos in a hooting snort, something in Mildred snaps. She brings her face right up close to her husband's and screams as loud as she can. With no need to pause for breath, her scream lasts for a long time, becoming louder as she puts every minute of lost sleep into it.

Car alarms join in from outside, as do dogs, then people shouting about the racket.

YEAR FOUR

Malcolm's eyelids flicker, then snap open. His eyes focus on Mildred's face, and he says, "Oh, bugger," and clutches his chest.

Mildred closes her mouth and watches silently as Malcolm's ghost floats out of his body.

He smiles lazily at her. "I'm awfully tired, love. I think I'll sleep for a hundred years."

Then he lies down, tugging an imaginary blanket over himself.

And starts snoring.

Ketrokur

by Don Money

Of the thirteen Yule Lads, Ketrokur was the most feared. While his brothers were known to slam doors, lick spoons, and other trivial inconveniences, Ketrokur lived up to his nickname, Meat Hook. When he came down from the mountains, the Icelandic night was bathed in blood.

Doors torn from their hinges, the iron hook in Ketrokur's hand grew bloodier with each house he visited. The greedy hook collecting a sacrificial toll.

With the sunrise, Ketrokur returned to his rocky crag; his sled was weighed down by the sacks stained from their bloody contents. A year's worth of meals on board.

The Christmas Angel

by Tracy Davidson

The Angel on top of the Christmas tree moved. Every time the boy looked, unwillingly, in its direction, it blinked. Or smiled. Once stuck out a tiny tongue. No-one else saw it. No-one believed him. They laughed.

Until... one minute past midnight, Christmas morning. The Angel's eyes turned blood red, its body grew and grew, until it dwarfed the tree. The parents' screams were silenced by tinsel, that wrapped around their necks. His brothers, silenced by the baubles filling their open mouths, choking them.

The boy didn't scream. Didn't run. He woke... shrunken, paralysed, on top of the tree. Blinking.

Dear Santa

by James Rumpel

Dear Santa,

I have been a good boy this year. Papa says I have been a wonderful helper. He says I am great bait and that I am getting strong enough that I will soon be able to help with the cutting.

For Christmas, I would like my own knives and a pair of handcuffs. If you can't get me the handcuffs, a bunch of zip-ties would be okay.

Thanks,

Billy.

P.S. You might not want to come down the chimney when you visit our house. Papa's been stuffing things into it lately. I wouldn't want you to get stuck.

YEAR FOUR

Crossing the Line

by Jameson Grey

New Year's Eve.

The day the last of my line dies. I've hired a boat for the occasion—a yacht, no less! Sailed out to the Line Islands. Currently sitting one second east of the International Date Line. Waiting.

I've requested the captain crosses the Date Line at midnight. Time it right, it *can* be beaten. The *curse*.

The crew's happy enough. They're getting paid either way.

The damn Barber family curse!

One dies at midnight. Every year.

It's 11.59. The boat is firing up. I feel it. I am heading up on deck.

Crossing the line one last ti—

Candy Cane Surprise

by C.L. Sidell

An elf hands us candy canes as we pass the greeting cards store.

Georgia snatches mine before I can unwrap it. “Nah, I want this one instead,” she declares, swapping them.

“It’s just dye,” I reply, trying to ignore the ache that’s been pulsing behind my eyes these last few hours. “They all taste about the same.”

“Whatever. I want the red one.”

Georgia yaps nonstop as we trudge through the parking lot towards our cars. One of the streetlamps is out, another flickering.

“So tacky—” *Suck-suck*. “Don’t they know people with standards won’t buy—” *Suck-suck*. “Adam’s going to *love* those tickets I got him—” *Suck-suck*.

I block out most of what she says, but hearing my boyfriend’s name stops me in my tracks.

Georgia turns. “What?” she asks, eyebrow raised. *Suck-suck*.

I’ve been sucking on my cane too. I pull it from my mouth, consider the pointed end.

“You know what, Georgia?” My head is pounding now. I grip the green-and-white striped candy in my fist, take a step forward. We’re blanketed in shadows, and there isn’t a single person in sight.

YEAR FOUR

"*What*, Kris?"

I lick the candy cane once more, test the sharpness on my tongue.

"You really suck."

Consequences

by Mel Andela

A dead mouse sat in sister's stocking, a toy car on the stairs for mother, and Jamie nestled with visions of destruction rather than sugar plums.

He sees you when you're sleeping…

Faint music made Jamie prickle with goosebumps.

Be good for goodness sake…

There was a creak at the door, and a hulking silhouette appeared.

"You're on my list," A not-so-jolly voice beckoned. "Time to go."

"N-no coal?" Jamie squeaked.

"No, when you've been really naughty—downright mean—you go to the workshop."

"Why?"

"Ho, ho, ho," The laugh was mirthless, merciless. "Who do you think makes the toys?"

Coal

by David D. West

Santa turned away from the plate of milk and cookies and saw the round rump of a boy digging through his sack of wonders. He frowned as the greedy boy wriggled to and fro, searching for hidden delights meant for others.

He set one soot-covered boot against the boy's ass and pushed. The boy fell into the sack with a gasp. Santa cinched it tight and the sack shrunk in on itself. The boy's screams died down as the sack compressed his writhing body.

When all was silent, Santa reached into the sack and pulled out a lump of coal.

Thrown Out

by A. Lily

There was an unfamiliar heftiness to the trash this morning. I wasn't accustomed to the weight, so I dragged it through the kitchen and to the front door. As I opened the door and hoisted the bag up, I noticed a tear beginning to separate the seam of the bag, and within moments, the entrails spilled out. Something stone-grey and cold fell wetly at my feet, slick with last night's leftover lasagne. I couldn't bear to speculate on what it could be, and yet, unwisely, I cast a furtive glance at the familiar shape.

I ran inside to grab another bag—something to cover up what that thing was, so I could toss it out of my life and out of my head. Going back out, I had hoped it would be gone. But it wasn't. It was still there, covered in marinara and looking vulgar and of place beneath the stone portico. Leaving it for last, I gathered the trash up, not paying any mind to the mess on my hands as glances turned into lingering stares. Having gathered the bulk of the trash up, I set the new bag aside and shook as I reached for the vein-marbled shape. I couldn't bear to throw it out with the rest of the trash, so I brushed the crystalline moisture off its little toes and cradled it in my day-old-food-covered hands.

I had blankets folded up in my receiving room. The kind that maintains their softness through limitless washes, and I bundled up that cold, and now wet, thing in my arms. Glistening droplets formed at the end of its pale eyelashes, and it almost looked alive. The lips were blue, but maybe with a little more warmth, the colour would return, so I wrapped it up in another blanket and propped the thing up on some cushions after setting it down by the stove heater.

A part of me ached at the thought of leaving it alone, but I *had* to make that phone call. It was the right thing to do. Any sane person with a semblance of humanity would have done it. I dialled a 9, and with my finger hovering over the 1, I realised I must have forgotten the number. In fact, I couldn't recall why I picked the phone up in the first place. Why was I wasting my time on the phone when there was so much for me to do?

It'll need a bath, clothes, and I hadn't even looked into these bland educational toys the mothers in social media groups swear by yet. But nothing small or it might choke.

What could I feed it? I looked through my cupboards and set aside two cans of sweet peas. They would be easy enough to mash into a quick meal when the cold little thing grows hungry. Now that the thought of food had come up, I swore I saw a little dribble on its chin.

Indeed, there appeared to be improvement in its health, as its cheeks had spread a mottled rosy hue. The blankets and the heat had done their job of melting away the frost. I picked it up and dabbed at the chin, then patted the moisture collecting and dripping from the soles of its feet. I thought to myself that I had responsibilities now. Something greater than myself to care for.

But, god, what was that smell? Of course, the poor thing

needs a bath.

I unwrapped the blanket and bile built up in the back of my throat, as I uncovered an array of putrid, weeping sores lining the soft flesh of its tummy. How could I have let it get this bad? I set my mind on that bath first, then I'd see about getting the little sweetie to a doctor.

Placing my hands underneath the stream of warm water, I noticed the stains I picked up from handling the garbage looked remarkably like blood as it spiralled down the drain. My heart seized at the sight for a moment, but then the terror passed. Dwelling on these thoughts, these sights, can't be good for one's own mental health. Fully unwrapping the bundle and holding it close to my chest is alarming because of how cold it still felt. Not a shiver passed between its body to mine. There are no whimpers or movement of any kind, yet this is not uncharacteristic of it. I was overwhelmed with a fondness for the quiet and still little thing.

When tepid water sat shallow in the tub, I turned off the tap. There was no baby cleanser, and I panicked at the thought of rubbing at the delicate skin with my own harsher soaps. I carefully considered the ingredients present in my shampoo and determined it to be a suitable replacement for baby soap. I felt so unprepared for all of this. I had to remember to make a visit to the store to pick up supplies.

It was awfully stiff, even in the water. Unable to keep its head from being submerged, I got into the tub as well and supported it on my chest, providing a little comfort to ease its fear of getting wet. The soap was lathered and applied to its skin. The fragrance floating from the suds did nothing to mask that distinct scent. I was getting quite used to it anyway. I actually couldn't recall a time when I smelled anything else.

I concentrated on the scalp, working my fingers through the cute fuzz on the top, and revealed a watercolour-like stain that spread along the top of its head. Bruises? I turned it around to face me, looked into those cloudy glass doll eyes for the first time, and apologised for being so rough. The guilt was still there, and a sob built in my stomach.

A layer of pink ooze sat with the bubbles, coating the surface of the tub. I washed the residue off by turning the shower on and gave the porcelain a good scrub with a clean rag to prevent any staining. It seemed like the bath hadn't done much to improve the poor thing's condition. I got up and towelled our bodies off. Bits of soggy flesh stuck to the fibres of the towel, and I chastised myself for rubbing too hard. I adjusted my method and gave the tiny thing little pats on the damp parts of its body, remembering to be especially careful with its head.

The sound of a door dragging open, then closing with a click, tugged my focus away from the thing in the towel. There is dread in those noises, an anticipation of being found out. Of losing whatever I had discovered today. There was the chime of keys being deposited on the plate and, along with that sound, came a rising panic. Holding its body in the towel on the journey from the bathroom to the bedroom became difficult, as skin sloughed off with every movement. I locked the door behind me and waited, my heart beating with a rapid flutter in my chest, for the familiar voice to call out my name. There is a questioning to his tone, which seemed to lie in the realm between familiarity and unfamiliarity, as the man approached the door. I couldn't place the voice with a name or face, and this served to heighten the fear.

Knuckles banged on the bedroom door, and I pulled the bundle closer to me with a grip so tight, blossoms of red bloomed on the towel. I lay beneath the blanket, screaming in a voice that could have been out loud, yet felt so quiet. *This is wrong. Why does it feel so wrong? He doesn't belong here. It's supposed to be just me and it, and no one else between us. Why won't he leave me and my sick little thing alone?*

A mechanical jolt within myself broke open my cries into wails, as a red-hot fire built itself in my belly. Whatever this agony was, I know *he* is the cause of it. And he's come to take away the only thing that ever mattered to me.

As my cries of pain ascended, so did the banging, with the latter ending with the door being knocked off a hinge, hitting the wall with enough force to intensity the suffering. The blanket was torn off me, exposing my swollen body, and I clutched at the cold, dead mass even tighter. I couldn't let him take it from me.

There was a shriek on the man's end, and I'm soaked. The sheets, the blankets, the decorative pillows with the delicate lace patterns, are dyed a sticky, wine-red. This man, who came into mine and my little thing's world without our permission, pressed his body against mine as he matched my sobs. The first words I had spoken out loud all day left my throat in a dry rasp. "You'll smother it."

He didn't hear me, and, with arms full of melting lead, I pushed him away, jerking back protectively, but there was nothing cold nor solid at my chest. My hands searched around me, but I couldn't find it. It was gone—dissolved into the stains on the bed.

The pain of loss is added to the nightmare within my womb. The tears stopped, but I wanted to keep crying until all that came out was as red as everything around me.

But all my mind can focus on is whether or not I remembered to take the trash out this morning.

Harmony, Like A Song I've Heard

by Ben Lockwood

Dear Mrs and Mr Brown,

I am writing to tell you that the story you've been told about your son's disappearance is not true.

I know, because I was there.

I believe I have some responsibility for the events that occurred. I know you've read this before, but please bear with me. Space changes the meaning of the words.

I remember when your son found the box. It was full of old sheet music and falling apart in the back of the Jacob's School of Music library. It was like me to be curious about things like that.

You would think it would have looked more ominous, or wrong in some way, given what was in it. But it didn't. It was just a box.

When he opened that box, though, it became clear enough. The inside was dark. Too dark. As if, to the box, the buzzing overhead light was only a pebble dropped in a vast, unending sea.

Your son—you know how he is when he sets his mind on something—he reached inside the box, despite its darkness. The music is what he pulled out.

It didn't look like any piece of music I had ever seen. For one, the colour was backwards. Instead of black notes on white paper, the notes were white on black paper. They looped in a strange pattern that should have made me uncomfortable. Just looking at it should have felt wrong.

I wish I could tell you I convinced your son to put it back in the box right then and there, to never think about it again, to never play it. But I can't, and I'm writing to tell you the story you've been told about your son's disappearance isn't true. I know.

Because I was there, I believe I have some responsibility for the events that occurred. I know you've read this before, but please bear with me. Space changes the meaning of the words.

I remember when he found the box of old sheet music. It was falling apart in the back of the Jacob's School of Music library. It was like me.

To be curious about things like that, you would think it would look more ominous, or wrong in some way, given what it was in it. But it didn't. It was just a box.

Over the years, I have come to understand what was really inside. I should be honest now and tell you that the letter you are reading, the one I am writing, has been written.

For me, it was ten years ago that your son opened that box. Ten years ago that he took out that sheet music, and all but ran to the practice room. I couldn't stop him.

By the time I caught up, he already had his violin out. The black sheet music sat on a stand in front of him, and he only hesitated a moment before playing that first note. The music had a harmony like a song I've heard before, like a song I've always known. Then the lights shimmered, and, by the time he finished the first fugue, I was five years away.

I remember thinking I could see the universe coming undone. That's what the shimmer looked like while he played. What it felt like is harder to explain. It was as if the space between my memories was expanding, like a dream you return to in longer and longer spurts until it's being awake that feels like the dream.

The shimmer grew wider as he played, and in the opening, I saw a room. It was the same room we were standing in, like a mirror. Except, in this room, *I* was playing the violin, not your son. I watched myself play the way I've always wanted to be able to play. The way your son plays. And then it was your son playing again, and suddenly I didn't know which room I was in.

The music was disorienting. I looked at him watching me, and me watching myself, and, in my confusion, I panicked. I stepped through that shimmer. I left your son behind.

It took me another five years to find him again.

When I did, it was a Tuesday. I found him sitting on a bench in a park, as if he'd been waiting for me. He looked the same, but spoke like a man who has crossed an ocean. He told me about the time he'd spend in a new land, and how space worked differently there. When I asked him where this new land was, he said here. I didn't understand.

I wanted to apologise for leaving him. He wanted to play the next fugue. I told him when he opened that box, though, it became clear enough. The inside was dark. Too dark. As if, to the box, the buzzing overhead light was only a pebble dropped in a vast, unending sea. Your son.

You know how he is when he sets his mind on something. He reached inside the box. Despite its darkness, the music is what he pulled out.

It didn't look like any piece of music I had ever seen. For one, the colour was backwards. Instead of black notes on white paper, they were white on black paper. They looped in a strange pattern.

That should have made me uncomfortable. Just looking at it should have felt wrong. I wish I could tell you I convinced your son to put it back in the box right then and there, to never think about it again, to never play it. But I can't, and I'm writing to tell you the story you've been told about.

Your son's disappearance isn't true. I know, because I was there. I believe I have some responsibility for the events that occurred. I know you've read this before, but please bear with me. Space changes the meaning.

Of the words, I remember. When your son found the box, it was full of old sheet music and falling apart in the back of the Jacob's School of Music library. It was like me to be curious.

About things like that, you would think it would have looked more ominous, or wrong in some way, given what was in it. But it didn't. It was just a box. Over the years, I have come to understand what was really inside. I should be honest now and tell you that.

The letter you are reading, the one I am writing, has been written for me. It was ten years ago that your son opened that box. Ten years ago that he took out that sheet music and all but ran to the practice room. I couldn't stop him by the time I caught up. He already had his violin out. The black sheet music sat on a stand in front of him, and he only hesitated a moment before playing that first note. The music had a harmony like a song I've heard before, like a song I've always known. Then the lights shimmered, and by the time he finished the first fugue, I was five years away.

Now I'm forty years away, and he's playing the third fugue while I stand in a hallway with carpet like in those old hotels. It's long, and one wall is all windows that overlook a vast, frozen wasteland. A man in a spacesuit is walking out there. I've found your son again.

I'm out there too, lying naked in the snow. Blood seeps from a wound in my neck and turns the snow a dark crimson. I stand here for minutes, or maybe years, looking out over the endless tundra, watching the blood pool. I don't know how long I've been here when I notice the drill.

It's large and your son is operating it. He's plunging it deeply, searching for meaning under layers of ice.

He sees me in the hallway and leaves the drill, walking towards me, past the dead me lying in the snow. When he approaches, I can see that he's saying something, but I can't hear him through the glass. I know what he is saying, though. Your son is telling me he is going to fix all of this. And I can see now that I am in the suit.

And I am writing to tell you.

Always Watching

by Sophie Wagner

As he rotted away, cheeks sallow, smile bloody, dreams of sugarplums died. Even magic couldn't fix him.

"Good morning!" piped a sing-song voice from the speakers in the padded room. Santa shot to his feet, camera's following his every move.

"Please!" he screamed. "I can't take this anymore. Let me go!"

"Tsk, tsk," came the voice. "Don't like being constantly watched? How's it make you feel?

"I want to die!" Santa shrieked.

"That's not very jolly..." the voice said. "Let's try again tomorrow." With that, he turned off the lights and left Santa in the dark, the cameras always watching.

A Song for Dorian

by Carol Ryles

Ta-da!” Lucinda gestured to her newest creation: a tree adorned with taxidermic hummingbirds, cygnets, sparrows, and ducklings.

Dorian chuckled, then guzzled his third goblet of merlot. “That takes stuffing the turkey to a whole new level. Is it finished?”

Lucinda almost lost herself to his hypnotic gaze.

“What the—” He dropped the goblet, staggered, collapsed.

Lucinda's camouflage faded, revealing the furry snout, reptilian tongue, and horns of a krampus. She knelt, lowered a talon to Dorian's eyeball. *The perfect bauble!*

Detaching the sclera, she broke into joyous, triumphant song.

“On the second day of Christmas my boyfriend gave to me...”

Log-in Failure

by S. Jade Path

It seemed innocent enough in the beginning.

Touted as energy efficient, time-saving, and of course, the all-important convenience factor. A single app to control our coffeepots, our lights, our security systems, emergency alarms, the very locks on our doors—everything at our literal fingertips. We eagerly embraced home automation.

It wasn't until after the second wave of carbon monoxide poisonings that people started suspecting something was amiss. When the fires started, the pattern emerged—houses with fully integrated automation had become death traps.

Whole families lost; bodies piled at the door. Fire alarms silent, doors locked, melted phones clutched in charred fingers.

Where Does the Time Go?

by Thomas J. Griffin

At 11:59 an orderly assists Patient 2022 onto the examining table. He's aged poorly, eyes sunken, back bowed. It's been a tough year.

"Perfect timing," says Dr Saturday, smiling warmly. "Your affairs are in order?"

"Affairs?" 2022 asks. "Isn't this a check-up?"

From the adjoining surgical suite, a woman screams.

"Is that what reception said?" The doctor *tsks*, prepping a syringe. "I'm afraid you're terminal."

2022 tries to rise, but the orderly restrains him. He struggles feebly until the syringe enters his carotid. At midnight, he sighs his last.

Next door, a newborn cries.

Dr Saturday beams. "Happy New Year!"

Black Hare Press

BLACK HARE PRESS is a small, independent publisher based in Melbourne, Australia.

Founded in 2018, our aim has always been to champion emerging authors from all around the globe and offer opportunities for them to participate in speculative fiction and horror short story anthologies.

Connect: linktr.ee/blackharepress

www.ingramcontent.com/pod-product-compliance
Lightning Source LLC
Chambersburg PA
CBHW030341310726
48979CB00001B/134